Death of a Romance Writer and Other Stories

Death of a Romance Writer and Other Stories

Includes the full-length novel
The Night-Blooming Cereus,
originally published under the name Joan Hadley

Joan Hess

Five Star • Waterville, Maine

Five Star First Edition Mystery Series.

Published in 2002 in conjunction with
Tekno Books and Ed Gorman.

Set in 11 pt. Plantin by Al Chase.

Printed in the United States on permanent paper.

Library of Congress Cataloging-in-Publication Data
Hess, Joan.
    Death of a romance writer and other stories / Joan Hess
      p. cm.
    "Includes the full-length novel 'The night-blooming cereus', originally published under the name Joan Hadley."
    ISBN 0-7862-3933-6 (hc : alk. paper)
    1. Detective and mystery stories, American.   I. Hadley, Joan. Night-blooming cereus.   II. Title: Night-blooming cereus.   III. Title.
    PS3558.E79785 D45 2002
      813'.54—dc21   2001059222

Table of Contents

Death of a Romance Writer

The young woman hesitated at the top of the great curving stair-case, grumbling rather rudely to herself as she gazed at the scene below. "Hell's bells!" she muttered under her breath. "Doesn't she like anything besides waltzes? A little New Wave rock, or at least jazz?"

In the grand ballroom ladies dressed in pastel gowns swept across the floor under the benevolent eyes of elegant gen-tlemen in black waistcoats and ruffled shirts. A stringed or-chestra labored its way through the familiar melodies with grim concentration. Servants moved inconspicuously along the walls of the vast room, their expressions studiously blank. The same old thing, down to the canapes and sweet sherry.

Gathering up her skirt with pale, delicately tapered fin-gers, the woman forced herself to move down the stairs. Her heart-shaped mouth was curled slightly, and her deep jade eyes flittered across the crowd without curiosity. He would make an appearance in a few minutes, she reminded herself glumly, but perhaps she could have a bit of fun in the mean-time. The fun would certainly end when he appeared—who-ever he was.

"Lady Althea!" gushed a shrill, nasal voice from the shadows behind her. "I was so hoping to see you this evening. The ball is absolutely delightful."

Lady Althea, the woman repeated to herself. A silly name, as usual, invoking images of moonlit gardens and scented breezes. Why not a simple "Kate" or "Jane"? Oh, no. It was

7

always "Desiree" or "Bianca," as if her bland personality must be disguised by alluring nomenclature.

The dowager tottered out of the shadows on tiny feet. In her seventies (hundreds, Althea sniffed to herself), the woman's face was a mesh of tiny lines, and her faded blue eyes glittered with malevolence. Her thin white hair was decorated with a handful of dusty plumes, one of which threatened to sweep across her hawkish nose with every twitch of the woman's head.

"Who're you?" Althea demanded bluntly.

The dowager raised a painted eyebrow. "I am your mother-in-law's dearest friend, Lady Althea. You had tea only yesterday at my summer home. Your first introduction to society, I believe. I'm amazed that it has slipped your mind."

"Yeah, sorry." Althea moved away from the woman's rancid breath and fluttery hands. Surely these people could be induced to brush their teeth, she thought testily. They didn't, of course. As far as she could tell, they had no bodily functions whatsoever. A few bouts of the vapors, a shoulder slashed by a duelling sword, a mysterious scar across the cheek. But nothing mundane to interrupt the flow of their lives.

Ignoring the woman's frown, Althea stood on her toes to peer around the room. He wasn't here yet. Good. Now, if she could only liven up the music and get these nameless people to loosen up a little bit, the evening might provide some amusement. A ball could be a ball, but it seldom was.

The dowager was not ready to allow Althea to escape. "Your dear mother-in-law has told me of your tragic history, and I must tell you how much I admire your courage," she hissed. Little drops of spittle landed on Althea's cheek, like a fine mist of acid rain.

"Sure, thanks," Althea said. "I'm a plucky sort, I understand. Personally, I'd rather watch television or read a confession magazine, but I never get the chance."

"Television? What might that be, my dear girl?"

Althea shook her head. "Never mind. Hey, which one of these ladies" (dames, broads) "is my mother-in-law? The one with the chicken beak or that fat slug in the corner?"

"Lady Althea! I must tell you that I am somewhat shocked by your manner," the dowager gasped. Her hand fluttered to her mouth. "I was led to believe you had been raised most properly in a convent; that you were of gentle birth and delicate nature."

"Is that so? I guess I'd better behave," Althea said dryly. She tucked a stray curl of her raven black hair into place, and checked the row of tiny seed pearl buttons on her elbow-length gloves. Now that, she told herself sternly, was the accepted and expected behavior. She glanced at the dowager.

"So which one is my mother-in-law?"

"Your mother-in-law is there," the dowager said, gesturing with a molting fan toward a grim-visaged woman sitting on a straightbacked chair. "But where is your dear husband, Lady Althea? I had such hopes of speaking to him."

"Beats me," Althea said. So she was already married, she thought with a sigh. These rapid shifts were disconcerting. Dear husband, huh! Gawd, he was probably a bodice ripper like the rest of them. And she had decided to wear her new gown—genuine silk and just the right color for her eyes. Perhaps there was enough time to change into something more expendable.

Frowning, Althea glanced across the coiffed heads of the guests to study her mother-in-law. A real loser, with a profile that ought to be illegal. Translucent blue complexion, hooded eyes, mouth tighter than a miser's purse. But the woman did have a smidgen of charm—all found in the garish diamond broach on her chest. From across the room, Althea could see the brilliance of the stone, and even the dull glow of the gold setting. Now that was charming.

Leaving the dowager puffing resentfully at the bottom of the staircase, Althea began to thread her way between the dancers. Despite her intention of finding the punchbowl, she found herself curtsying in front of her mother-in-law. Damn.

"Althea, dear child," the woman said frostily. She extended a limp white hand, as though she expected Althea to clasp it to her bosom—or kiss it, for God's sake!

Althea eyed it warily. At last she touched it timidly, then snatched her hand away and hid it behind her back. "Good evening," she said, swallowing a sour taste in the back of her throat. The diamond broach. It would keep her in penthouses and champagne for the rest of her life, if only . . .

"Excrutia, this child is charming!" the dowager said, shoving Althea aside. "But where is your son? Dear Jared must be eager to present his charming bride to his friends . . ."

Jared, huh. Althea brushed a black curl off her eyebrow as she checked the crowd. She was destined to be stuck with an elegant moniker, and so was he. Once, she remembered with a faint sigh, she had particularly liked a chap named Sam— but of course he had become a Derek. Sam had had bulging biceps and a busted nose, but it hadn't kept him from stirring up a bit of inventiveness between the covers. Derek, on the other hand, had spent hours gazing into her eyes and murmuring (bleating) endearments that were supposed to sweep her off her feet. Sam's approach was brisker—and a hell of a lot more interesting.

The mother-in-law was snivelling down her nose. "Where is my son, Althea? Have you already managed to . . . distract him from his duties as host?"

Althea thought of several snappy remarks but again found herself in an awkward curtsy. "No, ma'am. I haven't seen him since—"

Since what? It was impossible to keep track of the convoluted framework. Since he rescued her? Married her? Raped her? Jared would never do such a thing, she amended sourly. No doubt he had kept her from being raped by one of the marauding highwaymen that accosted virgins. Considering Jared, it might have been more fun to be accosted . . .

"Well, Althea," the mother-in-law snorted in a well-bred voice, "you must feel most fortunate to have snared my son. He is, after all, the owner of this charming manor and of all the land from here to the cliffs. And you, a penniless orphan, destined to become a scullery maid—had not heaven intervened on your behalf."

Sam's mother was a cheery drunkard who was still producing babies on an annual basis. This one had probably produced Jared by virgin birth. Forget that; birth was messy. Jared had no doubt simply appeared one day, lisping French and nibbling cucumber sandwiches under his nanny's approving smile.

Althea swallowed an angry response. Fluttering her thick lashes, she murmured, "Yes, ma'am, I was most fortunate to have met your son. When my father died, leaving me a penniless orphan at the mercies of my unscrupulous uncle, I feared for my life." Melodrama, pure and nauseating. Why couldn't she have been a barmaid? A bit of slap and giggle in the shadows behind the stables, a feather bed to keep warm for a guy like Sam. But instead she had to hang around with the aristocracy. Snivellers and snorters, bah!

But there was no point in worrying about this Jared fellow. Maybe he was a Sam in disguise. Maybe chickens had lips, and the moon was made of green cheese. Maybe it was time

11

to start expecting the Easter bunny to show up with a bunch of purple eggs.

The mother-in-law person stood up imperiously and held a lace handkerchief to her nose. "I am going into the garden for a bit of fresh air," she announced. "Send Jared to me when he appears, Althea. I must speak to him; it is of the greatest importance."

Hmmm? Had the old bat noticed her repeated glances at the diamond broach? If she were to tattle to this Jared person, Althea might find herself scrubbing pots after all. It seemed prudent to assume the dutiful role.

"Please don't take a chill, Lady Excrutia," Althea said in a solicitous whine. "Shall I fetch a shawl for you from your dressing room? Allow me to bring it to you in the garden."

The dowager with the plumes beamed approvingly at Althea's meek posture. "Charming child, just charming. But look, here's Jared!"

Oh, hell. Althea tried to forget about the promised encounter in garden—for a few minutes anyway. Forcing herself into a semblance of pleased surprise, she lifted her eyes to meet those of the unknown Jared.

Oh, my God, she thought with a scowl. Another arrogant one. There went another bodice, ripped into shreds. Endless lovemaking, nothing but simmering frustration as the result. And those granite gray eyes boring into her, for God's sake! It was more than anyone should have to bear . . . it really was.

"Damnedest thing I've ever seen!" The lieutenant leaned against the kitchen counter, watching the body being wheeled out of the tiny office. For the first time in his career even the paramedics were subdued. The two men waited for the medical examiner to finish wiping the inky smudges off his hands, then crowded into the room. The desk was cluttered with notebooks, chewed pencil stubs, and an over-flowing ashtray. A lipstick-stained coffee cup lay on the floor in a dried brown puddle. A typewriter hummed softly, and with a snort the second of the plainclothes detectives leaned over to switch it off.

"How'd you discover the body?" the medical examiner asked. Like Lady Macbeth, he seemed obsessed with the invisible marks on his hands, rubbing them against each other nervously.

"The woman in the next apartment called the super. It seems the woman who lived here was a writer, and the neighbor was used to the sound of the typewriter clattering all day long. She told the super the last couple of days there was no sound, and it was driving her crazy," the first detective said.

The second snorted again. "If I lived next door to one of these writers, and had to listen to that noise all day, I might have strangled the broad myself. As it is, I have to listen to my wife screaming at the kids every night and—"

"Damnedest thing," the first repeated, shaking his head. "In twenty-nine years on the force, I've seen a lot of weird things—but I've never seen anyone strangled with a typewriter ribbon."

The medical examiner laughed. "As good as a wire or a rope, but a hell of a lot messier. All you have to do now is find someone with ink-stained hands."

The second detective was reading the titles of the paperback books on the shelf above the desk. "Look at this, Carl. Do you know what the victim wrote? Romance novels, by damn! You know the things: *Sweet Moonlight*, *The Towering Passion of Lady Bianca*, etc., etc."

"My wife reads that stuff," the first admitted. He shook his head. "I dunno why, though. Gimme a good ball game on television and a six-pack to keep me cool. That's my idea of romance—me, Budweiser, and the Yankees."

The medical examiner raised his hand in a farewell gesture. "I'll get back to you in a day or two, Carl. Don't waste your time reading the victim's books—unless you think the intellectuals of the world conspired to do her in!" Chuckling to himself, he left the two detectives exchanging glances.

"Naw, Carl," the second said, "don't get your hopes up. It was a prowler or something. Let's go talk to the doorman and the elevator operator."

The first sighed, thinking of the tedious interviews that would prove necessary, the trivial gossip that the neighbors would feel obliged to share, the dinner he would not have a chance to eat that night.

"Too bad it wasn't a suicide," he grumbled. "My wife always makes meatballs on Mondays and then goes bowling with a bunch of the girls. Good game on tonight."

"Then we'd have our note," the second added, pointing at a piece of paper sticking out of the typewriter. "But nobody, not even dippy romance writers, can strangle themselves. My money's on the neighbor; she's probably half-deaf from the noise. She just couldn't stand the sound of the typewriter any longer and went berserk. I would've."

"She's eighty-three," the first one said. He leaned over to read the manuscript page, then straightened up. "My wife will get a kick out of this, you know. Yours will, too. All women think this stuff is great—all the damned moonlight and wine and deep soulful stares! It spoils them for the real world, Marv."

"Yeah, my wife wanted me to take her out to dinner for her birthday. Hell, the babysitter drives a damn Mercedes! I can't see spending half a week's salary on fancy food."

"So what'd you do?" Carl asked as they went out the door

of the office and started for the living room.

The one named Marv shrugged his shoulders. "I brought home a real nice pizza."

Lady Althea wrapped her arms around Sam's stocky waist and snuggled against him, ignoring the black smudges on his back from her previous caresses. For a long time, the horse's rhythmic clops were the only sound on the road. The moon illuminated the trees on either side of them with a silver haze, and the light breeze had an earthy redolence. At last the horse and its two riders were gone into the darkness, although a faint giggle seemed to linger in the air.

Back at the cold and lifeless manor house, the ball was over. The nameless gentility had disappeared, the orchestra vanished, the vast room as quiet as a tomb. In the center of the room lay a body. Two arrogant eyes stared at the darkened chandelier, unblinking and glazed with faint surprise. Blood had long since coagulated on the gash across his neck.

There was more blood in the garden. The figure there had the same surprised expression, and a similar slash across the neck. The bosom no longer heaved, although it had the appearance of a mountain range arising from the manicured lawn. The surface of this alpine region was smooth, except for a tiny rip in its surface where a broach had been removed hastily and without regard for the crinoline fabric.

His majesty's guards remained puzzled by the scene for a few weeks, then dismissed it from their minds. One or two of the younger ones sometimes mentioned it over pints of ale in the new roadhouse, but the older officers usually ignored them. The barmaid, always full of throaty laughter and ready for a frolic, kept them more amused on the feather beds upstairs.

Too Much to Bare

"My husband is going to kill me," Marjorie announced. It was not the first time she'd suggested the possibility. Anne had lost count. "Oh, honey," Sylvia said soothingly, "it's not as if we're taking the merchandise home, or even having a chance to do more than study it from a respectable distance. Not that I wouldn't object, should the opportunity arise—if you know what I mean!"

The three other women at the table obligingly giggled at Sylvia's comment. Marjorie, already damp with perspiration in her rumpled polyester pantsuit, flapped a pudgy hand as if to dispel any lingering aura of naughtiness. "You are such a joker," she said. "I don't know how you think of these things."

"I would imagine it comes from hanging around outside the locker room," Bitsy said. Her eyes, heavily accented with mascara and undulating ribbons of blue and gray shadow, closed for a moment as a curtain of black hair fell across her face. She took a sip of beer, wrinkled her nose, and pushed aside her cup. A Christian in the Colosseum could not have looked less delighted.

"Better than hanging around inside," Sylvia said, "unless we're discussing some little jock's strap."

Anne busied herself replenishing their plastic cups with beer from the pitcher, keeping her face lowered in order to hide her expression. Sylvia's jokes were always crude. Most of the teachers at the school avoided the lounge whenever Sylvia

16

sailed in for coffee and conversation; Anne had discovered she preferred to stay in the library rather than listen to the barrage of gossip and off-color humor. A thermos of coffee sufficed. But tonight she found herself taking a certain pleasure in Sylvia's company. A certain pleasure, yes.

The Happy Hour Saloon was swelling with a large and raucous crowd. The music blared from omnipresent speakers, too loud and senseless for Anne's taste, forcing voices to compete in shrieks. The throbbing, repetitive beat seemed to stir the two hundred or so women, however, with promises of erotica, of good times to come. Lights flashed in a dizzying pattern that lacked discernible organization, changing faces from red to green to blue as if they were hapless chameleons. The tables were littered with cups, pitchers, ashtrays heaped with cigarette butts, and spreading wet circles that glittered like kisses as the lights swept across them.

"Isn't this a hoot?" Sylvia demanded of the table. "I went to one of these last year, and it was beyond my wildest imagination." She flung her blonde hair over her shoulder and studied the barnlike room with a complacent smile. "This crowd looks a lot worse. We are in for quite a time this evening, ladies. Quite a time."

Marjorie drained her cup and pushed herself to her feet. "If Hank's going to kill me, I might as well die happily. I'm going for another pitcher, after a trip to the can to powder my nose. Anyone else interested?"

Bitsy picked up her purse and tucked it under her arm. "I'm tempted to stay in the ladies' room until the show is over," she said acidly. "I cannot believe I'm actually here. I don't know why we let Sylvia coerce us into this low-class display of vulgarity, although I can understand why it might appeal to her."

Waggling a finger at her, Sylvia said, "It's time you saw

something more exciting than a kindergarten classroom, my dear. You're beginning to look like one of your five-year-olds."

Bitsy pursed her lips into a pout. "This whole thing is nauseating. I should have stayed at my apartment and washed my hair. Let's go, Marjorie. The ladies' room is probably filthy, but I'm not accustomed to beer. Scotch is less fattening, and so much more civilized than this swill."

Once Marjorie and Bitsy found a path through the crowd of women and vanished around the far corner of the bar, Anne gazed across the table. "I can't believe I'm here either. It's a good thing Paul's out at the cabin this weekend. Maybe by Sunday night I'll have worked up enough courage to tell him about it." Or perhaps she might whisper it in his ear, while he lay in a coffin at the funeral home. Even tell him she'd changed her mind about the divorce—he could file it in hell or wherever he ended up. She bit her lip to hide a quick smile. The irony was delicious.

"What's he doing at the lake?" Sylvia asked. She lit a cigarette and inhaled deeply.

"He said he had a lot of work to do and wanted to put fifty miles between himself and a telephone. He's been under such stress lately; I hope he has a chance to relax."

"You still don't have a telephone out there? God, Anne, it's halfway to the end of the world."

"That's why Paul bought it. I don't really enjoy staying there, but he seems to find ways to amuse himself. I haven't been there in months." She crossed her fingers in her lap. She'd been there two days ago, when she'd called in sick and then taken a little field trip, although hardly in a fat yellow school bus. "He asked if I would drive up this weekend. I told him I absolutely had to finish the semester inventory at the library, but that's only partly true. In all honesty, he's been in a rotten mood for several months, and I have no desire to be cooped up with him in the middle of the woods."

"Maybe he's in mid-life crisis. My ex went crazy when he hit forty. His shrink said he'd get over it, but I divorced the bastard on general principle. When men get to that age, they don't seem to know what they want—unless it's a combination of cuddle and sizzle."

"He's not having an affair," Anne replied firmly. "Paul is much too straitlaced to do anything to threaten his stuffy law practice. I do wish he didn't have to work so hard; we haven't had a proper dinner in three months." He had, though. She'd opened the bill from the credit card company. Lots of restaurants, but she hadn't been invited for any cozy little dinners with elegant wine. She'd been at home, putting gourmet meals down the garbage disposal.

"The old working-late-at-the-office bit?" Sylvia raised two penciled eyebrows. "Well, if you're not going to worry about it, then neither am I, but I think you'd better keep an eye on him. Paul's an attractive man, and he knows it. Did you hear what happened this morning in the teachers' lounge when the toilet backed up?"

Anne forced a smile as Sylvia began to relate a bit of gossip that would, without a doubt, end on a crude bark of laughter. The music drowned out a major part of the story, but she didn't care. Sylvia didn't require more than a superficially attentive audience. The bitch. So she was surprised there was no telephone at the cabin. As if she didn't know. Of course what she and Paul did at the cabin didn't require a telephone—only a mattress. Or any flat surface, for that matter. Her smile wavered, but she tightened her jaw and willed it into obedience.

"Hank is going to kill me," Marjorie said as she set the pitcher on the table and sat down beside Anne. "So when do we see the boys?"

Sylvia consulted her watch. "In about ten minutes, I would guess. The management wants to give all of us time to drink ourselves into a cheerful mood."

Bitsy slipped in next to Sylvia and glared at the rowdier elements of the crowd. "*Cheerful* is hardly the adjective, Sylvia. Nasty and foulmouthed might be closer to the truth. Where do all these women come from? I've never seen so many women about to burst out of their jeans or pop buttons off their blouses." She shifted her eyes to Sylvia's ample chest, which was distorting a field of silk flowers.

"This isn't a Sunday prayer meeting," Sylvia said, grinning. "Now you and Marjorie could sneak in the back door of the church if you wanted to, but Anne and I came to have fun. Isn't that right, Anne?"

"Oh, yes," Anne murmured. Oh, no, she added to herself as she once again held in a smile. She had come to put the plan in motion. Sylvia needed to know where Paul was, and how lonely he might be for his cooperative slut. She decided to reiterate the information once again, just in case Sylvia had missed it. "You should have convinced Hank to go fishing with Paul, Marjorie. The poor baby's out at the cabin all by himself for the entire weekend, with no one to entertain him. And he's been acting very odd these last three or four months; I'm worried he might be on the edge of a nervous breakdown."

"So worried that you felt obliged to come to this horrid show instead of bothering to be with him?" Bitsy said coolly.

Anne winced as she struggled to hide a flicker of irritation. It was, she lectured herself, an opening to produce her alibi, even if it had been provided in a self-righteous tone of voice. "He told me he preferred to be alone, Bitsy, and I can't go to the cabin this weekend, in any case. I'm going to spend the next two days locked in the library with Bev to do the semester inventory. We agreed we'd work until midnight Saturday and Sunday if we had to, and send out for sandwiches. Paul will enjoy a chance for relaxation and total solitude."

"Total solitude?" Sylvia echoed, laughing. "Maybe he's having an affair with some nubile specimen of wildlife."

"That's not a very nice thing to say," Bitsy said. "Just because your husband chased every skirt in town doesn't mean that—"

"Paul's banging a raccoon? My ex would have; he banged everything that breathed." Sylvia laughed again, then finished her beer and lit another cigarette from the smoldering butt in her hand. Next to her, Bitsy coughed in complaint and pointedly fanned the air with her hand. Anne covertly studied Sylvia's face, searching for some sign that the blonde's thoughts were centered on the poor lonely husband in the conveniently remote cabin.

Marjorie had managed to mention her impending demise three more times before the music abruptly stopped. A middle-aged man in a pale blue tuxedo bounded onto the stage, a microphone in one hand. The crowd quieted in expectation, as did the four women at the table next to the stage.

"Are you ready?" the man demanded.

"Yes!" the women squealed.

"Are you ready?" he again demanded, leering into what must have resembled a murky aquarium of multicolored faces.

The crowd responded with increased enthusiasm. The ritual continued for several minutes as the emcee warmed up the audience. Anne could not bring herself to join the frenzied promises that she was indeed ready, even though, at a more essential level, the decision had been reached and the plan already set in motion. This man seemed too manipulative to merit response, too crassly chauvinistic—too much like Paul. Sylvia had no such reservations, of course. Marjorie was mouthing the sentiments of the crowd and clapping; Bitsy stared at the tabletop as if she were judging kindergarten finger paintings for potential van Goghs.

"Do you want to meet the men?" the emcee howled. The crowd howled that they most definitely did. The emcee mopped his forehead, assured them that they would in one teeny minute, but first they were going to have the opportunity to order one more round of drinks. Waving good-bye, he bounded off the stage and the music rose to fill the void.

Sylvia began to dig through her purse. "Damn it, I just had that prescription refilled last week," she said as she piled the contents on the table. "Tranquilizers aren't cheap."

But the gaunt blonde divorcée was, Anne thought. Too bad she couldn't find her pills, but they had been removed earlier in the week, when Sylvia had negligently left her purse in the lounge. They were a part of the plan, a major part of the plan that would end with a wonderfully melodramatic climax. The other climaxes would occur earlier—in the bed, under the kitchen table, wherever the two opted to indulge their carnal drives.

She really didn't care anymore. Her marriage was a farce, as silly and shallow as the night's entertainment. It would be over by Sunday, and she would be free from Paul's overbearing hypocrisy and Sylvia's treacherous avowals of friendship. A colleague had told her about seeing the two of them at a restaurant. Although the news had initially paralyzed her, she had begun within a matter of days to devise the plan. It had taken several weeks to perfect it; the invitation from Sylvia to the male revue had seemed such a lovely, ironic time for the countdown to begin.

"You really shouldn't mix barbiturates with alcohol. The combination can be lethal," she said, hoping she sounded properly concerned. The advice was based on many hours of research, after all, done while sipping coffee from her thermos. An elementary school library held so many fascinating books and magazines. From both sides of the table, Bitsy and Marjorie nodded their agreement.

Sylvia shrugged and began to cram things back in her purse. "It'd take a handful of the things to do any damage. I must have left them in the bathroom at home, or in another purse. Damnation, I feel a really ghastly tension headache coming on; I'll have to drown it in beer."

Just wait, Anne added under her breath. By Sunday night, Sylvia and Paul were going to be far past the point of feeling anything. The bottle was in the liquor cabinet at the cabin, a brand she knew Paul always kept well stocked. The drifting sediment at the bottom would not prevent the contents from being savored, and the effects would take several hours to be felt. By then, it would be much too late.

Sunday night, or perhaps Monday morning, she would telephone the sheriff's department and in a worried, wifely voice ask them to check the cabin. The suicide note she had typed on Paul's typewriter would be found in her bedside drawer, his illegible signature scrawled across the bottom. It was really quite nicely written, with pained admissions that he could no longer bear a life without Sylvia, that he had taken her pills earlier in the week so they could gently pass away in each other's arms. A bittersweet postscript to his wife, begging her forgiveness. She suspected she would shed a few tears when the police showed it to her. Her friends would all assure her that he had had a nervous breakdown, that he hadn't known what he was writing. They would be right, but she wouldn't tell them that.

"Oh, my lord," whispered Marjorie. "Hank really is going to kill me if I have to call him for bail."

Anne yanked her thoughts to the present moment and turned to the stage. A young man had appeared, dressed in a police uniform. His face was stern as he slapped a billy club across his palm. She felt as if it were slamming against her abdomen. Had Paul found the note and realized what she had arranged for the lovebirds?

"I should arrest all of you," he said, scowling as his eyes flitted around the room. "Run you in, book you, and take you to a cold, dark cell. Fling you across the cot and interrogate you until you beg for mercy. Is that what you want me to do?"

"No," screamed a voice from the crowd. "Take it off!"

His mouth softened; dimples appeared in his cheeks. "Is that what you want me to do?" he demanded of the crowd.

"Take it off!"

Like a prairie dog, the emcee popped up on the platform at the back of the stage. "Do you want Policeman Dick to take it off? You'll have to tell him what you want!"

"Take it off!" the crowd howled in unified frenzy.

The music began to pulsate as the young man toyed with the top button of his shirt, his hips synchronized with the beat. The crowd roared their approval. Sylvia leaned forward and said, "You turned absolutely white, Anne. Did you think he was a real cop?"

Anne kept her eyes on the man in the middle of the stage. "Don't be absurd, Sylvia. I don't have a guilty conscience," she said distractedly. The first button was undone, and the graceful fingers had moved down one tantalizing inch. A few curly chest hairs were visible now; she felt a sudden urge to dash onto the stage and brush her hand across them. "Is he going to take it all off?"

"I can't believe you said that," Bitsy sniffed. "I think this is disgusting."

Anne had expected to feel the same way, but now, with the

darling young blond man who looked so wholesome, so boyish and innocent and pleased with the response from the crowd—it wasn't disgusting. It was very, very interesting.

Marjorie put her cup down, her eyes wide and her mouth slightly agape. "I don't think it's disgusting," she said in a hollow voice.

Bitsy leaned back in the chair and crossed her arms. "The three of you are slobbering like dogs."

Anne barely heard the condemnation from across the table. Policeman Dick was easing out of his shirt, letting each sleeve slide down his arm so slowly she could feel the ripple of his biceps, the hard turn of his elbows, the soft skin of his forearm, the mounded base of his hand, the long, delicate fingers. She heard herself exhale as the khaki shirt fell to the floor.

His hips still moving with the music, the man flexed his arms and turned slowly so the women could appreciate his flat stomach and broad shoulders. He swaggered across the stage to Anne's table and curled his hands behind Sylvia's neck.

"Unbuckle my belt or I'll run you in," he said, smiling to take the menace from his facetious threat. He noticed Anne's stunned expression and winked at her, sharing the joke in an oddly private message.

"You can run me in anytime you want!" Sylvia smirked as she fumbled with the buckle of his belt. Beside her, Bitsy was almost invisible below the table. Her face was stony, and her mouth a pinched ring of scandalized disapproval.

When the buckle was freed, the man backed away to tease the crowd with his jutting pelvis and bare chest. His trousers began to slide down his hips. Again Anne could feel his skin, now so taut with smooth, muscular slopes. It's been such a long time, she thought, panicked by the intensity of her reaction. If only Paul hadn't lost interest when he began the affair with Sylvia . . . It was his fault she was responding like a silly, breathless, hormone-driven adolescent.

The uniform was off now; only a small triangle of khaki fabric acknowledged the limits of legality. The young man, Policeman Dick, she amended with a faint smile—began to dance with increased insistence, turning often so that all the women could have an equal opportunity to admire that which deserved admiration. The colored lights flashed across his body in silken hues, shadows to be stroked to find their depth.

As he moved toward the table, Sylvia creased a dollar bill and waved it over Anne's head. "Over here!" she called.

Perplexed, Anne frowned across the table. When Sylvia grinned and pointed, she turned back to see the young man dancing directly in front of her. Blue eyes crinkled in amusement. The dimples back again. And the wondrously unclad body, close enough that she could see the faint sheen of sweat. Feathery blond hair. Muscles that swooped like snow-covered hills. Hard thighs. The mysterious khaki bulge.

Despite the sudden grip of numbness, a wave of Novocain that flooded her chest and froze her lungs, she felt the dollar bill in her hand. The man slowly pulled her to her feet. All around them, women were bellowing in approval, their hands banging the tabletops and their feet pounding the floor. The music seemed to grow louder, a primitive command from a wild and unknown place. The young man curled a finger for Anne to move closer to him. Then, before she could consider her actions, she found herself sliding the bill under the narrow strap that supported his only item of clothing. Her fingers brushed his skin. A baby's skin.

He leaned down and caught her head in his hands. His deliberate kiss caught her by surprise, stunned her into acquiescence, and then, as his lips lingered, into unintentional cooperation. When she felt as if she were losing herself in a tunnel of heat, he eased away and met her eyes. After another disturbing wink, he danced away to collect the dollar bills that now waved like pennants all over the room.

"Sit down!" Bitsy snapped. "Everyone's staring at you. I want you to know that I am simply disgusted with you, Anne. And both of you too," she added to Sylvia and Marjorie. "I've had more of this than I can bear. I'm going home."

Anne wiggled her hand in farewell, but she could not unlock her eyes from the young blond dancer. Coals had been lit deep within her; they flamed and glowed, painfully. Her body ached for him. And he seemed to remain aware of her even as he accepted dollars and gave kisses to the screaming women crowding the edge of the stage.

Then, with a dimpled smile and a wink she felt was hers, he left the stage. The emcee introduced a dark-haired young man in a sequined cape, who began to produce gyrations with his hips as he paraded around the stage.

Anne looked at the dressing-room door in one corner of the room. "Will he be back?" she asked Sylvia.

"Probably. I could see you liked what you saw, Anne. You'd better not tell Paul too much about this when he gets home Sunday. He may not approve of his wife kissing a male stripper."

Marjorie sighed. "What was it like, Anne?"

"Just a kiss." But such a kiss. Soft lips and a faint hint of af-ter-shave. A kiss more innocent than a high-school sweetheart's, but promising more than any boy could offer. A cherub without a robe. Every mother's son, every woman's lover. The ache increased until she felt as if she might slip into a fantasy of such erotic delight that she would never willingly return.

"Looks like our Annie is in love," Sylvia said. She pulled

out another dollar bill and waved it over Marjorie's head. "Let's see if we can share the good fortune."

While Marjorie laughingly protested and tried to hide, Anne forced herself to watch the man on stage, who was nearing the same state of undress his predecessor had achieved. It did nothing to distract her from the memory of the kiss. She was startled when a waiter tapped her on the shoulder and handed her a folded note. He nodded in the direction of the dressing-room door and left.

Would she wait for "D" after the show?

There was a bit more, but she could hardly see the written letters. Would she? Did she dare? Anne Carter, wife of a lawyer, respected librarian at the neighborhood elementary school, gracious hostess for countless cocktail parties and elegant buffets designed to charm Paul's clients, was hardly the sort to hang around stage doors for male . . . dancers, dimples or not. She had never . . . done such a thing. It was . . . unthinkable. She simply . . . couldn't.

Men continued to dance on the stage. Dollars were waved; women were kissed and convinced not to pull too strenuously on the elastic straps that kept the show marginally legal.

Anne watched it all, sipping beer that had no taste, clapping to music that had no beat, hearing catcalls that had no meaning. Could she be in the blond man's arms while her husband and his mistress unwittingly poisoned themselves with the bottle she had left at the cabin?

Dick appeared during the second half of the show, this time dressed in tight pants and a shirt with flowing sleeves. As he danced at the table next to hers, Anne caught his questioning smile. She nodded. There really was no choice.

She survived the rest of the show, counting the minutes until the room would clear and he would emerge from the dressing room. At last, after a finale of flesh, the emcee thanked the crowd and told them when his show would return to the Happy Hour Saloon. Once the stage was empty, most of the women started for the exits, babbling excitedly about the relative merits of each performer.

"Hank's going to kill me," Marjorie said happily, then pulled herself out of her chair and left.

Anne glanced at Sylvia. "Don't you have a date?" she asked. At a cabin, with a bottle of scotch and a husband who had strayed too far to ever merit forgiveness. She wanted it to be done.

"I do, and here he comes," Sylvia said, putting her cigarette case in her purse. "But what about you? This is hardly the place for librarians to sit alone and drink beer."

"He's here?" He couldn't be here—he was at the cabin.

Sylvia waved to a man waiting near the door. "My accountant, actually. I've been after him since April, because he saved me an absolute fortune on my taxes this year. If he can get me a refund next year, I may break down and marry him."

"Your accountant?"

"Somebody has to do my taxes. What's wrong with you?"

"I thought—I thought you and Paul—" Anne gasped through a suddenly constricted throat.

"Not me, Annie. Your husband's attractive, but he's more interested in the younger set. Or those who teach them." Sylvia looked at the chair beside her, where Bitsy had sat until she had made the indignant exit. "You'd better ask Paul about his late nights at the office. I didn't want to say anything, but Bitsy's been awfully concerned the last few months about your schedule."

"Bitsy?" All she could manage was a croak. It couldn't be; the suicide note named Sylvia—not Bitsy. Her literary masterpiece would fool no one, not with the wrong name. The police would realize Paul hadn't written it. They would show

29

it to her, ask her if she had been to the cabin lately, demand to know if she had taken barbiturates from Sylvia's purse and left the empty vial under the note in the night table drawer. She hadn't worried about fingerprints, or mud on her tires, or any such trivial details. The investigation wouldn't have gone that far. The plan was too good.

She searched wildly for a way to prove Sylvia wrong, to catch her in some horridly devious lie. "But you had dinner with him!"

"He wanted to ask me how I thought you'd react to a divorce," Sylvia said gently. "He made me swear not to mention it to you. It's been Bitsy all along."

"No, it can't be. It can't be Bitsy." She rubbed her face, unable to believe it. "You're lying."

"Sorry to be the one to tell you," Sylvia said as she stood up. "I have to run; my gentleman friend's waiting to hear about the strippers. Don't stay here too long."

As Sylvia left, Anne felt her stomach grow cold with fear. Bitsy had left more than an hour ago, no doubt on her way to the rendezvous Anne herself had suggested. There was no way to telephone Paul, to tell him that the scotch was filled with barbiturates, that she would no longer contest a divorce if he would quietly pour the bottle down the drain and tear up the damning suicide note.

Perhaps she could drive up there in time to stop them from consuming too much of the scotch. The two wouldn't start on the bottle immediately. Surely they'd spend a few minutes greeting each other, and Bitsy would relish telling Paul all the details of the vulgarity to which she'd been exposed. Tell him how his wife had actually kissed a stripper. Offer righteous comments about the cheapness of the bar and the ill-bred behavior of the spectators.

Yes, she had time to rush to the cabin and prevent the

scotch from carrying out its lethal assignment. If she left at once. She grabbed her purse and shoved back her chair. She had enough gas in her car; the route to the cabin was still fresh in her mind. She'd have to confront the two and admit what she'd done, but maybe—

"I'm glad you waited for me," a voice murmured in her ear. A hand touched her elbow and pulled her back down to her chair. "You're the sexiest woman I've ever seen, with your lovely dark hair and little-girl eyes."

"I—I have to leave. Now."

His hand tightened around her elbow, sending a flow of electricity up her arm. As disappointment crossed his face, she said, "An errand has come up, something I really and truly have to do. I'm sorry. I'd like to stay for a drink, but I have to go. Right now. There isn't much time. I'm sorry."

"We leave in the morning and won't be through here for at least six months," he said with a sigh, his blue eyes lowered. "I was very excited about getting to know you, if only for one night. I couldn't believe you'd actually waited for me, but I suppose you've changed your mind." He looked up with a wistful smile. "I wanted to make you happy this one night."

Anne took a deep breath as she studied the sweep of his eyelashes, the faint frown that managed to provoke his dimples, the haze of moisture on his neck from a hurried shower. She knew what his shirt and jeans covered, and she could envision what the khaki triangle had hidden. This—or a frantic drive down a dark, rutted road to the cabin to save two treacherous people from a fate they well deserved?

As the lights swept across the room, her face changed from red to blue to green. "The errand's not all that important," she said in a soft, slow voice.

Death in Bloom

"The thing is," Ruby Bee announced before Estelle could once again start in squawking like a bluejay, which, for the record, she'd been doing for the last ten minutes, give or take, "Beryl makes superior apple pies. I'm thinking she might be inclined to share her secret. That's why we're doing this."

Estelle adjusted the rearview mirror and made sure her beehive of red hair was securely pinned and ready to withstand anything short of hurricane-strength winds. "I still don't see why the both of us should close up shop and go over to drink coffee, eat a piece of pie, and be so bored we're gonna wish we'd joined a book club. Beryl's pies take the blue ribbon every year at the county fair. That doesn't mean I want to spend an hour admiring her begonias and zucchinis."

Ruby Bee sighed as she drove up County 103. "Did you hear what I said, Estelle? Beryl's apple pies have a certain something. I've been trying to figure out for most of thirty years what her secret is. Times I think it's an extra dash of nutmeg or cinnamon, and then I think it must be ginger. I realize this sounds odd, but there are nights I toss and turn until dawn."

"Odd," Estelle echoed in a voice meant to irritate Ruby Bee, which it most certainly did. "You're saying you can't sleep on account of Beryl Blanchard winning the blue ribbon at the county fair every year on account of ginger? I spend a lot more hours worrying if the IRS will come after me—or if a slobbering serial killer will bust into my house."

Ruby Bee turned up the gravel driveway to Beryl's house. "I suspect you're losing sleep over something less likely than Idalupino Buchanon's face appearing on the cover of *People* magazine. We're gonna have pie and coffee, spend a few minutes with Buck, and dutifully admire the garden. If Beryl wants to give me her secret recipe, so be it. If not, no one has yet dared to criticize the apple pie I serve at the bar and grill."

"Not if they want to live to see the dawning of another day," Estelle muttered, then looked at the weedy pasture as Ruby Bee's car bounced up the rutted driveway. The house was, at best, serviceable. The garden, on the other hand, was enough to suck the breath out of any soul's body. Yellows and reds and fuchsias and oranges and pinks and purples—every glorious color on the spectrum—exploded from all sides. Blooms stretched to meet the sun; others cascaded like iridescent waterfalls.

"You got to admit," Ruby Bee said solemnly, "that this is something. Beryl may not be on the top of my list of favorite people, but you'd almost think she gets seed catalogs direct from the Garden of Eden."

"Then we'd better keep an eye out for the serpent," Estelle said as she unbuckled her seat belt.

Ruby Bee frowned but held her peace as they got out of the car. Maggody was a quiet little town most of the time, although things seemed to keep happening. Today, however, held no undertones of menace. Arly, who just happened to be the chief of police as well as Ruby Bee's daughter, had last been seen napping at her desk at the two-room police department, most likely dreaming of an escape to a somewhat more invigorating lifestyle that precluded moonshiners and dim-witted locals. There were no banks in Maggody, so the odds of a robbery-in-progress were limited. Anyone who imprudently ran the sole stoplight was in luck for the next hour or so.

"Ruby Bee, Estelle!" shrieked Beryl as she arose from a bed of exceedingly tall purple perennials. "I am delighted that you came! This is such a treat for me. So few people drop by these days. Buck and Sylvie are as excited as I am."

Ruby Bee pasted on a smile. "You know I'm always in the mood for pie and coffee. How's Buck doing?"

Beryl, whose gray hair held a tint of the same purple as the flowers surrounding her, wiped her face on her shirt cuff, leaving a smudge of dirt on her otherwise properly schoolmarmish features. "The wheelchair's not been easy for him, but he knows he has to be careful. He gets all these crazy ideas about European tours and African safaris and how we can travel to all these places like he never had the heart surgery. Sylvie's forever bringing home brochures about cruises and the like. Silliness! You name another place on earth more beautiful than where we're standing." She spread her arms as if embracing nature in its entirety. "What more could anyone want?"

"Something more exciting than Maggody," Buck said as he wheeled onto the porch. "I just want to go while we can. A few years from now, maybe I'll be content to sit here, watching the turkey vultures circle in on me. I was in the United States Navy, as you ladies must know. We had shore leave in Athens and Naples and a whole lot of fascinating places. I keep trying to persuade Beryl here to take a gander at them while we can. I drank a little ouzo in my time, I did, and climbed to the very rim of Vesuvius. One night when I was on the Isle of Capri—"

"We don't have any reason to travel," Beryl cut in. "We've got a vegetable garden, an orchard ripe with peaches and apples, and flowers that could dazzle a blind man. Why would I want to go to some foreign place where I'm likely to

get a disease? Home is where you get meat loaf, mashed potatoes, and apple pie."

Buck made a gesture that indicated he'd heard the argument more times than he could count. "Just thought I'd mention it," he said darkly as he spun around and went inside.

"He doing okay otherwise?" asked Ruby Bee.

Beryl shrugged as she picked up a muddy trowel and
stacked together several empty plastic pots. "He'd do better if
he did away with all his foolish ideas about traveling. Taking
care of the property is a full-time job, what with planting in
the spring, tending in the summer, harvesting in the fall, and
pruning and planning in the winter. It's not like Sylvie could
step in for even a week or two. I'd be terrified that she'd make
such a mess of everything that it'd take me two or three years
to recover."

"I just love your hollyhocks," Estelle said tactfully.

"Me, too," Beryl said. "Now let's go inside for pie and
coffee, and then we'll have a nice stroll. I'm particularly
pleased with the dianthus along the back fence. It has a wonderful cinnamon scent."

Ruby Bee smiled with all the subtlety of a fox teetering on
the henhouse roof. "Speaking of cinnamon, Beryl . . ."

They went into the house. The living room was dark and
sparse, what with the drapes drawn and the wood floor unadorned. The obligatory crocheted doilies were spread across
the arms of the sofa. Photographs of dyspeptic ancestors
glowered from the walls. Tables that might have held vases of
nature's glories were bare, with the exception of the odd
crystal dish that most likely had arrived as a wedding present
and had never since held so much as a mint. The only book in
sight was a family Bible.

"Sylvie!" Beryl called as they went down the hall. "We
have company. I hope you're not sulking in your room." She

35

lowered her voice and looked back at Ruby Bee and Estelle. "Sylvie's not always fit for company. She did insist on baking the apple pie this morning, though."

The baker under discussion trudged into the kitchen. She was thick, pale, somewhat sallow, and clearly unhappy. "You didn't mention company, Ma."

Ruby Bee managed a smile. "And how are you doing these days, Sylvie? Still attending the community college in Farberville?"

"No," Sylvie muttered. "I did for a year, but now I'm here, taking care of things. Maybe down the road I can get some kind of degree." She put on an apron and began to shove pots and pans into the gray dishwasher in the sink. "How's Arly doing?"

"Real fine," Ruby Bee said, looking at Estelle for help. A bullfrog caught in a spotlight might have appeared less panicky.

"Yeah, real fine," said Estelle. "Why, Arly's just happy as a hog in a wallow. I'm sure she'd like to be out and about with men of an acceptable persuasion, but she's willing to settle for a grilled cheese sandwich and happy hour at the bar and grill. How about you, Sylvie? You ever think about coming by for a beer? Things start jumping on Friday afternoons."

Rather than responding, Sylvie grimly set a pie on the dinette. "Coffee'll be ready in a minute," she said, then disappeared down the hallway.

Beryl sighed. "I just don't know what to do with that girl. I've made it clear she can take a class or two at the community college, as long as she can work around Buck's needs. I'm just not strong enough to deal with him. I can't help him in or out of his chair, or see to his basic needs in certain matters. I want you to know I've tried, Ruby Bee and Estelle; the spirit is willing, but . . ."

"How about I pour the coffee?" Ruby Bee said. She waited until Beryl nodded, then found cups and saucers in a cabinet and filled each cup. "Shall I cut the pie?"

Beryl sighed. "These days, the complaints are enough to wear me out. Sylvie acts like we should find a way to pay a private nurse to see to Buck, but we can't. He spends his days whining about trips to foreign places. He needs the wheelchair, for pity's sake. I can't see myself lugging it up the gangplank of a ship or through the streets of some nasty place like Rome. I've been told that men"—her voice dropped to a whisper—"urinate in the streets. Can you imagine?"

"What about a cruise?" said Estelle as she accepted a plate from Ruby Bee. "Seems like there'd be one that caters to folks with disabilities. If Sylvie went along, you could visit some exotic ports and Buck might feel better."

"Some of the brochures say they do," Beryl said, "but most likely all they offer is wide bathroom doors. Besides, who'd look after my hybrid tea roses and prune the flowering crab apples? My garden means everything to me. I can't leave it to amateurs."

Ruby Bee was trying to come up with a rebuttal as she took a bite of the blue-ribbon pie. It was not easy to swallow. "A bit tart," she mumbled.

"I'd say so!" Beryl banged down her fork. "Sylvie! You march yourself in here right now, young lady. Here I invited guests for a nice dessert! This pie could pucker a face inside out. I'm so embarrassed I could just crawl under the table. I would never have served this if . . ."

Sylvie came into the kitchen. "Sorry, Mother. We ran out of sugar, and I thought I could adjust the recipe with honey. We've got some oatmeal cookies in the freezer. Maybe I can—"

Beryl rose with the menace of a summer squall. "That's

37

quite enough, Sylvie. Give your father his bath, then remain in your room until I call for you."

"Now, Beryl," said Estelle, "it isn't like this was submitted to the committee at the county fair. All of us have substituted ingredients on occasion, although I can tell you molasses and Karo syrup just don't—"

"Shall we go outside?" Beryl said coldly.

Ruby Bee could tell it was not the moment to broach the most delicate topic of ginger versus an extra pinch of cinnamon. "It isn't that bad," she said to Sylvie, who was hovering in the doorway with a very peculiar look on her face. "The crust is very flaky and light, and nicely browned. Sometimes, mine are so soggy I feel like I plucked 'em out of a swamp."

Sylvie stared at her mother. "If I'd known we were expecting company, I would have tried more honey."

"Be sure to give your father's back a good scrub," Beryl said. She went across the kitchen, picked up a plastic bottle, and squirted cream into her palm. "I never go outside without a good slathering of sunscreen. We can't be too careful about skin cancer, can we?" Without waiting for a response, she began to apply it to her face, neck, and bare forearms.

Ruby Bee gave Estelle a hard look, then said, "We can't stay for long, Beryl. I'm supposed to be open for lunch, and I believe Estelle has an appointment before too long."

"That's right," Estelle said brightly. "Elsie McMay gets mighty testy if I keep her waiting for so much as a butterfly's flitter. We'll just take a quick gander at your garden and be on our way."

Beryl finished rubbing the lotion onto her skin. "Sylvie, you get busy with your duties. Tell your father I'll be in to see to his lunch after I've cut back the verbena. There are times when it feels like I'm the only person in this family able to take responsibility. You might as well have made that pie with green persimmons."

Ruby Bee gazed longingly at her car as they went outside. In a few minutes, she assured herself, she and Estelle could bounce down the driveway and turn on County 103. Not even the most delectable apple pie this side of heaven could warrant putting up with Beryl Blanchard and her mean-spirited tongue. The pie might have needed more honey, but Beryl needed an infusion.

Buck was seated in his wheelchair on the far corner of the porch. "Leaving so soon?" he called.

Ruby Bee sat down on a wicker chair beside him. "I was thinking how much I'd like to hear about your adventures in Naples and Athens," she said, wishing she had the gumption to grab his hand but keenly aware of Beryl's glare. "I'll bet you have all sorts of souvenirs and trinkets from your Navy days. Would you mind if I came by at another time?"

"If it works out," said Buck. "I may be gone."

She couldn't stop herself from clasping his bony arm. "Now, Buck, it can't be that bad. Beryl's feeding you a healthy diet of fresh fruits and vegetables. You're as nice and pink as"—she waved vaguely at the yard—"those blossoms over by the gate. Once you get back your strength, why, you might just be arm-wrasslin' at the bar and grill come Friday night. I seem to recollect you were pretty darn good at it once upon a time."

Beryl loomed over them. "Before he got sick, there was a lot of things he could do. Now all he's good for is sitting and complaining. Estelle's around back, looking at the dianthus. You want to see them?"

Sylvie came out of the front door. "There's something I should tell you, Ma."

"I don't want to hear one more word from you, young

lady," said Beryl. "You just take your father in and see to him, then go to your room and read your Bible until I call you. See if you can find any recipes using milk and honey."

"I'm warning you—you should hear me out."

Beryl's cheeks turned red. "Maybe I'll hear you out of house and home if you don't obey me. If I find so much as a single travel brochure on the table when I come back inside, I'll pack your bags myself and throw them at the end of the driveway. As for your father, he can learn to wear diapers and suck soup through a straw. Do you understand?"

Sylvie grabbed the handles of Buck's wheelchair and took him into the house. Ruby Bee was too appalled to do more than follow Beryl down the steps to the yard.

Beryl stopped at a trellis covered with sweet-scented, creamy blossoms. "This is an antique variety of honeysuckle called Serotina that blooms all summer. In the fall, it will be laden with lovely red berries that draw in our feathered friends. We are all nature's guardians, are we not? As opposed as I am to disorganization, I allow the butterfly weed just beyond the fence to thrive in order to nurture our winged visitors."

Ruby Bee was steeling herself to make a remark about nurturing those a mite closer to home when she saw a yellow jacket light on Beryl's arm. "You got another friend," she said, pointing.

Beryl flicked it off. "They never bother me. Out here in the splendors of . . ." She stopped to flick off another one. "Why, I haven't been stung since . . ."

"Take it easy," advised Ruby Bee, backing away. "Don't slap at 'em."

Beryl was staring in horror as several more yellow jackets began to crawl up her arm. "I'm allergic to them. Up until three years ago, I didn't know I was, but then I got stung and had to be taken to the emergency room. Why are they doing this? Make them go away!" She gasped as one lit on her cheek. "Away!"

Ruby Bee had no idea what she was supposed to do. "Don't make any sudden moves. They're just—"

"What?" shrieked Beryl as several more alit.

Estelle came dashing around the corner. "What in tarnation's wrong?"

"She must have disturbed a nest," Ruby Bee said, still not willing to move in any closer. "All they're doing is investigating thus far. As long as she doesn't . . ."

Beryl began to slap at her arms. "What are they doing? Why won't they leave me alone?" She ducked her head and stumbled backward. "Make them go away! Oh my Gawd! I've been stung! Get these things off me!"

"What should I do?" demanded Ruby Bee. "Call for an ambulance?"

"Do you have one of those kits?" Estelle said, grabbing Beryl's arm despite the yellow jackets descending like ants at a picnic. "Can you give yourself a shot?"

Beryl fell onto the grass. "Kit's in the refrigerator." Her voice thickened. "Need it now."

Estelle nodded. "I'll get it right away. You just rest easy for a minute."

"I can barely breathe," Beryl gasped. She rolled over and weakly attempted to brush the yellow jackets off her face and arms. "Help me!"

Estelle ran into the kitchen and jerked open the refrigerator door. A carton of milk, a covered dish with leftover pot roast, a bowl of green beans. "Sylvie!" she called as she pawed through bowls. "Where's the kit?"

"Kit?" said Sylvie as she came into the kitchen, rubbing her eyes and yawning.

41

"Your mother has been stung!"

Sylvie paused. "Oh, dear."

"She says there's a kit in the refrigerator!"

"Then let's have a look, shall we?" Sylvie opened the refrigerator door, pondered the contents, and then closed it. "No, I don't see any kit. Why don't you ask Mother which shelf she put it on?"

Estelle went back to the yard, where she found Ruby Bee twisting her hands. Beryl was still, white, and to be real blunt, as dead as a doornail. "I don't know if this so-called kit might have helped, but I feel like we should have done something," she said as she stared down at Beryl's body. Yellow jackets seemed to be feasting on her as if she were a crumb of cake at a Sunday school picnic. "You'd almost think . . ."

"When they collect the body," Ruby Bee mused, "ain't nobody going to test her skin. She was allergic to bee stings. She went into shock, and she died before she could give herself a shot. Yellow jackets are nasty critters. When riled, they attack. They're a sight smaller than hornets, but they're meaner and more willing to attack."

"Why did they?" asked Sylvie as she sank down on the grass.

"I reckon you know," Ruby Bee said as she folded Beryl's hands over her chest. "You and Buck are gonna have to live with it. I won't say anything. You'll have to decide if a Caribbean cruise is enough to wash away your sins. You have to live with what happened, not me. If the sugar that was meant for the pie ended up in the sunblock lotion, that's not up to me."

"You won't say anything?" said Sylvie.

Ruby Bee gazed at Estelle. "We need to go. If I don't put an apple pie in the oven before long, the truckers will be squawking like jays long about noon. Maybe I'll try an extra pinch of ginger."

"Do that," murmured Sylvia as she went inside the house and closed the door.

Time Will Tell

"Mary Frances was so excited I could barely get her hair rolled," Estelle said as she reached for the basket of pretzels on the bar. "She was as jumpy as a long-tailed cat in a room full of rocking chairs, and I finally had to threaten to get a towel and tie her down."

Ruby Bee smiled as she envisioned Mary Frances Frank, who wasn't even five feet tall but had more energy than one of those nuclear power plants. "Well, you got to admit being named Teacher of the Year is an honor. I don't know how she's faced those teenagers every morning for forty years and tried to get them interested in poetry when they were more interested in one another's britches. Back in my time, we sat on opposite sides of the room, and—"

"The award is gonna be presented at the cafeteria this Friday evening. I told her to come by that morning and I'll recomb her hair for free. She was real pleased." Estelle nodded smugly at her reflection in the mirror, real pleased by the undeniable generosity of her own gesture.

Harrumphing under her breath, Ruby Bee came out from behind the bar to take another pitcher of beer to the only customers, a trio of truckers in the back booth. Business at Ruby Bee's Bar & Grill was slow these days, but so was everything in Maggody, Arkansas (pop. 755). These days, at least, everybody knew where Arkansas was on the map on account of the new president (not between Oklahoma and Texas, as the old president had said), and Ruby Bee was hoping that tourists might start flocking like cowbirds now that summer was approaching. Jim Bob Buchanon seemed to feel the same, since he'd repaired the dryers at the Suds of Fun Launderette and put a fresh coat of paint on the front of Jim Bob's SuperSaver Buy 4 Less. This very morning she'd watched Roy Stivers setting out brass lamps and cracked washbowls in front of his antique store, and Brother Verber down at the Voice of the Almighty Lord Assembly Hall had changed the letters on the portable sign to read: STRANGERS WELCOME; FREE ADMISSION TO HEAVEN. This wasn't to say the collection plate wouldn't be passed under their noses several times, but at least he wasn't selling tickets at the door.

"I already knew about all the details concerning the ceremony," she said disdainfully as she returned. "Benjamin called me yesterday to say he wants to have a surprise party afterward at their house. He was supposed to come by at two to talk about the menu." She consulted the neon-trimmed clock behind her. "It's already after four. I wonder if he's still coming."

Estelle snorted. "I wouldn't hold my breath. Poor Mary Frances had to wait most of an hour before he picked her up. I'd have been hotter than a pepper mill, but she said she was used to it after all these years. She admitted he was always late when they were dating in college and she should have known there was no way to change him. The only reason she didn't wait at the altar was that she told him the wrong time for the wedding. He was at the hospital when Sara Anne was born, but Mary Frances was in labor so long her mother had time to drive down from Saint Louis. When Ben Junior was born, he didn't get there until she was back in her room and the baby was in the nursery. Imagine it taking him more than three hours to get to the hospital!"

"She's a saint to put up with him all these years. Maybe I

ought to call him at his office and remind him about our meeting. Do you recollect the name of his insurance outfit in Starley City?"

Estelle did, and pretty soon Ruby Bee was asking to speak to Benjamin Frank.

The secretary's sigh hinted at years of frustration. "He's not here yet, Mrs. Hanks. He called more than an hour ago to say he was on his way, so I'm hoping he'll be here before Mr. Whitbread gets fed up and leaves. There's a lot of business at stake." She sighed again, but most likely not for the last time.

"It don't take an hour to get to Starley City," said Ruby Bee, feeling sorry for the secretary and the unknown Mr. Whitbread. "I could be there in fifteen minutes."

"Mr. Frank has good intentions, but he'll think of errands along the way and pretty soon he'll be on the other side of the county talking to a client or over at the cafe drinking coffee. He won't even notice that he's late."

Ruby Bee asked her to remind him of the meeting, then hung up and mentally adjusted Mary Frances's halo. "How can someone be like that?" she asked Estelle. "If I was Mary Frances, I'd have long since ripped out my hair and taken to wandering around town in my underwear like Cornwallis Buchanon did before they packed him off to the county old folks home."

"She said they've never heard the opening hymn at church or seen the credits at the picture show. She used to invite folks for supper, but she finally stopped on account of Benjamin getting home about the time everybody was saying good night. Last year they were supposed to visit Ben Junior all the way up in Alaska, but they got to the airport late and missed the flight. She cried for a week because she was gonna see their new grandbaby for the first time and Ben Junior had booked them on a three-day cruise as a Christmas present. Of course the airline wouldn't refund the money for the tickets because it wasn't their fault, and Ben Junior lost the deposit."

"There ought to be one of those twelve-step programs for folks like that," Ruby Bee said with a trace of tartness, "but they couldn't hold their meetings. Everybody'd show up too late."

They were busy commiserating with Mary Frances when the door opened and Benjamin Frank came striding across the dance floor. He was a big man, his face crinkled, his gray hair clipped short, his grin stretching from ear to ear, his teeth as white and even as could be bought anywhere. He had an unfortunate fondness for plaid and polyester, but the overall effect was dapper, if not chic. "How're the two prettiest ladies in Maggody today?" he called. "I keep waiting to hear you've both eloped with handsome millionaires from Farberville. If Mary Frances didn't keep me on a short leash, I'd be showing up on your doorsteps with flowers and candy to beg for a peck on the cheek."

Ruby Bee gave him a pinched frown. "You said you were coming at two o'clock, Benjamin, and your secretary was expecting you an hour ago."

He winked at Estelle as he sat on the stool beside her. "You sure worked magic on Mary Frances's hair this morning. You ought to open a hair salon in New York City and run those fancy boys like Vidal Sassoon right out of business."

Estelle patted her own festive red beehive. "That's right kind of you, Benjamin," she said, unable to stop herself from simpering. "A lot of folks don't realize that cosmetology is an art, and—"

"About the party," inserted Ruby Bee. "What kind of food do you want me to fix?"

He beamed at her. "Everybody knows you're the best cook

47

west of the Mississippi, Ruby Bee. You decide on the menu, and don't think twice about the price. I'm so proud of Mary Frances for being the Teacher of the Year that I get misty just thinking about it. I want this party to be real special. The ceremony starts at seven, so we'll most likely leave by six-thirty. You can bring the food then and get everything all set out in the dining room. I'll leave some balloons and crepe paper streamers in a sack on the back porch and be eternally grateful if you could tape 'em up."

"We'd be delighted," Estelle said just as if she were the one catering and not just tagging along out of habit. "Mary Frances will be downright thrilled when she steps through the door."

"But we aim to be at the high school at seven," said Ruby Bee. "Mary Frances won't get her award until everybody's done making speeches, but I don't want to miss a minute of it." She paused to give him a piercing look. "And you don't, either."

"I'll be sitting in the first row," Benjamin said as he slid off the stool. "I promised her I'd be home and in the shower by six o'clock, and ready to escort her whenever she's finished getting gussied up. I guess I'd better head on to my office. My secretary gets irritable if I'm late."

Ruby Bee waited until he was gone before she said, "I'd get homicidal, myself. Do you realize he never once apologized for being late?"

They resumed commiserating with poor Mary Frances, who'd taught countless teenagers to recite poetry but couldn't seem to teach her husband how to tell time.

I'd given up trying to whittle a chunk of wood into something remotely resembling a marshland mallard and was dozing away the day in the Maggody PD, where I was the one and only P. Once upon a time I'd had a real live deputy, but now I had a beeper. I also had an answering machine, but I'd quit checking messages after I realized the only person using it was my mother, Ruby Bee, and every last one of her messages began with a treatise on how much she disliked talking to a machine. What I really needed was voice mail, I decided as I monitored the progress of a spider across the ceiling. "To gripe about my schoolmarm hair, Press One. To gripe about my aversion to lipstick, Press Two. To gripe about my lack of a social life, Press Three." It would never work; there weren't enough buttons to handle Ruby Bee's litany of my sins.

The telephone interrupted my whimsical reverie. After a few scowls in its direction, I picked up the receiver and reluctantly conceded that the caller had reached the PD.

"Arly, this is Mrs. Jim Bob," said a familiar but not welcome voice. "I am fed up with those junior high boys cutting across the back of my yard on their way to Boone Creek. Not five minutes ago they tramped right through my begonias, and when I went onto the porch and told them to get off my property, one of them used an obscenity."

"No kidding?" I said with the proper degree of incredulity. "Do you want me to shoot 'em? I've still got four bullets in a box in the back room."

"No, I want you to go down to the creek and give them a lecture about trespassing and disrespect for their elders. I'd do it myself but I have to fix a green bean casserole for Eula Lemoy, whose back is bothering her. It won't keep me from watching for your car to go down the road within the next five minutes, Miss Chief of Police."

"I'll probably go ahead and shoot 'em," I said, albeit to the dial tone. Mrs. Jim Bob's a royal pain, but Jim Bob's the mayor and therefore, at least technically, my boss. In order to avoid a tedious lecture at the next town council meeting, I hung the CLOSED sign on the door and drove down Finger

Lane to the swimming hole to see if I could persuade the miscreants to find another shortcut.

Said miscreants had moved on. I gazed at the bubbly brown water, remembering some moonlit nights of my youth when hormones had bubbled as loudly. The sun was warm, the breeze laden with earthy rawness of spring, the birds twittering and flitting in the branches, the squirrels nattering at me. Manhattan, where I'd led a tumultuous married life, has art galleries and opera, but there are some scenes that are a sight more elegant.

It occurred to me that I needed to stake out the swimming hole for an hour or two, just in case the miscreants returned. In order to survive the ordeal, I needed provisions along the lines of a ham sandwich, potato salad, a bag of cookies, and a big cup of iced tea. All of this was available at the SuperSaver deli, where I could also find a tabloid filled with wondrous stories of alien lobbyists and sexual aberrations.

Such are the exactitudes of law enforcement in a town where nothing ever happens, I told myself as I parked in front of the store and started inside. I detoured to greet the figure almost hidden behind a cart piled high with sacks of groceries.

"Congratulations, Mrs. Frank," I said, resisting the urge to scuffle my feet and duck my head as if I were telling lies about uncompleted homework. She hadn't been a tyrant in the classroom, but even fifteen or so years later, with white hair and faded blue eyes, she radiated a measurable dose of the same authority.

"Thank you, Arly. I must say I'm tickled pink, although I don't know if I'm more excited about the award or my retirement. Forty years is a long time to attempt to instill a lively interest in dead poets."

I couldn't argue with that. "Well, congratulations again,"

I said, edging toward the door.

"Forty years of bells and tardy slips," she continued in a musing voice, "to be followed by who knows how many years of waiting for Benjamin. That's what I'm doing now. My car's in the shop, so I'm at his mercy. Do you know how long I've been standing here?" Her voice tightened and her eyes narrowed as she regarded the rows of parked cars. "Over half an hour, that's how long. Benjamin promised to pick me up at four sharp, which is why I went ahead and bought ice cream and frozen orange juice."

"Would you like me to give you a ride home?"

"That's thoughtful of you, Arly, but surely Benjamin will be here before too much longer. It simply never occurs to him that other people dislike waiting for him. I've grown accustomed to it after all these years, but now that I'm retiring, I wonder if I'll be able to handle it."

I was eager to get back to the creek, take off my shoes and let the mud slip between my toes, stuff my face, read about two-headed babies in the Amazon rain forest. "I'll be clapping for you on Friday," I said in one last attempt to extricate myself from the conversation.

"But Benjamin won't," she said, talking more to herself than to yours truly. "It won't matter how many times I tell him how important this is, how many times I beg him to be there at seven o'clock. He'll cross his heart and swear he'll be there, but he won't, and he'll be wondering where everyone is when he arrives two hours later. This may be the most important event in my life—an acknowledgment of all my years of teaching and the beginning of what's supposed to be our golden years together. He really should be on time." She took an orange from a sack and squeezed it until the skin burst and juice dribbled down her white fingers. "He really should."

Something was dribbling down my back that wasn't a

source of vitamin C and I was ready to forget about my picnic and flat out flee to my car. I'd known Mary Frances Frank for a good many years, but this was my first glimpse of her as a vindictive Munchkin. "I'm sure he'll make it this one time," I said.

"He'd better," she said. "Otherwise, he'll be very, very sorry . . . this one time."

By Friday I'd corralled the miscreants and bawled them out, cleaned the back room of the PD in a paroxysm of seasonal madness, and given some consideration to dustbusting my efficiency apartment above the antique store. Only my penchant for chicken-fried steak and cream gravy saved me, and I was devising ways to idle away the afternoon as I went into the bar and grill.

"Thought you said you'd be here at noon," Ruby Bee said in an unfriendly voice.

I didn't much worry about it, in that she's no more predictable than the weather—and this was hurricane season, after all. "Did I say that? I could have sworn I said I'd be here around noon." I appropriated a stool and gave her a beguiling smile. "How about the blue plate special and a glass of milk?"

"How about you learn to be on time?" muttered my mother, although she did so while stomping into the kitchen.

I sat and waited, listening placidly to the wails from the jukebox and the conversations from the booths along the wall. Now that it was no longer legal to shoot helpless birds and hapless mammals, the hot topic seemed to be the slaughter of large mouth bass and crappies. At least it was preferable to brands of toilet bowl cleaners.

Estelle sat down beside me as Ruby Bee came through the kitchen doors. "I guess we're all excited," she said.

"I guess we are," I said, although I had no idea what she

assumed was exciting us. I myself was a little choked up at the sight of the plate Ruby Bee was carrying, but I'm a patsy in such matters.

Ruby Bee banged down the plate in front of me. "Has Mary Frances decided what she's going to wear tonight?" she asked Estelle.

"Her beige linen suit. She wanted to buy a new dress, but her car's still at the shop and Benjamin didn't get home yesterday in time for her to drive to Farberville. I wouldn't have liked to have been him when he finally got there. Mary Frances's eyes were flashing when she told me about it this morning, and I can imagine what all she said to him. They may have been married for forty years, but his lateness is starting to get on her nerves."

"I heard something interesting," Ruby Bee said. She glanced at me to see if I was listening, then moved down the bar so she and Estelle could share the big secret. The two often mistake me for someone who cares. "I heard," she continued with the muted subtlety of a chain saw, "that Mary Frances made up with her brother just two days ago. After all these years of not speaking, she upped and called him, and then borrowed Elsie's car for the afternoon and went to visit him."

"She didn't say one word to me," Estelle said, clearly stunned by the magnitude of the revelation. "Not one word, and there I was recombing her hair for free!"

"Elsie promised not to tell anyone, but we were talking about the award ceremony tonight and she let drop that Mary Frances invited her brother and his wife."

"What about the credenza?"

Ruby Bee nodded somberly. "She gave it to him. Here they've been fighting like dogs and cats over it since their mama died ten years ago, refusing to speak to each other at the family reunions, paying lawyers to file lawsuits, and sitting on opposite sides of the church at weddings and funerals. All of a sudden she's willing to give him the credenza just to make peace with him. He went to her house and picked it up last night. I was flabbergasted when I heard that."

I halted a forkful of mashed potatoes halfway to my mouth. "I don't understand why you're treating this like the collapse of the Soviet Union. Maybe she wants to begin her retirement without any lingering feuds."

Estelle pondered this while she ate a pretzel. "Nope, this credenza is mahogany and it's been in the family for three or four generations. We're not talking about a sewing box or an end table worth a few dollars. Roy Stivers appraised it back when Mary Frances and her brother were dividing the estate, and he said he hadn't come across a nicer one in all his born days."

In that I wasn't sure I'd recognize a credenza if it nipped me on the butt, I resumed eating.

Ruby Bee resumed gossiping. "Elsie was miffed when Mary Frances brought the car back all covered with mud. It seems her brother is working on that new stretch of highway that's supposed to replace Highway Seventy-one if they ever finish blasting through the mountains. Mary Frances wanted to hose off the mud, but Elsie said not to bother on account of it wasn't right for the Teacher of the Year to be washing cars. They almost had an argument over it, but Mary Frances insisted Elsie come over for coffee and homemade doughnuts this morning. Elsie ain't all that hard to mollify."

"Mary Frances is gonna be real hard to mollify if Benjamin's not on time tonight," Estelle said. "She told me she was going to teach him a lesson once and for all. Do you reckon she'll say something in her speech?"

"She can't say anything folks don't already know."

The discussion wandered at this point, and so did I. Not off to the trenches, mind you, or even off to determine the dimensions of the credenza and delve into the mystery of why a woman might want to make peace with her brother after ten years of estrangement. The grapevine was more than capable of producing a tidy solution sooner or later.

Where I wandered was out to the skeletal remains of Purtle's Esso station, where I could run a speed trap to make a little money for the local coffers and, more importantly, read a magazine. At five o'clock, I went back to the PD and tucked away my radar gun, called the dispatcher at the sheriff's office to find out if I'd missed anything newsworthy (I hadn't), and was halfway out the door when I noticed the blinking red rat's eye of the answering machine.

Approach-avoidance reared its ugly head. Was it the man of my dreams offering an escape to a Caribbean island? Was it a lawyer in Manhattan calling to tell me my ex-husband was so overcome with remorse that he was sending the money he owed me? Or was it the pope?

I pushed the button.

"This is Ruby Bee Hanks, and I don't know why I bother to call over there when all I ever get is this rude machine. I don't know what the world's coming to when people can't bother to answer their own telephones." There was a sharp inhalation before she took off once more. "Estelle and I are going out to Mary Frances's house just before the ceremony to get everything ready for the party. We won't get to the cafeteria until right at seven, so you need to go over early and save us seats on—"

The machine cut her off before I could, although it was close. I locked up and walked across the road to my apartment, having been warned much earlier that Ruby Bee's Bar & Grill would not be serving supper to the likes of me or anyone else. I could survive on a can of soup, since I'd be having chocolate cake and champagne punch within a matter of hours, I assured myself as I showered and changed into a skirt and blouse in honor of the honoree.

I figured I'd best get to the high school fifteen minutes early in order to secure the best seats. Would Benjamin Frank be thinking the same thing? From what I could gather, the only place he'd get to on time was his own funeral—unless Mary Frances Frank did indeed teach him a lesson as she'd vowed. The adage about old dogs and new tricks came to mind, along with her comment that he would be "very, very sorry."

Abruptly I got it—credenza and all. My fingers felt numb as I finished buttoning my blouse, grabbed the car keys, and sprinted down the stairs and across the road. Mary Frances had not been making peace with her brother; she'd been making a deal. It was nearly six-forty, which meant Ruby Bee and Estelle were in as much danger as Benjamin Frank, and if my car balked, all three were in for one helluva surprise party.

I squealed out in front of a pickup truck and jammed down the accelerator. The Franks lived in a farmhouse several miles out of town on a passable county road. Six forty-two. Ruby Bee and Estelle might already be there, taping up streamers and setting out the punch bowl. Benjamin might be there, or still at his office in Starley City. Six forty-five. Mary Frances had no idea Ruby Bee and Estelle might be in the house. Six forty-eight.

I turned off the highway and tightened my grip on the steering wheel as I bounced down the road. Six-fifty came and went. Biting down on my lip, I went even faster and therefore came within inches of crashing into the back of Ruby Bee's car in the middle of the road. Dust caught up with me as I leaned my forehead against the steering wheel and waited for the adrenaline to abate.

Ruby Bee stood up on the far side of her car. "What in tarnation's going on?" she squawked. "You liked to kill the both of us! Driving like a madman on a narrow road!"

I got out of my car and clung to the antenna until my knees quit knocking. "Where's Estelle?"

"As any fool can see, I had a flat tire. She went on ahead to see if Benjamin can come help us change it and get all the party food into the house. At this rate, there's no way we'll be at the cafeteria on time."

Six fifty-eight. "How far is it?" I demanded.

"You're antsy this evening," she said, her hands on her hips and a disapproving look on her face. "It's nearly a mile further, and Estelle's wearing high heels, but she should be getting there by now. If you'd stop *gawking* and loosen these lug nuts, we won't need Benjamin's help."

"Is he there?"

"Now how on earth should I know a thing like that?"

We both turned and looked up the road a split second before an explosion rocked the sky, the sound reverberating across the valley like distant cannon fire. Black smoke and an orange haze appeared above the trees. It was seven o'clock.

Mrs. Jim Bob stood behind a podium, her hands clutching the edges as she leaned into the microphone. "And our only hope for the future lies in the moral education of our youth, who need to learn about respecting their elders and staying out of their begonias," she was saying as I came into the room.

"Excuse me," I said, "but there's been an accident. I need to speak to Mrs. Frank." Scanning the faces in the audience, I hurried up to the front row as Mary Frances Frank stood up. I asked her to accompany me to the back of the room.

"There was an explosion at your house," I said, then stopped, ignoring the murmurs of uneasiness and Mrs. Jim Bob's shrill comments about being interrupted.

"I thought I smelled gas," she said without hesitation. "I mentioned it to Benjamin this morning, and he said he'd call the gas company. It's a good thing nobody was home."

"Then your husband is here?"

"Well, I believe he ought to be on his way by now. He called from his office at six and assured me he'd go by the house to take a quick shower, then come right here. I made a point of reminding him how important it was for him to be here at seven, then arranged for Mrs. Jim Bob to give me a ride." She regarded me with a level expression. "He may be running a few minutes late, but he should be here any minute."

"It's already seven-thirty," I said. "I had to wait at your house until a sheriff's deputy arrived to take over. The volunteer fire department is on its way, but I'm afraid there won't be anything to save. It was a powerful explosion. My first thought was dynamite."

"Why were you out that way?"

"I went to warn Ruby Bee and Estelle to be away from the house at seven o'clock. Benjamin arranged a surprise party for you after the ceremony, and they were delivering the food on their way here."

Her face turned as white as her hair. "Oh, no . . . I didn't know. I had no idea. Were they injured?"

I gave her the look she'd given me years earlier when I'd tried to explain that my dog ate my term paper. "You're damn lucky they weren't. Ruby Bee had a flat a mile from your house, and Estelle went ahead to ask Benjamin to give them a hand. If she hadn't lost a heel, she might well have lost her life."

"Thank God," she whispered.

"Benjamin's car was in the driveway," I continued coldly. "He must have been running late. If he'd been here as he promised, no one would have been hurt in the explosion."

She looked up at me, her eyes welling with tears, her lips trembling. "I told him over and over how important it was that he be here at the cafeteria at exactly seven o'clock. I really did."

I believed her. I really did.

The Night-Blooming Cereus

I think the most important thing to tell you, the potential readers, is that this book was written in 1985. That's right—sixteen years ago. In today's context, this book may seem naive, although I do believe the essence of my interpretation of the political situation was as accurate as any one of us could be at that time. It certainly was as accurate as I could make it. It was written after a trip to Israel in August, 1985. During that trip, I was exposed to a great deal of information in the media there that was never reported here. Bits and pieces were, of course, but much of the conflict between the Israelis and the Palestinians was being swept under the carpet, so to speak. Too sensitive, too complex, too confusing for the American public. The average American. You and I. We received the sanitized version in order to protect our delicate (and less than perspicacious) sensibilities.

This book, however, is most certainly not a scathing assessment of the social and political mores of that moment. That I left to the pundits and the scholars, the politicians, those who inhabit think tanks and proffer dire analyses of simmering unrest and social injustice. I did the research there, and came home with maps, newspapers, editorials, writings, and all that one must pile on one's desk before one ventures into a piece of fiction that does vaguely intend to reflect the author's experience and interpretation. But I was nothing more than a tourist, as was Theo Bloomer, and could only reflect on what I saw, read, and felt.

(Whenever I see the phrase "think tank," I always imagine a bunch of guys in suits sitting around a table in the deep end of a drained swimming pool. Aides skitter down the incline from the shallow end with printed faxes and pots of coffee. And maybe bagels. Brain power, you know.)

So why was I in Israel in 1985? Not by choice, I assure you. The ex-in-laws announced that, in honor of their fiftieth wedding anniversary, the entire extended family would be present for a command performance in Jerusalem and environs. The two of them, four highly competitive and neurotic siblings, four spouses (none of us Jewish), and six children ranging from ages one to nine. August, in the Middle East. My children were six and nine at the time, and subsisted for three weeks on soda pop and ice cream, being a bit young for hummus and all things odd. I slipped them vitamins.

And then there was Walter, our guide. Every morning we reported to the mini-van to be transported to various truly fascinating historical sites. Or I suppose they might have been, had Walter not insisted that he have everyone's attention (did I mention six children?) in order to lecture us on the historical and biblical significance of same. Walter was knowledgeable, but my son was more interested in teetering on the walls or scaling the nearest hillside. As one ex-sister-in-law murmured, "When you've seen one Herodian rock, you've seen them all."

But on we went, gritting our teeth. The four spouses, who bonded like the Four Horsemen of the Apocalypse, spent many hours hiding out upstairs, drinking vodka and orange soda pop and calling El Al to inquire about the next flight. Every member of the group, with the exception of the ex-in-laws, was visited with the Hebraic version of Montezuma's revenge.

There were many wondrous moments. I myself am not re-

Joan Hess

ligious, but I was moved when we visited sites that have had a profound influence on our Judaic-Christian culture. Bethlehem. The Mount of Olives. King David's tunnel that brought water to Jerusalem during sieges. The Dead Sea (where you really, really shouldn't shave your legs before you go for a swim). The River Jordan. Camels. Bedouins in tents with TV antennas. We spent several nights at the kibbutz that I wrote about in the book, and I managed to speak to many of the committed residents, American and Israeli.

So my message is that I was there, that I saw the diversity of the conflicting cultures, as well as the soldiers on the roof and the footage of the bulldozers flattening sad little houses of suspected terrorists. I loved prowling around the Old City, buying souvenir tiles that read "Shalom, Y'all," and gazing at the Temple Wall. Being allowed to glimpse inside an Orthodox Christian church and savor the incense and slivers of sunlight capturing the swirling smoke. Slipping off my shoes and being admitted to the Muslim temple to see the rock that Mohammed purportedly stepped on before being transported to heaven.

Theo is there with no more insight than I could give him. He is a tourist, a reasonably objective observer, doing his best to assimilate this very alien culture as did I. The political climate has accelerated in its intensity, but in ways that seem an extension of what I saw in 1985. Sadly.

Joan Hess, 2001

Chapter 1

"This is entirely your fault, Theo," came the voice over the telephone. "As you very well know, Dorrie has idolized you since the day she was born, and if you hadn't told her—"

"How are you, Nadine?"

"—about your shady history with that dreadful communist organization, she would never have even considered this crazy scheme. Now what are you going to do about it, Theo?"

"How is Charles? Has he pulled off any quadruple by-passes worthy of the front page?" Theo Bloomer asked in a mild attempt at diversion. Not that it would succeed, he thought gloomily. He could almost see his sister on the distant end of the telephone line, with her hennaed hair, substantial bust, and aristocratic nose. Like an aged racehorse, she was inclined to snort. A particularly loud one brought him back to the conversation.

"Charles is distraught, Theo. As am I. Dorrie has always listened to us and respected our opinions, despite any encouragement to the contrary from her dear Uncle Theo. I just cannot imagine what's gotten into the child. I tried to be understanding but the situation is well beyond understanding now. Do you realize that the fall semester begins in less than three weeks?"

"Did I tell you about my night-blooming cereus, Nadine? I've nurtured it for four-and-one-half years, and now I do believe it's finally going to bloom."

The ensuing growl gave him a flicker of satisfaction.

Nadine Bloomer Caldicott (matron extraordinaire, bridge player of noted viciousness, guiding force of the hospital auxiliary, chairperson of the country club entertainment committee) rarely allowed her well-powdered demeanor to slip. Self-indulgence was, as she was fond of saying in more than one situation, symptomatic of the underprivileged classes. Caldicotts were hardly underprivileged.

Theo made an apologetic (if insincere) noise and said, "What has Dorrie done?"

"Dorrie is living on a kibbutz in Israel—if you can imagine such an absurd thing! She called last night to tell us how utterly fascinated she was with the socialist structure, and how she intended to remain there in order to further observe the social interactions of the community. She said it would make a divine thesis. I told her in no uncertain terms that she was to cease this silly little ploy at once and return to Connecticut on the next flight. I had intended to take her to New York for a bit of shopping before school starts, but if she continues to espouse this radical—"

"Dorrie living on a kibbutz in Israel? Nadine, I do agree that the idea is absurd. Have you taken to martinis before breakfast?"

"No, Theo, I have not." Snort, snort. "She even asked her father to see if he could get a refund on her dorm room at Wellesley. You can imagine how Charles feels, especially now that he's the treasurer of the county Republican party. He would be quite pained if someone were to suggest that we had actually permitted Dorrie to participate in a left-wing variety of lifestyle. I hope you're prepared to bring her to her senses, Theo—and bring her home!"

While the telephone continued to sputter in his ear, Theo gazed at the night-blooming cereus on the windowsill above the kitchen sink. Four-and-one-half years of fertilizer, repotting, and high-spirited conversation. A despondent voice from a corner of his brain told him it was futile to argue with his sister's ironclad determination. Still, it would have been nice to see it bloom. Very nice, indeed.

The TWA 747 hit the tarmac with the squeal of chalk on a blackboard, followed by a series of heart-stopping shudders. A few of the passengers in steerage cheered, but most were too tired and grimy to do more than contribute to a collective sigh that told of preprocessed fodder and unfocused movies. The stewardesses, as disheveled and grim as their unruly charges after the twelve-hour flight, sternly warned them not to unbuckle their seatbelts until the plane reached a complete halt and an appropriate message flashed above their heads. Almost everyone rose to yank canvas totes and bulging plastic bags from the overhead compartments. Crackling threats ensued from the intercom, but the passengers knew it was too late to be evicted in mid-Atlantic or mid-Mediterranean.

Theo cautiously flexed his knees, which had locked into position hours earlier. The knees, sixty-one years old and lately turning rebellious, popped and creaked as they were forced to unbend. His back and neck were no less coopera- tive, but eventually Theo coerced his body into a functional state and joined the line of passengers jostling down the narrow aisle.

Once Theo was on the tarmac, a wave of heat washed over him with all the fury of an unfettered sauna. Without stop- ping to analyze the consequences, Theo did something he had never before done in public—he loosened his necktie and unbuttoned the top button of his white shirt. Seconds later, he slipped off his jacket and folded it over his arm.

"The heat, you see," he explained, although no one was near enough to hear his confession and forgive him. He stood patiently as buses arrived to shuttle the passengers to a squatty building in the distance. He was a tall, balding man with the aura of a retired school teacher or an accountant. His blue eyes were faded behind the thickness of round, wire-rimmed bifocals, and his clipped beard was more gray than brown. The beard was his one concession to vanity, grown in hopes it would divert eyes from the creeping pink circle on the top of his head. No one had ever commented on the beard, nor had anyone commented on his receding hair; thus he had not yet been able to determine if the ploy was successful.

Theo was accustomed to being categorized and dismissed, and his mildness reinforced the image. He was not a school teacher or accountant, however. The unmitigated (he could not bring himself to say "bald") truth was that he was a retired florist, a subject he judiciously avoided if ever it threatened to arise. There were no fresh jokes about the coincidence of name and occupation. Everyone seemed to think he would be amused by stories of Dr. Wolfe the veterinarian or Hatchett the IRS agent. Theo had heard them all.

After a brief bus ride, a not-so-brief wait for luggage, and an amazingly brief trip through customs, Theo found himself once again swamped with heat as he was carried with the crowd out of the airport. He waited until most of the throng had hugged, kissed, shrieked messages, and finally dispersed. Then, blotting his forehead with a handkerchief, he found a cab driver willing to take him to Kibbutz Mishkan—for a price. The thousands of shekels mentioned, although initially alarming, computed to less than fifty dollars. Nods were exchanged, and Theo's sole piece of luggage tossed in the trunk. The cab squealed out of the airport much as the 747 had done in New York.

Theo gazed out the window with interest. So this was

Israel. Dry, as expected in late summer, and slightly scruffy from thousands of years of use. The traffic had been heavy: nomads from the Fertile Crescent, barbarians from the East, conquering armies from Europe. The Jews had been through several times, driven by an affirmation from their God that they were the chosen people and this their Promised Land. The Egyptians, the Romans, the Crusaders, the Turks, and now the Arabs had begged to differ; Theo wondered if the Jews' current hold on the country was any stronger now than it had been two thousand sand years ago. For their sake, he hoped so.

The basic brownness of the coastal plain was interspersed with irrigated fields. At first cotton plants covered the gently rolling land, the pods heavy with fuzz. Then, to Theo's amazement, the cotton gave way to sunflowers. The blossoms were sere, their heads drooping like despondent children. He made a careful note on the back page of his travel guide. Perhaps the horticulture hobbyists' club at home might be intrigued.

By what was surely divine intervention, Theo's driver had none of his Brooklyn counterpart's desire for incessant chatter as they drove down the highway toward Jerusalem and ultimately the kibbutz on the shore of the Dead Sea. With a silent prayer of gratitude, Theo sank into the upholstery for a much-needed nap. The guidebook slipped out of his hands and between two fastidiously polished shoes.

When he next opened his eyes, he saw desert on all sides. It was not his idea of a desert, which included such mundane images as undulating sand dunes and robed Arabs atop plodding camels. Here he saw only uncompromising rock and scattered clumps of dried plants, species unfamiliar. Jagged cliffs that disappeared into waterless riverbeds. Skeletons not of bleached bones, but of rusted trucks, abandoned tanks and tumbled fortifications. It had none of the romance of Lawrence's domain. He spotted a bedouin campsite, but it too was disappointing. The tent was made of burlap bags and bits of printed cotton, with a television antenna poked through one end. The only sign of life was an emaciated goat. No doubt the family was inside the tattered tent, watching reruns of Gilligan's Island. He wondered what they would make of it.

The taxi driver caught Theo's eye in the rearview mirror. "Hot enough for you?" he rasped as he flashed two rows of brown teeth that brought to mind dried marigold pods.

Theo quickly closed his eyes.

He opened them when the taxi stopped. Wincing at the glare, he studied a fence topped with concertina wire and beyond it rows of date palms. The harshness of the desert still lay behind him, but ahead lay an attempt at greenery. The florist in him felt comforted—until he saw a sweat-stained khaki uniform approaching the taxi, a rifle dangling at one side.

The driver conversed with the guard in what Theo presumed was Hebrew, and they were waved through the gate without further ceremony. On one side the rows of palms held formation; on the other, low buildings were surrounded by small areas of grass and flowers. Theo rolled down the dusty window for a better view, but immediately rolled it up as he deduced the unmistakable proximity of poultry houses.

As the taxi swung around a low metal building, Theo leaned forward for his first glimpse of the famed Dead Sea. Beyond two concrete-block bathhouses, a stretch of sand sloped gently to the water's edge. The sea was obscured by a haze that danced above the surface like ghostly ballerinas. In the distance was a hint of mountains, insubstantial silhouettes that seemed to drift above the haze. The water had a curious blank quality, the restrained ripples disturbing no darting schools of fish, no tentacles of algae, no beds of shell-fish. The Dead Sea did look dead, he decided, pleased by the punctiliousness of its name.

The taxi once again stopped. The driver climbed out to remove Theo's suitcase from the trunk, while Theo followed more slowly. The heat here, at the lowest area of land on the face of the earth, was worse than he had imagined it would be. At the airport, the heat had been dry. Now he was grasped by blistering, humid arms, his lungs squeezed by searing fingers, his face slapped with a mask of invisible, suffocating heat.

Resisting the urge to take off the last items of his clothing, he dug out his wallet, tipped the driver for his silence, and carried the suitcase toward a low building with the words GUEST HOUSE in English, among other languages, displayed on a wall.

More than five thousand miles away, a petal deep inside the bud on the night-blooming cereus felt a primeval tickle.

Chapter 2

The lobby was as cool as the storage room of a florist shop, although hardly as colorful. Theo gulped down several lungfuls of the air before advancing toward an unoccupied reception counter. The equipment was standard for a hotel: a cash register, a display of postcards, and several tiers of boxes, all with keys dangling over the lips. Everything but a desk clerk or a round bell with which to summon one.

Not for a second did Theo Bloomer consider barking a demand for service, nor did he presume to bang on the counter to make his presence known. Instead, slipping on his jacket and affixing his necktie, he turned around to study the lobby until someone might find it convenient to accept his money in exchange for temporary lodging.

The room held several groupings of sofas and chairs, all arranged for an optimum view of a television on a high shelf. Beyond those was a padded bar with stools to buffer the selection of liquor bottles and upturned glasses. Alas, there was no bartender to offer advice or a sip of chilled soda water.

On one side of the bar was a shrouded gift shop. On the other side was a set of French doors, curtained to obscure whatever lay beyond them. Theo briefly toyed with the idea of tapping on the door, but instead turned back to the desk to see if there might be written instructions for an unexpected visitor.

As he did so, a face rose up from behind the counter, halting when the chin grazed the edge. Their eyes met with equal alarm; Theo swallowed a yelp of surprise as he stepped back. The face belonged to a young woman, he realized, a young woman on the brink of a blood-curdling scream. The idea was appalling.

"If it isn't too much trouble, I'd like a room," he said quickly. He gestured at his suitcase near the door in hopes its presence might lend credibility to what sounded, even to him, like an improbable request. "If it's not too much trouble," he repeated, feeling increasingly pessimistic about his chances.

The woman's mouth fell open. Her eyes rounded and unblinking, she slowly began to sink, as if her knees were in a pool of quicksand hidden by the counter.

"Please wait," Theo implored. "Are you the desk manager? I'm Theodore Bloomer, from Connecticut. I sent a telegram that I was coming, but perhaps it failed to arrive?"

Only two large brown eyes were visible now, topped by a high forehead and flat black hair. Gradually they too disappeared, leaving Theo to gaze once more at an unoccupied counter. It was extremely unsettling. He supposed he could lean over the counter to see what the mute creature was doing, but that seemed presumptuous and apt to send her into hysterics. Then again, it was disheartening to lose the only person he had thus far seen in the lobby.

As he pondered his options, a door opened and a more substantial woman came into view. Theo eyed her warily, prepared for her to vanish also should he dare inquire about a room.

"May I help you?" she said in a pleasantly husky voice. She smiled as she stepped behind the counter.

After a pause, Theo tentatively said, "I'm Theo Bloomer." When she continued to smile, he decided to throw caution to the wind. "I sent a telegram that I was coming, but I may have

71

preceded it by a day or two. In any case, I'd like a room for a few days."

"I'm Miriam Adler, Mr. Bloomer, and I'm afraid we have not yet received your telegram. However, all but one of our rooms are unoccupied, so we'll be delighted to have you as a guest at Kibbutz Mishkan. A single room?"

Encouraged by her failure to dematerialize, Theo studied her with the same seriousness he gave an unidentified seedling or a yellowed maidenhair fern. Her face was deeply tanned and covered by a sprinkling of honey-colored freckles. Hair that had once been a glowing auburn was now flecked with gray, but neatly done in gentle waves that softened her high cheekbones and straight, elegant nose. Her mouth was generous, curled slightly at each corner in a perpetual smile. Her eyes were dark brown, flecked with tiny arrowheads of gold and regarding him with amused tolerance.

Redness crept up his neck as he cleared his throat. "Yes, a single room, please. I don't know how long I'll be staying, Mrs. Adler, and I hope that won't cause any inconvenience. I'm here to visit a relative."

"Please call me Miriam. We're all quite informal on the kibbutz, and I hope you'll enjoy yourself and feel at home. I can see that you're more interested in a cool shower and a long nap at the moment, so I'll sign you in and have someone take your luggage to your room immediately. You'll be in the building behind this one."

Theo filled out a form, allowed his passport to be locked in a small wall safe, and agreed to a second-floor room with a view of the Dead Sea. He insisted that he could manage the suitcase without assistance, and accepted a key on a plastic tag.

"Thank you, Miriam," he said with his usual graveness. "If I may presume to delay you further, I am curious about a woman who appeared here before you came. She has black hair, and she seemed frightened by me. I hope I did nothing to upset the young woman, and I would dearly like to assure her that I meant no harm."

Miriam wrinkled her nose. "That was Essie. She must have been cleaning the floor when you startled her, Theo. We're rather used to her, but our guests do find her peculiar. You'll encounter her often during your stay, so I'd best explain that she—ah, inhabits a world of her own making. It's a creative sort of mental disorder, but I can assure you that she is both harmless and a very efficient maid. Now, let me walk to your room with you."

They left the coolness of the lobby, but Theo kept his jacket and necktie in place despite the heat. Miriam was an attractive woman, he heard himself commenting in a smug, manly voice. He had not permitted such a thought for more than thirty years, and he briskly squelched it as he would a mealybug.

"You mentioned that you have a relative here," Miriam said as they strolled down a sidewalk lined with orange bougainvillea and clipped grass. She was not, he noted in admiration, the least bit damp with perspiration.

"Yes, my niece Dorrie Caldicott. She telephoned her parents several days ago to inform them that she intended to remain at the kibbutz. In that school starts soon, her mother asked me to speak to her about it," Theo said, wondering why he felt apologetic.

"Dorrie is your niece? How interesting," Miriam said. "She's a delightful girl, but I'm not at all sure why she has remained on the kibbutz these last few weeks. Is Judith also a relative?"

Theo shook his head, now feeling as if he were disappointing Miriam by his inability to answer in the affirmative.

Jet lag, he scolded himself, was responsible for this un-Bloomerish behavior, which seemed to resemble pubescent hormonal turmoil. Disgraceful.

Miriam smiled as she pointed at a flight of stairs leading to a balcony and row of doors. "Your room is in the middle, and Dorrie's is at the end. I imagine you'll find her in residence. Good luck, Theo."

"Thank you, Miriam." He started for the stairs, then stopped to blink over his shoulder. "Will I see you and your husband at dinner?"

"Not unless you and Essie have a great deal in common. I've been a widow for twelve years, and I eat in the communal dining hall with the kibbutzniks. The main building of the guesthouse has a restaurant for tourists and our guests. However, I'd be delighted to give you a tour of the kibbutz tomorrow if you're interested."

"Oh, dear, I'm sorry if I've alluded to painful memories," Theo said hastily.

Miriam shrugged. "Please don't apologize. Many of our kibbutzniks were killed in that war and the others, and the Arabs have yet to apologize. Twelve years is, as I have learned, a very long time."

Theo felt much as he had when, as a small boy seated before a grand piano in the center of a vast and drafty stage, he had searched the audience for a parental smile of encouragement. An absurd feeling for a somewhat bald widower. Thoroughly amazed, he heard himself continuing, "Perhaps you might join me after dinner for coffee or brandy in the lobby to discuss this proposed tour?"

Her smile was more like a grin. "Why, that would be lovely. Shall we say nine o'clock, Theo?"

He managed a nod and escaped before he compounded his disgrace. Theo had dealt with people all his life over the counter of his florist shop, determining their desires from bridal bouquets to funeral memorials. He had done so with dignity and reserve. He had never stooped to personal comments, even to those who had chosen orchids for a gardenia event. Or vice versa.

He entered the room and centered his suitcase on a small table. The bed looked adequate, the bathroom modern, the air conditioner capable of arctic breezes. Dorrie would have to wait until he had showered and rested, he decided. A card proclaimed, among other things, that dinner would be served between six and eight. With practiced efficiency, Theo unpacked his bag, placed neatly folded shirts and underwear in drawers, and hung creased trousers in the closet. Shoes were placed beneath cuffs in parallel precision. He then set his alarm clock for seven-thirty, took a brisk shower, and collapsed on the bed for a few hours of heavenly oblivion.

At which point the door opened.

Chapter 3

Theo Bloomer did not sink to uttering expletives, having decided decades earlier they were an indication of both a base mentality and a limited vocabulary. He was therefore quite surprised at the speed with which one such particularly succinct word flashed across his mind.

Firmly dismissing it, he said, "Who's there?"

The response was an explosive exhalation and a jangle of keys.

Theo sat up and put on his glasses. The door and entry were not visible from his bed, but he was certain who his visitor would prove to be. "Essie, you may come in," he said softly, as if speaking to a wounded animal of unknown ferocity.

The head, tilted to a peculiar angle, appeared around the corner. The familiar brown eyes stared without blinking, and the mouth formed a circle of leery indecision. When Theo remained silent, she edged forward and held out an armful of towels. Her black hair hung to her waist, which looked no bigger than Theo's wrist. Her rib cage was visible under a cotton dress that draped unevenly several inches below her knees. Her feet were large, bare, and dusty.

"Thank you, Essie. You may leave them there if you wish."

"You can't use theb there. Supposed to go in the bathroob." Her voice was flat and adenoidal, as if the words bounced about an echo chamber high in her nose. It was very

76

difficult to understand. He could hear no accent in her statement, only petulant challenge.

"I promise that I shall transfer them to the bathroom later. Thank you for bringing them."

She unclasped her hands and impassively watched the towels tumble to the floor in an avalanche of white terry cloth. Theo disguised a wince as she suddenly looked up at him. "Why did you cob here?"

"I came to visit my niece, Dorrie Caldicott."

Essie's head swiveled as she studied the room. "Not here. Not her roob. Her roob's down there." Her head jerked to one side.

"Ah, yes, thank you. After I rest, I intend to locate her roob—ah, room, so that we can have a visit," Theo murmured. Her unblinking eyes made him uncomfortable, as if she were a gardener and he a hapless clump of crabgrass. Reminding himself of his age—and rapidly declining physical condition—he added, "Is that all, Essie? I was hoping to take a nap before dinner."

"Fish."

"I fear I failed to bring the proper equipment, but I do appreciate the suggestion. Now, I would like to—"

"Fish for dinner. I saw it in the kitchen. Left over from last week. Put tobato sauce on it so it won't smell." The last came out in an accented, shrill voice. She began to sway back and forth, her painfully thin body responding to an interior tornado, then abruptly jerked herself to a halt. "I don't like fish," she announced flatly.

Theo could not halt a yawn. When it had run its course, he blinked leaden eyelids. "Neither do I, any more. I'm going to have to ask you to leave, Essie; I am exhausted."

"Take a stroll at ten." No discernible accent, but this time in a low growl that sounded like a man's voice.

"I prefer a nap at the present, but I will certainly take a stroll later. Good-bye, Essie." He took off his glasses and watched a blurred shadow waft out of view. The door banged closed seconds later.

Once again Theo sank back for a nap.

The alarm woke him from an unpleasant dream of stewardesses armed with whips and drunken pilots who pirouetted in the aisles. He fumbled for his glasses and managed to shut off the alarm. After a few minutes of befuddlement, he remembered where he was and why. Dorrie Caldicott was busily breaking her mother's heart and ruining her bridge game while he wasted precious hours in self-indulgent sleep. The more quickly he cleared up the situation, the sooner he could return to his bungalow and his unattended night-blooming cereus. If only it could wait until he returned.

Minutes later, clad in a light gray suit and somber tie, Theo walked to the last room on the balcony and tapped on the door. Perhaps the whole mess could be resolved before dinner, and he could meet Miriam Adler with an unsullied conscience. And take Dorrie home on the next available flight.

The theory evaporated when his knock was unheeded. Sighing, he walked along the sidewalk to the lobby, bravely opened the French doors, and entered the restaurant. An aroma of fish and tomatoes stopped him in the doorway.

"Oh, my God, Uncle Theo?" Loud, amazed, very much prep school à la Connecticut. "Is that really and truly you? I can't believe it!"

Theo squinted myopically across an atoll of round white tables to find his niece and namesake, Theodora Bloomer Caldicott, who was on her feet and hopping about like a cheerleader with a full bladder. She looked very much as she had when he last saw her in the Caldicott manor. Her long blonde hair cascaded down her back in artful disarray, and her eyelashes were carefully smudged to achieve an image of startled innocence. She wore her standard outfit: a cotton shirt with a discreet emblem and prewashed designer jeans, chopped off centimeters short of a semipornographic length. Her sneakers, Theo knew, cost more than many an entire floral bill for a wedding.

He hurried across the room before she could shriek another greeting. They hugged for a minute, pleased with each other, then Theo disengaged her and gestured at the three empty places at her table.

"May I join you?"

"Oh, Uncle Theo, of course you can join me. This is such a shock—it really is! Why on earth are you here? I simply cannot get over it! I am just totally floored."

He allowed her to continue in that vein as he took a sip of water and unfolded his napkin. There were no other diners in the room; the waitress near the kitchen door seemed unimpressed by the barrage of girlish squeals and giggles. At last Dorrie ran out of protests of incredulousness and gave him a calculating look.

"Mother sent you, didn't she? I can just hear her: 'Theo, this is all your fault for corrupting that innocent child with your nasty old stories about those filthy communists.' She probably tied you up with wire, tossed you in the trunk of the Mercedes, and delivered you to a porter at the airport to be checked straight through."

"That is a fairly accurate reconstruction, Dorrie. Nadine is perturbed by the situation, and pointed out several times that you are, among other things, an Episcopalian. Some well-meaning bridge player told her that Israel is, among other things, a Jewish state. The information was distressing.

Terrorist attacks, bombings, and leftist economic theories were also mentioned, as was your senior year at Wellesley. Charles is two strokes off his handicap; Nadine trumped her partner's ace at a tournament. I was indeed sent to investigate."

Dorrie's blue eyes flashed between thick, curled lashes.

"Well, I don't care about Daddy's golf scores or Mother's mortification. They refused to listen to me when I called. All they cared about was the dorm deposit at Wellesley and the back-to-school dance at the club. I mailed Biff a postcard to explain why I couldn't go with him. I'm not a barbarian." She emphasized her avowal with a delicate sniff of her upturned nose. The infamous Caldicott jaw inched forward.

"I'm sure you're not, Dorrie. Despite your mother's orders, I did not come to drag you home in time for the dance at the country club. If you feel it vital to remain in order to analyze the social structure of the kibbutz, you may do so. Your dorm room may lie fallow this year if you wish."

"Thanks, Uncle Theo. Now that we've cleared things up, what do you want for dinner?" Her voice fell to a dramatic whisper that could be heard across the Dead Sea in Jordan. "The food is not terribly good. It's what they call 'kosher,' which has to do with some law about meat and milk. The waitress literally wigged out when I ordered a simple cheeseburger."

Theo glanced at the menu. "Not the fish, I think. All the traveling may have upset my stomach. I believe I'll have a salad and a piece of fruit, and club soda to drink."

"It's not even Perrier, Uncle Theo. It's some local brand with an unpronounceable name. I don't know how I've survived this long."

"I shall risk it just this once." He gave his order to the waitress, and listened as Dorrie ordered soup, salad, fish, pota-

80

toes, and whatever else she could find on the menu. She was twenty years old, he reminded himself with a bemused smile, and oblivious to exterior pressures when the subject of food arose. Nadine had despaired loudly when Dorrie had munched steadily through all childhood diseases, an appendectomy, and a series of pubescent depressions due to traitorous boyfriends and catastrophic tennis tournaments. He suspected his sister would have preferred a slight and fragile rosebud to an exuberant snapdragon with the appetite of a venus flytrap.

Yet Dorrie was still very much a Caldicott, with a dose of Bloomer blue blood thrown in. The pacifier had been sterling silver, the bibs Irish lace, the petticoats starched, and the hair ribbons neatly bowed. White gloves had been donned without a whimper. Dorrie had been instructed in piano, ballet, ballroom dancing, watercolors, tennis, golf, and all other skills deemed vital for a meaningful life in Connecticut. She had finished her junior year at Wellesley with an admirable gradepoint in her chosen field, sociology. Of all her beaming relatives, only Theo wondered what simmered beneath her gracious smiles and bright chatter.

Now he wondered more than ever.

They ate, or rather Dorrie did, while Theo watched. Essie's editorial on the fish still haunted him, and even the salad had a suggestive odor of piscatory longevity. After Dorrie had packed in the last bite, he placed his napkin beside his plate and surreptitiously glanced at his watch. Two fifty-three and ticking. It felt much later.

Dorrie giggled at his frown. "You have to add a bunch of hours, Uncle Theo. Do you have a date?"

Theo cleared his throat, willing the blush to stay under his collar. "No, but I did arrange to meet Mrs. Adler in the lounge to discuss a tour of the kibbutz tomorrow. You and I do need to talk, however, and I'm sure Mrs. Adler would not mind if I were to cancel our discussion."

"A date with Miriam, hmmm?" Dorrie gave him an impertinent smile rarely seen in Connecticut. "That's okay; I was planning to wash my hair right after dinner. This heat is so barbaric that, if I don't condition my hair every single night, it just frizzes out of control and I look exactly like Frankenstein's bride—or worse. We can talk later, or even tomorrow. And you'll need to meet Judith, too."

"Miriam mentioned her earlier, but I failed to recognize the name. Who is this Judith, Dorrie?"

"Judith Feldheim. She's the reason I'm here, Uncle Theo, and the reason I can't go home. Have a lovely time with Miriam."

Before Theo could protest, Dorrie tossed her napkin on the table and left the restaurant.

Chapter 4

Miriam was sitting on one of the sofas in the lobby, talking to a young man whose scowl was almost audible. A second young man watched from behind the sofa. Unwilling to intrude, Theo moved to the bar, now tended by a rotund and rubicund man, and requested two brandies. After he had signed a ticket, he turned back to see Miriam waving for him to join them.

"This is my son Gideon and his friend, Hershel Waskow," she said, clearly struggling to overcome annoyance. "This is Theo Bloomer, Dorrie's uncle. He arrived today for a visit."

Gideon made no effort to respond to his mother's social cues. His face would have been a study in chiseled male beauty had it not been distorted with sulkiness. His broad shoulders were hunched, and taut muscles were visible under his dusty T-shirt and brief shorts. Even his tousled auburn hair seemed to bristle as he glanced up and snorted a terse acknowledgment of Theo's nod.

Hershel produced a weak smile above a weaker chin. He was taller than Gideon, but with none of the latter's physical assurance or sense of muscular density. A curtain of black, oily hair hung over his forehead in an unsuccessful attempt to hide a splay of old pockmarks. His large hands dangled at either side as he ducked his head and muttered something inaudible. A brayish laugh followed.

Theo again nodded, unable to reply to that which he had not been able to hear.

Gideon turned back to his mother. "No one is planning to

Joan Hess

go anywhere tonight, so there's no reason to get so damned upset about it. Hershel has a hot date with his rich little Jewish American princess. Ilana's mad at me because she thinks I'm fooling around with someone else. I couldn't get away if I had a jeep—which I don't. But if there's one more unprovoked attack against one of our shopkeepers, you can forget my promise to stay away from—"

"Gideon!" Miriam interrupted. "Mr. Bloomer has no interest in your political tantrums, nor do I. If you were twenty years younger, your *metapelet* would spank you and send you to bed. I suggest you work out your difficulties with Ilana, then come by my house later for another talk."

Gideon stood up and stalked away. Hershel trotted after him, mumbling sympathetically and flapping a hand in an attempt to pat his friend's shoulder. Theo offered one of the brandies to Miriam and sat down across from her. The brandy sloshed in her glass as she fought to control her hand, but at last she won the skirmish and looked up with a grimace that Theo found appealingly wry.

"Children can be difficult," she said, "even when they're twenty-five years old and supposedly capable of mature behavior. I hope you'll accept my apologies for Gideon's rudeness."

"I'm sure he intended no rudeness, Miriam."

"That hardly excuses it. He's—he's been under a great deal of stress these days. I had hoped his vacation in Athens would relax him." She sighed, then took a swallow of brandy. "Actually, he's been worse since he and Hershel returned."

"And you have no idea . . . ?"

"Well, he's obsessively concerned about the political situation in the Administered Territories, as many of the young people are. Those of us who've managed more or less to co-exist with the Arabs are somewhat more cautious in our deal-

84

ings with them. There've been too many deaths."

"Then we're near the Administered Territories?" Theo said, glancing over his shoulder. No silent, heavily armed figure glided through the shadows, but circumspection couldn't hurt.

"Gideon insists on calling them Judaea and Samaria, but we are very near. You drove through the West Bank on your trip from the airport, and the line is only a few miles to the north of here. Jerusalem is surrounded on three sides. The Gaza Strip is to the west and the Golan Heights are to the north, on the border of Lebanon. The entire country is less than three hundred miles long, so nothing is very far."

Theo decided to avoid further discussion of the contiguity of hostile neighbors. "Gideon seemed upset over an incident . . . ?"

"He's more upset about Ilana's jealousy. She's very important to him, although he forgets it upon occasion. They grew up together, studied, and stirred up mischief until they went into the army. They also went to the university together, and graduated just a few months ago. 'Wither thou goest, I will go; and whither thou lodgest, I will lodge.' If Ilana is a modern-day Ruth, then Hershel and Gideon are my Jonathan and David. The three have been a triple threat since their first day in the children's house."

"They were all three reared in a children's house?"

"It's on your tour tomorrow," she said. "All the children are reared together, by the community rather than by their parents. The new mothers stay home with their infants for six to twelve weeks, depending on individual needs. Then the babies are placed with peers in the children's house so that the mothers can return to work as productive members of the kibbutz. We're a bit old-fashioned; some of the newer kibbutzim encourage the children to sleep at home until they reach adolescence."

Theo tried a timid smile. "Surrogate parenting must have its advantages. Between the ages of fourteen and seventeen, Dorrie provoked quite a few thunderstorms at home. Her mother would have cheerfully packed the child's bags and enrolled her in a Swiss finishing school, had she trusted her to stay away from seedy counts and cheap wine."

"You have no children of your own?"

"No, I do not. Dorrie is very dear to me, despite her periodic pouts and rebellions, but I doubt I know very much about the parent-child relationship." Theo busied himself with brandy for a moment, then added, "Tell me more about the Kibbutz Mishkan, Miriam. What does Mishkan mean?"

"Mishkan is the Hebrew word for tabernacle, the receptacle for the Torah. Even though we were not terribly religious when we founded the kibbutz, it seemed appropriate. That was thirty years ago; now it doesn't seem at all appropriate, but we're too stubborn to change it. Besides, we'd have to order new stationery."

Theo blinked. "You founded the kibbutz thirty years ago? Your accent is still very American, Miriam."

"I grew up in New York City. My husband Sy and I came here when we were newly married, motivated by a dream to replenish the barren soil and help form a Jewish state that could assimilate immigrants from all over the world. We slept in tents, worked from sunrise to sunset, wrapped our blisters with rags, and literally willed crops to grow. When it was too dark to farm, we sat around a lantern arguing about equality, direct democracy, and social relationships within such a tight community. My God, we were so very young and idealistic."

"The kibbutz is still flourishing, from what I've seen. You and the others have succeeded in your dream. I admire that."

"It will always be the most important thing in my life," she said. "I sacrificed a predictable, prosperous life of dinner parties and carpools for a life of fear, hard physical labor, and intimacy with death. I sacrificed my youth and my husband. It's hard to understand, even for me at times. And it's different for this new generation of kibbutzniks. On one hand, they're not so willing to sacrifice their personal goals for the good of the community. On the other, they're feverishly committed to a Jewish state. All of our young people go into the army, and some of them don't come back. Wars and terrorism never seem to stop, no matter what the newspapers report and the politicians claim."

"But it was worth it, was it not?" he asked gently.

Her quick smile returned. "I hope you'll think so tomorrow after the tour. Is your room comfortable?"

"Very comfortable, thank you. Essie came by with clean towels and some—ah, enlightening suggestions about leisure activities, if I understood her. Fishing and strolling were among her first choices."

Looking exasperated, Miriam asked him to repeat Essie's comments. He did so as well as he could, but his confusion must have been apparent, for she began to laugh at his expression and his hesitancy.

"Essie has been known to offer obscure advice from time to time, and I shall have to speak to her about it once again. I can't have her spooking our guests," she said as she rose. "Tomorrow I'll be around the lobby from seven o'clock until noon. Sleep as late as you can, enjoy a leisurely breakfast, then ask someone to fetch me."

Miriam left through the French doors, and Theo walked out of the lobby and down the sidewalk. When he reached the balcony, he continued down the walkway to Dorrie's room and tapped on the door. Dorrie opened it immediately, her hair hidden under a toweled turban and her face, for once, devoid of makeup. She looked much as she had before her pubescent onslaught.

"Uncle Theo, do come in," she giggled. "I feel like I'm back in the dorm and ready for a gossip session with the girls. We ought to put on our pajamas, slap on mudpacks, and raid the kitchen for potato chips and diet sodas. Wouldn't that be hilarious?"

"Quite hilarious," he said as he accepted the unnerving invitation to come in. He supposed her room was furnished like his, but it was impossible to ascertain. What furniture there might be was invisible under drifts of clothing, bottles of unknown content, and scattered books and brochures. The floor was equally cluttered, and the bathroom was, he decided with a prim frown, impassable to all but the bravest explorers. Armed explorers.

Dorrie hastily moved an armload of clothes off a chair. "Could I offer you a glass of water?" Connecticut etiquette had not been forgotten.

"No, thank you." He had glimpsed the encrusted glasses on the bathroom counter. "We do need to talk, Dorrie. Although your mother was amusingly distraught, she does have a reasonable cause to be concerned. What are you doing here—at a kibbutz in Israel? And why on earth did you announce that you were planning to stay?"

Dorrie perched on a corner of the bed and gave him a mischievous grin. "Well . . . I'm not actually planning to spend my life in this hot, humid outback, surrounded by turkey houses and dewy-eyed idealists. It hardly fits into an upscale lifestyle. I just told Mother and Daddy that I was going to do it."

"And why did you do that?" Theo said, mentally sighing with relief. "It did cause an uproar."

"So that you'd come."

Theo had suspected as much, but he saw no reason to mention it—or to discuss the inconvenience her little ploy had produced. Caldicotts were not interested in inconvenience. "Then I must extend my congratulations, for here I am. Surely my physical presence is not the extent of your scheme?"

She folded her legs under her with enviable ease and pushed a lock of hair out of her eyes. "As Mother probably told you, Judith and I were on a tour of Greece with Simmons, who's the classics prof at school. Simmons is without a doubt the most—"

"Judith?" Theo inserted softly.

"Judith Feldheim was my roommate at Wellesley last year. She's scholarship, and absolutely brilliant—in academic matters. Socially, she was a tad fringy, but I tried to help her with a few of the more important details."

"Perrier and polo shirts?"

"When I first moved in with her, she had no idea about wines, or the difference between salad and dessert forks, or anything else that's absolutely critical. Her clothes were more appropriate for a vocational school that emphasized welding as the key to success. I rushed her to Mr. Robert the very first weekend to have him do something about her hair. He was still apoplectic three months later."

"I trust he's since recovered," Theo said dryly. "But let us return to the subject of your presence in Israel."

"I'm doing my best, Uncle Theo. Judith's parents were killed when she was a child, and she grew up in foster homes. From what she's told me, some were okay and others horrid. In any case, she had no advantages." Dorrie shuddered at the unthinkable.

"Then she did well to obtain a scholarship. She sounds as though she had a difficult childhood, but is intelligent and determined enough to overcome it."

"Yeah," Dorrie agreed, "but it wasn't easy to wean her away from polyester. Anyway, last year she collected a couple of thousand dollars from an annuity her parents left her. We decided to go on Simmons's tour, even though we knew that it would be unbelievably tedious to be stuck on a bus with Simmons for eight weeks. Judith is majoring in classics, and she wanted to see the sights before they were corroded with acid rain. When she graduates, she's going to teach Greek and Latin to ghetto children."

Theo closed his eyes for a second. "An admirable goal. But why did you agree to accompany her, if Simmons is as distasteful as you claim?"

"The truth is that last summer Mother insisted that I work, if you can imagine that. I very reasonably pointed out that I did not care to disrupt a perfectly civilized summer, but she was beyond reason. It was so execrable that I simply couldn't face it again."

"A salt mine? A poultry-processing factory?"

She made a face and toppled over like a domino. "The gift shop at the hospital," she said in a hollow voice. "I had to wear this silly little pink pinafore and peddle confession magazines and candy bars until three o'clock almost every single day. If I mentioned my so-called salary, I'd choke to death while you laughed yourself into a stroke. And it gets worse. By the time I arrived at the club, everyone had already gone home. I played all of three tennis sets the entire summer, and Biff played other games with every female under sixty-five, except Mother. She's too much for him."

Theo ignored the digression. "So you discovered an inner passion to tour Greece with Judith and Simmons, despite the anticipated tedium and discomfort? That doesn't explain Israel and Mishkan."

Dorrie lifted her head to wrinkle her nose. "Mishkan?"

"The name of your present abode," he explained gravely.

"Oh," she said, letting her head fall back. "Well, the tour was as awful as I had expected. We stayed in hotels that hardly merit a twinkle, much less one star, and ate in restaurants that specialized in eggplant. Simmons lectured at the drop of a visor, and all the other girls carried grubby notebooks in order to write down every pedantic pearl of wisdom from Simmons's tight lips. I diligently tried to take an interest in the archaeological ruins, but to be frank—when you've seen one old rock, you've seen them all. I have now seen somewhere in the range of eleven thousand of them."

"So you and Judith decided to escape to Israel?"

Dorrie sighed at the ceiling. "I thought we ought to detour for Paris. One of the girls at school knows an artist with a divinely quaint studio on the Left Bank, and I'm sure he would have been thrilled to let us stay for a week or two. I almost had Judith convinced, but then Fate struck."

"Fate?"

"We were sitting at a sidewalk cafe in Athens, trying to decide if Judith had enough money to fly to Paris—the trains can be dingy—when these two guys asked if they could join us. Judith almost died in her seat, but I told them they could. Three hours later Judith was In Love. The capital letters are hers."

"With Gideon Adler?" Theo said, surprised.

Dorrie politely overlooked his faux pas. "With Hershel Waskow, Uncle Theo. Gideon's not exactly her type. Hershel is."

"The thin young man with the stooped shoulders?"

"The chinless, spineless, mindless wonder. He's hardly the sort one imagines in the role of an Israeli Romeo, but he and Judith found each other more quickly than Simmons could recite a passage from *Ulysses*. It was sort of sweet, I suppose, and I presumed that they'd hop in bed, exchange addresses, and forget about each other. Silly me." She rolled her eyes and sighed.

Theo tried not to sound disapproving as he said, "That may be a standard form of romantic fulfillment among your friends, but it hardly seems to be, shall we say, adequate."

"That's exactly what Judith thought," Dorrie said irritably. She sat up and pushed the errant curl off her forehead. "Judith was convinced that she'd found her true love. After a teensy argument, we went back to the vile structure loosely termed a hotel, packed our bags, and left Simmons a note at the desk. And here we are." She flopped back once more. Another sigh was aimed at the ceiling.

"I understand Judith's motivation, but not yours, Dorrie. Why did you come with her?"

"Judith is totally immature about men. Every one she's been involved with turned up with a prison record, a pregnant wife, or a job in a garage. Leechley was on academic probation; Bruce had a secret predilection for panty hose and black brassieres—and I don't mean on women. Poor Judith has yet to pick anyone remotely resembling a winner. Her choices don't even place or show, for that matter. Three legs and hoof-and-mouth disease is more like it."

"So you came along in order to supply advice?"

"Somebody had to, and Simmons is a virgin. Judith is my best friend, and I'm going to stay until I convince her to come back to Wellesley with me. Or you do, Uncle Theo." The voice drifting toward the ceiling was immensely smug.

Chapter 5

Once in the safety of his room, Theo undressed and prepared for bed. Then, with a vague hope his travel guide would vanquish his unease over Dorrie's complacently presented plan, he began to read. And read. And read.

It was becoming absurd, he thought as he alertly plowed through one chapter after another. At last he tucked a bookmark between the pages and placed the book on the bedside table. His watch, now set to local time, indicated it was nearing midnight, but it felt more like the middle of the afternoon. Sleep was out of the question. No greenhouse to putter in, no potted plant to listen to a report of his silly flutter around Miriam, as if she were a candle and he an obscure species of hairless moth. She had been polite, but she was undoubtedly polite to everyone, including the boring, the presumptuous, and the bald.

His mental lecture lasted for only a minute or two. Then, unable to bring himself to return to his book, he slipped his feet into slippers and began to wander around the room. By twelve-thirty, he suspected he had logged nearly a mile. For his effort, he felt more alert, if such a thing were possible, and less inclined to sleep.

At last he admitted the impossibility of further exploration of the room, dressed, and pocketed the key. Outside, the stars were muted by the evaporation rising from the Dead Sea even in the middle of the night. Darkness had brought no relief; the air was as thick and suffocating as it had been twelve hours ago.

After an indecisive moment, Theo went down the stairs and strolled along a path he hoped might lead to the beach. A metallic redolence grew stronger as he passed between two dark bathhouses and down a rough walkway. As he neared the edge of the water, the acrid air began to sting his eyes and overpower his nose and throat. He was gasping when he finally halted with his toes inches from the gently lapping waves.

"An apropos name," he murmured, taking out his handkerchief to wipe his eyes. "It's likely to have a terminal effect on anyone foolish enough to actually bathe in it."

There were no lights across the water to indicate the presence of a Jordanian village or even a guard post. There was nothing except diaphanous mist and blackness. He looked back at Kibbutz Mishkan, lit by a few sparse lampposts and strategic floodlights. In the distance an engine rumbled to a halt. Turkeys gobbled briefly in alarm, then subsided into gallinaceous grumbles.

He turned back and bent down in order to dip his finger in the water, then touched it to the tip of his tongue. "Vile," he said thoughtfully, "and oily. I do wonder why anyone—"

A noise from the shadows stopped him from further speculation. He hastily dried his finger on the handkerchief as he peered for a sign of movement. He saw nothing.

When the noise was not repeated, Theo started up the path toward the bathhouses, smiling at his momentary and old-maidish alarm. Israel, as Mr. Baedeker had assured him, was rife with dogs and cats, along with mice, lizards, birds, and other benign creatures that prowled the night. A voice in the back of his mind mentioned that there were also terrorists.

Although he knew it was foolish, he quickened his pace.

Once in his room, he vowed, he would order his eyelids closed, and sleep whether he liked it or not. The midnight stroll was a silly way for a silly old man to escape his thoughts, and he would have no more of it. For that matter, he—

Two figures stepped into his path. Theo caught a glimpse of khaki and guns as he stumbled forward onto the hard concrete walk. What little air was left in his lungs went out with a pained whoosh that left red circles in front of his eyes and an erratic rhythm in his chest. Pain shot up from his knee. The pebbles on the concrete bit into his palms like thorns. Above him he heard the sound of a rifle being cocked. Breathing heavily, he looked up at a sardonic smile and two hard, glittering eyes.

The woman aimed her gun at the center of his forehead. She growled something in Hebrew. Nevertheless, the message was more than clear.

"Don't shoot, please," he said, hoping the response was appropriate to the question.

A second figure leaned over to stare at him. "Mr. Bloomer?"

With a bark of laughter, a third khaki-clad figure appeared from the shadows. "It seems Dorrie's uncle is more than a simple tourist from the States."

Theo struggled to his feet and took out his handkerchief to wipe the dirt off his hands. Although he admitted to a few fears, children in khaki playing soldiers were not on the list. Their guns merited a degree of respect, however. And the young woman, whom he presumed was Ilana, seemed very near utilizing hers in a manner perilous to his hopes for longevity.

"Dorrie's uncle?" she echoed incredulously.

Theo bowed slightly. "I do have that honor, but not the honor of your acquaintance. I am Theodore Bloomer of

Handy Hollow, Connecticut. I have already been introduced to Gideon and Hershel."

She stepped back and glanced at her companions. "Dorrie's uncle? Are you sure?" With visible disappointment, she lowered the rifle.

Gideon scowled. "That's what my mother told me. Hershel was there, too. What do you think?"

Hershel's gun was trembling against his knee. "It's the man from the lobby. I guess you're right, Gid."

Ilana (or so Theo still presumed) stepped forward to stare. In the dull light her cropped hair was as streaked and unruly as a haystack, but her round eyes still glittered like black buttons.

"So what are you doing on the beach after midnight, Mr. Theodore Bloomer? Expecting to meet someone in a *kaffiyeh?*"

Theo explained his insomnia to three stony faces. "And I followed the path to the edge of the water, at which point I heard you," he concluded with an apologetic shrug. "You could say that I was taking Essie's advice," he added, hoping to introduce a bit of levity to the situation.

"What did Essie say?" Gideon demanded.

If the levity were there, it hadn't made a significant dent on the beach patrol. He opted for a retreat. "She just mumbled a few suggestions about possible activities. Strolling was one of them. I'll just return to my room now, if you don't mind, and try to sleep."

"Good night," Hershel mumbled, looking abashed.

Ilana (or so he continued to presume in the absence of an introduction) was less than abashed. "I shall file a report about this," she said sternly, her English accented but concise. "Your passport is in the safe; the gate is closed for the night. Better you should not plan to cut short your stay at the Kibbutz Mishkan guest house, Mr. Bloomer."

Gideon opened his mouth as if to emphasize the warning, but settled for a scowl. The three exchanged nods, then faded into the darkness near the path.

"Interesting," Theo said in an underbreath, once more using his handkerchief to wipe his hands. He repeated the word several times on the return trip to his room, where he carefully bolted the door before tumbling into bed.

Chapter 6

The next morning, after a restive but satisfactory bout of sleep, Theo went to the restaurant. Without an editorial about the menu to daunt his appetite, he ate a substantial breakfast at a corner table. When he was finished, he asked the waitress where he might find Mrs. Adler. He was told that she often worked in the office behind the reception desk. It proved to be true.

"Did you manage any sleep?" she asked with a solicitous frown. "You look in need of a nap in the sun and a swim rather than a guided tour."

"Perhaps later, although I have reservations about the therapeutic value of the waters of the Dead Sea. It has a peculiar odor, and it tastes quite unpleasant." He did not add that he had not made a public appearance in bathing trunks in more than three decades.

"It's famed for its effect on arthritis and such ailments, but I won't play the Jewish mother. Come along, then," Miriam said, as she sailed past him and through the lobby. She stopped in the doorway and glanced back at him with a critical eye. "Wait a moment, Theo. You're likely to burn your head if you stay outside without protection. The sun is intense here."

As he formulated a protest, she leaned over the counter and found a white cloth hat with a narrow brim. She saw his expression and burst into laughter. "It's a typical Israeli hat," she managed to sputter, unable to halt the lilting laughter. "You'll look like a *sabra,* Theo. I—I promise."

"A *sabra?*" he said. He gingerly took the hat between his thumb and index finger, wondering if a *sabra* were a species of bald marine animal.

"A native-born Israeli. It comes from the name of a certain kind of cactus fruit. Tough and prickly on the outside, but rumored to be sweet on the inside. Try on the hat, Theo."

"If you feel that it is necessary." He was painfully aware that he was going to look peculiar in the thing. It was—well, it was jaunty, a word rarely used in conjunction with a retired florist. Then again, his head was likely to resemble a tomato if left unprotected. He put on the little hat and adjusted it until it seemed secure, if not rakish. "How do I look?"

Miriam tilted her head to study him. "Very proper, considering. Are you ready for an hour or so in the sun?"

Theo nodded. The hat inched forward, but he staunchly ignored it, despite the intrusive and unsettling image of a myopic turtle that flashed across his mind.

"The kibbutz movement originated in nineteen oh-nine," she told him as they wandered down the sidewalk, "with the establishment of a group near Lake Kinneret. The precedent, however, was set about one hundred BCE, Before the Common Era, when a sect of Jews left Jerusalem to create a new community in the desert. The Essenes survived until the Roman legions destroyed them in sixty-six CE, but we've learned much about them from the Dead Sea Scrolls. They seem to have had the same problems we have today: equality of work, participation in a direct democratic process, balancing the requirements of the group with the needs of the individual."

Theo stopped to admire a striking scarlet vine growing on what was, without a doubt, a bomb shelter. Which, unless it were strictly for decoration, implied the necessity of taking shelter from bombs. After a brief glance at an innocent blue

sky, he said, "You mentioned earlier that your second generation of kibbutzniks has experienced some difficulty . . . ?"

Miriam pulled off a flower and crumpled it in her hand.

The petals drifted to the sidewalk like droplets of blood,
then skidded away in the breeze. "For the most part, those of
us who founded Kibbutz Mishkan came from the worst slums
of New York City. Our immigrant parents had learned that
the streets weren't paved with gold; they were barely paved at
all. Nazi Germany taught us that we needed a homeland, a
place to establish ourselves as Jews and as citizens of the
world. We came to Israel not with stars in our eyes—but with
fire and fury. We never paused to wonder if we should plant
date palms here or squash there; we arrogantly said, 'There
shall be date palms and there shall be squash.' When the time
came to add an industry, we did. Like all naive young parents,
we conceived, delivered, and instinctively protected our hostile offspring."

She paused to point out the scattered concrete-block du-
plexes and two-story apartment buildings that housed the
adults, mentioning that hers was one of the first built. It was,
Theo noted, fronted by a row of annuals that were bleached
by the sun, yet still cheerful. Petunias had always been a favorite of his.

"Our children," she added as they resumed their walk,
"have a difficult time feeling the passions we felt. Having
spent their lives here, they can't understand the struggle we
had to establish our structure, define our goals—and then
force it to happen. They contend that they've been asked to
continue in the shadow of a past ideal. Some leave the kibbutz; others, such as my son, struggle with themselves to discover a new passion. I was a dreamer; Gideon is a pragmatist
who—" She stopped herself with an unhappy shrug. "That
was a digression from my standard talk, and I apologize. You

mustn't think the second generation is unemotional. Although kibbutzniks represent less than four percent of the population, they accounted for more than twenty-five percent of the casualties in the last war. These kids care deeply about Israel."

She stopped to wave at two young women who came out of a building that clanked and steamed as if it housed a locomotive. Miriam introduced them as Hadassah and Naomi, adding that they worked in the laundry facility. They giggled at Theo's grave bow, then excused themselves and scurried down the sidewalk like oblivious young housewives headed for lunch at a shopping mall.

Theo watched them as they turned a corner and disappeared. "I would think," he said hesitantly, "that those girls would resent having to do the work they do. It must be terribly hot and tedious."

"They know that their work is as important to the kibbutz as meal preparation, factory production, or agricultural duties, and they receive equal shares of the goods and services. When the kibbutz was first begun, we all demanded the most arduous assignments and argued for the privilege of being the most exhausted, sore, sunburned kibbutznik to collapse on a cot every night." Miriam bent over to scoop up a handful of dirt from a flowerbed. "This is what matters," she said softly, lifting her gaze to include the buildings, clumps of trees, and distant fields. "This."

Theo was rescued from the necessity of a response by a horde of school-aged children. They swept by in a dusty cloud of knees, elbows, and loud explosions of laughter elicited by incomprehensible comments aimed, he suspected, at his appearance in the peculiar hat. Three teachers trailed after them, chatting among themselves.

"A field trip," Miriam explained with a smile that did

much to ease his discomfort. "Let's visit the factory. I think you'll find it quite impressive, or at least very noisy and bustling. We have contracts with several manufacturing firms to design and produce their cartons. Personally, I'm fond of the ice-cream boxes."

The factory was more than very noisy. Theo resisted an urge to pull his hat down over his ears as they walked between enormous machines that inked, chopped, cut, slammed, and spewed forth a bright river of flattened cardboard corpses.

"Tuna today," Miriam yelled over the din. "Let me introduce you to the line supervisor. He'll be delighted to explain the intricacies of tunafish cartons, if you're interested."

Theo felt obliged to feel fascinated by the workings of the cacophonous cavern. The supervisor, a sturdy young man with black hair and a broad smile, enthusiastically shook Theo's hand and shouted a highly technical explanation that would have been enlightening had Theo been able to understand any of it. The workers glanced up briefly, but most seemed to find their work of greater interest.

When the supervisor at last finished, Theo mouthed a word of thanks and gratefully followed Miriam out the door. "A nice young man," he said, shaking his head to stop a shrill whistle that originated from the inside of his bruised eardrums. "How long has he been in charge of the factory?"

"A few weeks, and he isn't really in charge. The workers make group decisions about production goals, machine assignments, and so forth. No one relishes the role of supervisor, however, and Daniel seems to be stuck for the moment. Most of us have to force ourselves to accept positions of authority; it somehow goes against the spirit of the kibbutz. A leadership hierarchy is inevitable, but not socially desirable."

"So everyone is willing to take whatever job is assigned?" Theo asked. "No one refuses to take a dirty or boring job?"

"There are no insignificant jobs. Each is vital, and each is filled on a voluntary basis. Many of our neophytes end up with a mild case of sunstroke—after they insist on working twelve hours a day in the fields. Personal sacrifice is the rule, not the exception."

They sat down on a bench under a tree. Theo fanned himself with his hat as he tried to assimilate the information his attractive—yes, attractive; there was no way of ignoring it—guide had given him. It would not play in Connecticut, he decided, trying to picture Dorrie pleading for a job that might chip her fingernail polish or cause her to miss a tennis tournament. Or sweat. The image of Dorrie's expression faded, to be replaced by an older and wiser face, with fine lines around the eyes and a mist of soft freckles.

"Hard to understand, isn't it?" Miriam said softly. He caught a glimpse of impish amusement before she looked away.

He opted for a safe subject and told her what he had learned from Dorrie about her avowal to remain on the kibbutz. "So Judith is at the root of Dorrie's nonsense," he concluded. "I am supposed to meet with Judith, convince her of her folly, and persuade her to return to the United States in time for the fall semester. Dorrie is not opposed to a brief stopover in Paris, but is willing to forego it if absolutely necessary."

"Judith is an intense young woman. She's been very enthusiastic about the kibbutz since she arrived, and has thrown herself into the work of the community. I realized that she and Hershel were seeing each other in their free time, but I didn't know it was quite so serious. It won't be easy to persuade her to leave with you."

"I can only do my best," Theo said. "What about Hershel? Does he seem to be the sort to make a commitment to Judith, to encourage her to stay and marry?"

"Hershel's hard to second-guess. Sy and I placed our son in the children's house by choice; Hershel's parents were killed in a terrorist raid during the Six-Day War, when he was not quite seven years old. All of us tried to make him feel a part of our families, and to support and nurture him as if he were our own. I'm afraid he never quite recovered from his loss, and has always been a sad, shy boy. His friendship with Gideon is the only thing that's kept him out of a permanent depression."

"Perhaps I ought not to disturb his relationship with Judith," he said. "If they can be happy together . . . ?"

"You'd better talk to her," Miriam said, still frowning. "In fact, we'll go by the children's house now so that you can meet her. It's an obligatory stop on the tour, between the carton factory and the turkey houses."

They resumed their walk until they reached a fence that enclosed a divided playground. In the distance, elementary school children played sedately underneath a tree. On the near side, several toddlers were struggling with a wagon, while a dark-haired young woman watched from the shade.

Miriam waved from the gate. "Judith, come meet Dorrie's uncle, Theo Bloomer. He's visiting Kibbutz Mishkan this week."

As she approached, Theo could see that Dorrie had faced a chore worthy of Hercules. Judith's round face was attractive, although devoid of makeup and as shiny as a holly leaf. Mr. Robert had not been notably successful; his artistic endeavor had been replaced by a pendulous braid, tied with a broken shoelace. Tortoise-shell glasses contributed to her aura of unsmiling earnestness. The blue work shirt was frayed at the collar, and a button dangled by a thread like a round white spider. A tarnished silver Star of David hung from a second shoelace around her neck. Theo found himself comparing her to the blossom of a meadow milkweed, which was not without unruly charm. It would look incongruous, however, in the centerpiece arrangement on a formal dining table.

"So Dorrie called in the cavalry," she said in response to Miriam's introduction. "I'm pleased to meet you, Mr. Bloomer, and I hope you have a lovely visit with us."

"Thank you, Judith. I am charmed to meet you. I understand that you and Dorrie were roommates at school last year."

"Poor Dorrie," Judith sighed, "was—stop that!" She ran across the playground to remove a rock from a small mouth, then returned with an apologetic look. "As I was saying, Dorrie was startled to find me in her room. I had not one shirt with an alligator, much less a bona fide polo player. No one's name stitched on my denim derriere or on my genuine leather purse—which was genuine plastic. Dorrie had to lie down for several hours, with a cold compress on her forehead."

Theo acknowledged her acumen with a brief smile. "She seems to have recovered nicely from the culture shock. I gather the two of you are close friends now."

Judith again dashed across the playground to rescue the rock. While he and Miriam waited, Theo murmured, "She's not at all what I was led to anticipate. Dorrie made her sound—well, compliant and capable of responding to persuasion. I believe I shall have no success with Judith."

"You need to talk to her," Miriam insisted in a low voice. As Judith returned, she said, "Why don't you and Mr. Bloomer have a soda in the lounge, Judith?"

"I'm on duty until nine o'clock. One of the other teachers has a cold, and Sarah asked me to cover the second shift. Sorry, Mr. Bloomer." Behind her a toddler war erupted amidst squeals and cries. Judith shrugged and turned away to separate combatants and soothe imaginary wounds.

Miriam raised her voice to compete with the uproar. "I'll speak to Sarah, Judith. I'm sure we can work out something so that you can have a break."

Judith waved over a screaming child that seemed determined to make chowder of his playmates. Theo and Miriam hurried away from the playground to the relative peacefulness of the sidewalk.

"Then Judith is doing work in the kibbutz?" Theo asked. "Is she already a member?"

"No, would-be members must do a three-month apprenticeship, and then, if they seem like potentials, a one-year trial stay. We have more applicants than we can begin to absorb, despite the proximity of the Administered Territories and Jordan eleven miles away. We can only take about twenty-five a year, unless they're spouses or relatives. As a rule, we won't consider singles unless they're under thirty and feverishly committed, but there's always room for volunteers. Judith volunteered ten minutes after she arrived."

"Dorrie didn't request an assignment to keep her busy?"

Miriam tried to hide a smile. "She was offered a position in the turkey house, and also in the date grove. She declined."

"Then what has she been doing for the last few weeks?"

The smile finally won. "You'll have to ask her, Theo. It's one of our local mysteries, and I haven't time to play detective. Let's go to the community dining hall so that I can speak to Sarah about Judith's break. Surely someone else can tend the battlefront for an hour or so, as long as it's not I. I prefer tourists to teething infants and dirty diapers."

Pleased that he interested her more than a squabble of children, Theo followed.

The community dining hall was filled with long tables that stretched toward the back wall like narrow formica runways.

The clatter from an invisible kitchen indicated the presence of massive, modern appliances and a great deal of industrious work. Most of the tables were uninhabited, but a few people looked up incuriously as Miriam scanned the room.

Slipping into her tour-guide role, she told him how the dining hall served as the center of kibbutz life. Although meals were provided three times a day, many of the older kibbutzniks often ate in their homes, she explained, adding that general assemblies were held several times a month, as well as chess tournaments and crafts classes. Theo learned there was a library on the second floor, along with meeting rooms and offices.

They went up a flight of stairs and through a carpeted lounge. They entered an office that would have been spacious had it not been filled with filing cabinets, a battered sofa, a coffee table, and an oversized desk covered with stacks of ledgers and officious forms. A silver-haired man, dressed in tight denim jeans and a loose shirt embroidered with vining flowers, closed a ledger and looked up with a scowl. It disappeared when he saw Miriam.

"Yussef," Miriam said, "this is Theo Bloomer. Theo, Yussef Nava." After the two men shook hands, she continued, "I'm sorry to interrupt you, but I'm looking for Sarah. Has she already gone to Jericho for the meeting?"

Yussef snorted like a certain Connecticut racehorse. "I have no idea, Miriam. Sarah rarely mentions her plans to me these days; for all I know, she may have run away to Baltimore with a PLO gunman. Which," he added with a second derisive snort, "would not overly distress me. It would, in fact, provide an opportunity to break out a bottle of that absolutely marvelous claret I picked up last spring in the south of France. Could I interest you in joining me in the privacy of my living room later?"

Theo did not care for the leer on Yussef's face, but it did not warrant an attack from a knight in rusty armor. He cleared his throat and said, "Shall I wait downstairs, Miriam?"

"No, Theo, I'm ready to leave. Yussef, if you happen to see Sarah, please ask her to call me at the guesthouse. By the way, I received a nasty call from a bureaucrat at the revenue office in Jerusalem. I told him that you'd sent the quarterly installment in weeks ago, but he grunted out a threat or two before he rang off. You did send the check in with the tax form, didn't you?"

"But of course, light of my life. The government must have decided to save money by using camels to carry the mail—or Arabs to deliver it. I shall call your nasty bureaucrat and warn him not to bother you with petty problems."

"While we're on the subject of petty problems, whatever happened to the towels I ordered six weeks ago?"

Yussef's daisy-covered shoulders rose. "I'll see if an invoice has come through, dearest Miriam, but you must realize these things take time."

"Guests take towels, along with ashtrays and soap. Remember to ask Sarah to call me, please."

"I shall, desert flower, I shall. Oh, and about an hour ago Anya called looking for you. Our mentally-deficient maid failed to do the floors in the lobby, and Anya is in a dither. I realize that we all agreed that Essie should have some responsibilities, but it may be time to retire her to a padded room. She'll enjoy it; the decor will match the interior of her head. Cotton batting and plywood."

"Now, Yussef," Miriam said grimly, "in a general assembly we all agreed that Essie was to have the assignment, even though we were aware that she does wander off upon occasion. Within a few hours she'll come back with a pitiful collection of aluminum foil and shiny feathers, offer some story about the call of the wild, and return to work. I'd suggest you stop criticizing her—unless you'd prefer to do the lobby floor on your hands and knees . . ."

"Only if I can kneel before you," he countered with a smirk.

Theo was not amused by the image, but he kept the acerbic comment that came to mind to himself. Miriam merely laughed as if she'd heard it before.

Yussef leered a farewell and returned to his ledger. As they went down the stairs, she said, "He's not as—as immature as he pretends. Yussef has done the ordering and kept the books for the kibbutz for nearly twenty years, and he has done a marvelous job. Now that we've prepared to computerize the operation, he's begun to feel less important. It's difficult."

"Sarah is his wife?" Rhetorical but necessary.

"Indeed she is, although I hope they behave much better toward each other in private. They've been married for nearly thirty years; something must be holding them together."

Theo dearly hoped so.

On the kitchen sill so many miles away, that which was holding the cereus bud together began to ease as the orange leaf patiently continued to prod.

Chapter 7

On their way back to the lobby, Miriam pointed out the odoriferous turkey houses, a factory constructed of corrugated iron sheets, a small infirmary with three rooms for ailing kibbutzniks, and the fields and orchards irrigated by snakish black hoses that zigzagged into scum-coated ponds.

"Surely the water does not come from the Dead Sea," Theo said, enchanted by the tidy, verdant rows. "I am astonished there is adequate water for all this and for the date palms."

"We can use brackish water for the palms, which is why you'll see so many of them in Israel. The other crops require fresh water, but as hard as it is to imagine, we have flash floods every year. Portions of the road are actually under water for hours at a time, although not from excessive rain. At the most, we get a few inches every year, but Jerusalem receives an average of twenty-one inches in less than three months. The Judaean desert is downhill all the way. The water reaches us in dry riverbeds called wadis, and we save every drop we can in cisterns and ponds. Would you like to see a wadi while you're here?"

"Is that safe?" Theo asked. "If a sudden surge of water should catch us, it could be dangerous."

"The wadis are dangerous only in the winter when the streambeds fill. If you'd like, we could take a jeep out one morning, and even a picnic lunch." A worried look crossed her face, as if she felt she were being presumptuous. After a moment of hesitancy, she seemed to arrive at a decision. "Although most of the Dead Sea Scrolls were found to the north, in the area near Qumran, a few were found in the caves near here. We could look in one or two of them. Who knows? We might stumble onto a perfectly preserved scroll and become known as world-famous archaeologists." The hesitancy returned and she shook her head. "How silly of me, Theo. You're here to see about Dorrie and Judith; I shouldn't suggest frivolous diversions."

"But I would very much enjoy a trip into the desert," Theo protested. "I am fascinated by the idea, and also by the premise of a picnic. I wish I had a bottle of marvelous claret to contribute, but I shall attempt to purchase one from the bartender."

They halted in the doorway of the lobby. "I'll see about a jeep and a basket for tomorrow," she said, "but often one has to wait. We have only a dozen cars and jeeps for over two hundred people. It's one of the minor details that drives Gideon crazy—but it's also an economic reality. Now I'd better see about Essie. If she's wandering in the desert, she may not turn up for several hours and I doubt Anya will scrub the floors in a burst of altruistic spirit."

"She wanders away often?"

"Does chicken soup cure the common cold? Yes, Theo, we lose her at least once a month, but she usually comes back on her own after she's found enough treasures. This is the first time she's left without doing her assignment, however, and that worries me. It really is unlike her. I'll have to talk to her about it."

Theo reiterated his desire to visit the desert. Miriam promised to let him know later and vanished through the door behind the registration desk. He gazed at the door for a few seconds, then went to the bar for a glass of soda water, brand unknown. The bout in the sun had tired him, he realized. The phenomenon of jet lag could no longer be ignored.

He returned to his room, closed the curtains, and slept.

A knock on the door roused him several hours later. Dorrie was dressed in a terry-cloth beach robe and sandals from which pink toenails protruded like gleaming lobelia petals. In one hand she held a bulging bag; in the other, a plastic water bottle and two of the glasses from her bathroom.

"Don't you want to swim, Uncle Theo? I usually wait until late in the afternoon to sunbathe. It's simply too hot during the middle of the day, and I cannot bear to perspire unless there's a legitimate purpose. But I must face the reality that my tan is not what it ought to be. I cannot return to school looking as if I'd spent the summer vacation in a tomb. No one would speak to me."

Theo edged back in alarm. "I did not plan to swim, my dear. I have several chapters in my Baedekers to finish, and—"

"Uncle Theo," Dorrie interrupted, sounding exactly like her mother, "are you being modest? The beach is totally empty; no one will peek at your paunch except me—and I intend to give all of my attention to the horrible white bikini line across my back. You can't protest that you're unable to swim. No one has ever gone under; the water's too buoyant. I insist you try it."

"I suppose I ought to try it this one time," he said. Dorrie not only had the acuity of her mother, but also the steel spine. It was hopeless. "Let me change into my bathing trunks and find a towel that isn't too damp. The maid has taken an unauthorized leave of absence, and we may have to suffer without fresh linens until she returns."

"Essie hasn't done my room, either," Dorrie said.

Wondering how she could tell, Theo let her wait outside

while he changed into his swimming attire. The paunch was—well, visible, but hardly overwhelming, he told himself in a show of bravado. He then put on his robe, picked up the guidebook and a towel, and followed her down the sidewalk to the beach.

"The mineral content of the water is twenty-seven percent, and the salinity is twenty-five percent higher than the Mediterranean," he informed her, the book held open to the appropriate page. "There are also measurable amounts of iodine, sulfur, potash, and bromine."

"Fascinating," Dorrie murmured. She pointed out a shower nearby, and then found a level patch of sand on which to spread her towel and other vital paraphernalia. When she was satisfied with the arrangement, which encompassed an area adequate for a battalion campsite, she said, "Don't let the water get in your eyes or mouth, Uncle Theo. It tastes like the punch the boys at Cornell serve on football weekends. Too nauseous for words!"

As promised, the beach was unpopulated. Theo left his rubber sandals at the water's edge and, wincing at the burning rocks, waded into the shallow water. Even there the rocks were hot, so he resolutely continued forward until the water reached his waist.

As he leaned back, his feet rose of their own volition to offer a view of ten toes and an equal number of unadorned toenails. His arms drifted to the surface as if he were ensconced in a recliner. The rest of him had no tendency to sink. Quite the contrary, he decided with an amazed smile.

"One does not sink," he called to Dorrie. "Mr. Baedeker was emphatic about the effect of the high salinity, but I assumed it to be an exaggeration. It most definitely is not."

Dorrie was supine for maximum exposure. She waved a bottle of lotion in response. "I've been in a few times, just to see if it would do anything for the dry skin on my heels. It's weird, isn't it?"

Theo bobbled like a cork, delightedly watching his feet. The water was tepid but refreshing, and as soothing as a massage. Oil swirled on the surface in undulating rainbows; the odor was not intolerable once he grew accustomed to it. It could well be therapeutic, he concluded as he let his head fall back.

He drifted about for a few minutes, until a tingle on the top of his head reminded him that he had failed to wear the odd native hat Miriam had given him. Which led his thoughts to Miriam. Which he firmly resisted as he made his way to the shallow water and the protection of his sandals.

After a brief shower, he found a shaded area near Dorrie and sat down on his towel. "I met Judith this morning, Dorrie. I found her polite but not at all an easy subject for coercion. She has the temperament and tenacity of a philodendron. You may have to return without her."

"No can do," Dorrie said through white-caked lips. Her eyes were invisible under squares of cotton; very little of the rest of her was, except for those parts dictated by law. "I can't leave her here. The climate will destroy her complexion and damage her hair beyond redemption. Besides that, she has only one more year at Wellesley, and a few more years somewhere else for a graduate degree. Then all the little ghetto children will learn to mug pedestrians in Latin. They can remind themselves that *fortuna favet fortibus*. I learned that much from Simmons."

"Judith did not sound as if she were concerned with her physical deterioration or her escape from academia. It is not unreasonable to permit her to decide for herself. She may elect to stay here."

"Then I'll have to stay, too," Dorrie said complacently. "You can tell Mother and Daddy."

Theo tugged at the tip of his beard as he searched for further arguments. Loyalty was an admirable virtue, but his niece's stubbornness seemed based on something else, something she refused to explain. She was not the sort to suffer, to jeopardize her tidy future or even her immediate comfort, unless she were deeply disturbed.

"What about Hershel?" he hazarded. "Don't you like him?"

"What's not to like? He's a nice man, in an awkward, inarticulate fashion that Judith finds especially endearing for reasons that escape me. Very sincere, very earnest about Judith staying here and eventually marrying him in some Jewish ceremony under a tent. With brand-X soda water and chopped chicken liver at the reception. Folk dancing done to music on a record player." A strangled noise slipped out as Dorrie envisioned the scene. It would not play in Connecticut.

"He recently graduated from the university?" There had to be something, if only he could isolate it.

"Yep, after the army he, Gideon, and Ilana all went to the university in Tel Aviv as if they were Siamese triplets. Hershel majored in archaeology, and Gideon in agro-economics. I don't know what Ilana studied—malice, probably. She is a colossal pain in the ass. She'd do well at Radcliffe."

"I believe I encountered the young woman," Theo said. He did not mention the circumstances, although he was within a few feet of the site of his embarrassment. "Small, blonde hair much the same color as yours but shorter, and with a squarish face?"

"My hair is frosted summer ash, Uncle Theo. Hers is strictly sandstorm and split ends, and chopped off at an unflattering length. I suspect she cuts her hair herself—in the dark, with pruning shears. I trimmed my bangs once for a party, and I thought Mr. Robert was going to have a stroke.

115

He made me swear to never, ever do it again. I had to Federal Express all my scissors to him."

"Oh," Theo said. Life in Connecticut was more perilous than he had thought. If Mr. Robert tired of styling hair, he might do well as a cabin attendant on overseas flights. "Then am I correct in saying that you and Ilana are not especially friendly?"

Dorrie yanked herself to a sitting position. "Ilana suggested that I work in the turkey house! Can you believe that? I had no idea how even to respond; I had to conclude she was attempting some sort of tasteless joke. Then she mentioned the date palms. People actually climb up ladders to hang bags around the dates to protect them from birds. I was floored, Uncle Theo. Floored." The memories seemed adequate to send her into well-bred hysterics, if the trembling lower lips and flashing eyes were symptomatic.

"Of course you were," Theo said hastily. "Those are hardly your species of dates. Ilana sounds like a most peculiar person."

The lower lip ceased its tremors and curled slightly. "Ilana is jealous of me," she confided in a demure tone. "As I told you, Judith and I met Hershel and Gideon in Athens, and came back with them on the same flight. Judith and Hershel wanted to crawl all over each other, so I was forced to sit with Gideon. Ilana jumped to some bizarre conclusion that Gideon and I were developing the hots for each other. She's been in love with him since she was old enough to tweak his diapers."

"Is that a supposition or a fact?"

"Everybody knows about her crush on Gideon. God, everybody knows when someone sneezes around her, and half of them come running to see if it might be detrimental to the welfare of the community. It's absolutely stifling."

"Does Gideon reciprocate Ilana's feelings?" Theo said, overlooking the aspersions on the kibbutz. Where Miriam lived.

"I don't know." Dorrie applied a sheen of lotion to her shoulders, replaced the bottle in her bag, positioned the cotton squares, and lay back. "It doesn't concern me, since I have a meaningful emotional commitment to Biff. His father owns a brokerage firm in New York, and Biff has already picked out a darling corner office. If we have to live in the city, I hope we can find something on the Upper East Side. Lofts may be quaint, but I think I'd prefer a more formal arrangement. What do you think, Uncle Theo? Should I sacrifice a guest room to be trendy?"

"Let me give it some thought," Theo said gravely. Judith loved Hershel, who loved her. That was tidy. But if Ilana loved Gideon, who was panting after Dorrie, who was more concerned about trendy addresses than his feelings . . . and if Yussef was lusting after Miriam rather than his wife . . . and if Miriam was overly sympathetic to the lecherous hippie . . . and if the purportedly efficient maid did not appear to clean the bedrooms in the guest house . . . it clearly wasn't tidy at all.

"How does Essie fit in with the other three?" he asked. "She surely did not go into the army or attend the university."

Dorrie giggled. "Isn't she interesting? I think I had her case history in Ab Psych my sophomore year. I'd love to see her in Simmons's lecture class."

"Have you had a conversation with her?"

"Who can tell? I tried again yesterday morning, but she kept blinking her eyes and muttering dire curses in that nasal monotone of hers. I doubt she knows whether or not she's supposed to have an accent. It comes and goes with the tide."

"I noticed that, too," Theo said, remembering the odd discussion of fish futures.

Dorrie sat up to smooth a dab of lotion on her nose. "I thought I'd be friendly and ask her where she lived, and she turned around and said she was going to run over and bite me or something equally absurd. I was terrified that I was going to hurt her feelings, so I nodded as if I'd understood and told her I had to wash my hair. Well, she made a face and said, 'Why?' and I just couldn't think of an answer. I suspect she's never washed her hair, much less applied a creme rinse and a conditioner. Can you imagine Mr. Robert's face if Essie strolled in?" She sank back in a flurry of giggles.

"Did she say anything about fresh towels?"

The giggles stopped abruptly. "She told me I was cheap. I hadn't even offered a tip, Uncle Theo. It was a total non sequitur. I certainly intend to drop a few dollars on the dresser when I leave, but I cannot make a daily habit of it. Daddy cut off my checking account last month because of some gross error the bank made. They actually had the nerve to return eleven checks in one week simply because I was a teensy bit late with a deposit. I've had my own checking account there since I was five years old; it's not like they don't know me!"

"Dreadful," Theo murmured.

"I should say so. Anyway, yesterday afternoon when I told Judith, Romeostein, the Marquessa de Sade, and Gideon, they all thought it was *trés amusant*. The vile squids!"

"You told them about your—ah, problems with the local bank?"

"We were talking about Essie," she reminded him huffily. "I would never tell anyone but a close family member about the ordeal with the bank. And Biff, of course, and his mother. Do you know what the very worst part of it was?" There was a dramatic pause during which Theo felt obliged to hold his breath, or at least look as though he were doing so. "It was the very week of my birthday."

"How insensitive of them."

"That's exactly what Biff said. He said I ought to sue them for defamation of character and then just pull all my money out and take it to another bank. Daddy wouldn't let me."

"No, I would imagine that Charles preferred to have a word with the banker in private. Discretion and all." Theo looked at the Dead Sea. The matte brown surface rather reminded him of Charles.

"They play golf every Thursday," Dorrie sighed. "But as I was trying to tell you, Judith, Ilana, and Gideon all howled like veritable banshees when I told them about Essie's dour comments. 'Essie and sex?' That's by far the silliest thing I've heard in months; Essie wouldn't know a bird from a bee if they both perched on her head to copulate. But all the same, it was not pleasant for me. Gideon was the only one who could understand how indignant I was—justifiably so—and he tried to tell me that Essie hadn't meant anything. At least he tried, Uncle Theo."

Theo could sympathize with the young man. It must have been decidedly trying.

119

Chapter 8

Miriam came by early in the evening to say a jeep was available if he were still interested in a jaunt and a picnic.

"Very much," he assured her, "but you are looking quite harried. Are you certain that this will not inconvenience you?"

"I can't find Essie, and it's worrying me more and more. She is one of the world's most irresponsible people, but she never has disappeared for such a long time. I'm trying not to think any ominous thoughts about what might have happened to her." She made the wry face Theo found so charming. "I don't want to bore you with the bitter truth about hotel staff management, so I shall see you tomorrow in the lobby around ten o'clock."

Theo saw her out, then turned around to frown at the unmade bed. It was all well and good to provide Essie with an uncomplicated assignment so that she could share in the work of the kibbutz. Well and good, yes; successful, no.

Grumbling under his breath, he made the bed to his satisfaction, draped the damp towels over the shower rod, and straightened the room. The gritty surfaces of the furniture irritated him, but he had no equipment to clean them properly. He was forced to use a handkerchief, but the result was far from satisfactory.

Dorrie joined him for dinner. They chatted about minor Connecticut matters, and when they were finished, went to the lobby for brandy and a perplexing dose of the evening news in Hebrew. Although the words were incomprehensible, the footage of the aftermath of an explosion was graphic. A policeman barked harshly into the camera as he pointed at a razed building and a huddle of weeping women dressed in long robes. Gurneys were wheeled past the camera, their occupants covered with white sheets already stained with dark patches. The news commentator expounded further, then turned his attention to tanks rumbling over hills.

"That was in Hebron," Dorrie said idly. "It's less than thirty miles from here, as the crow flies. Do they have crows in Israel?"

Theo raised his eyebrows. "I do not know why they wouldn't. I'm impressed that you've been learning Hebrew in your spare time."

"Hardly, Uncle Theo, it's all I can do to keep my hair conditioned. Gideon told me about the bombing."

"It looked serious. Thirty miles from here, you say?"

"It's three times further if the crow drives. Gideon said that four children were killed when a wall fell on them this morning. The building was a community center, and the children were there for some kind of scout meeting. Arabs, Gideon said. I think it's horrid that someone killed those little kids by mistake, even if they were Arabs."

"I agree," Theo said. He was aware of the tension between Arabs and Jews, but his fear of finding himself between grenade-wielding combatants had abated since his arrival. He was not delighted to be reminded of the situation, especially when it was a mere thirty miles away. "Have the police arrested the terrorists yet?"

Dorrie glared at a chipped fingernail. "They aren't terrorists, according to Gideon. Some group has already claimed credit. Gideon said the people who do these things are Jewish defense fighters, retaliating for earlier incidents. I don't suppose you have a nail file, do you?"

"I regret that I do not, Dorrie. I must admit that I am perplexed by Gideon's choice of nomenclature. If Jews were responsible for the death of four children, Arab or otherwise, do they not merit a title of 'terrorists'?"

She shrugged. "Gideon told me about it all the way from Athens to Tel Aviv, if you can imagine. He thinks that the retaliation is necessary in order for the Jews to keep their hold on Judaea and Samaria. He says the Arabs have to be taught that they can't get away with anything; otherwise, they'll keep murdering innocent people. The Arabs have pulled some pretty ghastly stuff, including killing women and babies, blowing up synagogues and so forth. All those terrible hijackings and airport bombings in the last year, the execution of hostages, the kidnappings and commando raids on border towns—it is fairly dreadful, Uncle Theo. Not that Gideon needed to froth about it for the entire plane ride, of course. I had hoped to read a magazine."

"But four children . . ." Theo said unhappily. "Surely Gideon cannot feel that the loss of innocent lives can in any way strengthen the position of the Jews?" When Dorrie again responded with a shrug, he put down his glass. "The bartender, I believe, would prefer us to leave so that he can close the bar. Shall we accommodate him?"

Dorrie was now frowning at all of her fingernails. "Yes, I need to go back to my room at once. I'm going to have to do something about my nails; this Israeli polish just disintegrates as fast as I put it on. It's been sheer hell trying to find a civilized color, and when I do, it chips off the moment I move my hand. I really don't know how I've avoided saying something tacky to someone about it."

Theo sympathized all the way back to their rooms.

The next morning he joined Miriam in the lobby. "I brought my hat," he said by way of greeting. "On the other hand, I was not able to purchase a bottle of wine from the bar last night. Apparently one can buy it only one glass at a time."

"We make more money that way," Miriam said, "but I brought a bottle from my house. Marvelous claret it isn't, but it does have a cork. Yussef prefers the imported variety, but I think it's a fairly good Israeli wine—and it cost about a fifth of what he pays. I don't know how he can afford to be a connoisseur."

Theo assured her that he preferred to try the local product. He gallantly insisted on carrying the picnic basket to a battered jeep, but prudently suggested to Miriam that she drive. They bounced through the gate and turned southward on a shimmering black highway.

Clinging to his hat as the hot wind tried to sling it away, Theo pointed at a dirt road parallel to the highway. It was protected by a fence topped with concertina wire. "What is the purpose of a second road?"

"It's a security road, maintained by the army. They smooth it down every few days so that they can determine if anyone has crossed it. We do have an occasional visitor from across the Dead Sea, and it's usually not anyone with benevolent intent. The road is a simple but effective way of controlling the border."

Theo peered at the pristine surface of the security road, wishing it made him feel more secure. "Did you hear of the bombing incident in Hebron? Four children were killed."

"I've heard it was the Sons of Light group," Miriam said her hands white around the steering wheel. "This country's been at war for four thousand years already; I wish everyone would take a holiday. The Administered Territories are somewhat peaceful, but this sort of nonsense simply stirs everyone up for another round of violence. The radical right-wing faction thinks the retaliation is justified, of course, and demands pardons and amnesty whenever a Jew is arrested for blowing up a West Bank mayor or schoolroom. Then the Arabs are enraged when the sentence is so light. But children . . ."

"What is this Sons of Light?" Theo said.

"The name comes from a manuscript found in one of the caves near Qumran. The official title of the document, which is roughly two thousand years old and from the Essene sect, is The War of the Sons of Light against the Sons of Darkness. Ironically appropriate, isn't it? It's one of the Dead Sea Scrolls now in the Israel Museum in Jerusalem. You can see some of the caves from the highway, although there are many more within the mountains that have yet to be explored."

Abruptly, she turned onto a road of dubious definition. Theo clamped one hand on the edge of his seat as he began to bounce about like a kernel of popcorn in hot oil. Further questions were impossible as the jeep roared in protest at the erose surface and tortuous incline. At last they reached a wide area on the side of the road.

"Here we are," Miriam said brightly. "A wadi for your inspection, and a cave reputedly nearby. Would you like a drink of water before we start hiking?"

Theo nodded through a cottony mouth, having experienced dust in intimate detail during the last few minutes of the ride. After a mouthful of water, he said, "This Sons of Light group sounds dangerous, Miriam. A bomb at a community center is more than mildly fanatical. Have the police been unable to find any clues to the identities of the members?"

She took a drink, then capped the bottle and placed it on the seat of the jeep. "Not that I know of. They've been playing their vicious pranks for the last three months or so, and although these are the first fatalities, they've done an effective job of incensing the Arabs. Retaliation is difficult to stop; no one is ever sure who owes whom the next lesson. But let's not get into a political discussion, Theo. Isn't the view magnificent?"

The wadi was indeed magnificent, reminding him of an angry slash left by a negligent giant. It was not difficult to imagine it filled with roiling brown water that might sweep an unwary hiker to a painful death. But now it was dry, and had been so for a very long time. The rocks were warm hues of brown and beige, a muted patchwork quilt that needed only to be smoothed down by the same giant to provide a cozy resting place. Not to mention warm.

"It is impressive," Theo said. For once, he wished he had a camera, although a flat image would never capture the harsh textures and glowing colors. Unlike the Dead Sea, it held a promise of life, adapted to the point of invisibility but present and watchful.

Miriam rewarded him with a slow grin. "I'm glad you're impressed with our admittedly hostile environment. Tourists are often appalled at the harshness and heat, and fail to understand how we can bear to live here, much less freely choose to do so."

Theo unobtrusively slipped his handkerchief back in his pocket. "The heat is noticeable," he said stoically, "but tolerable. I am beginning to grow accustomed to it." And to the freckles on her cheeks, and to the fine lines around her eyes, and—"Did you say that there are caves in this area? I'm not prepared for any serious spelunking, but I would be interested in examining one."

"They're all over the mountains. Gideon told me of one not too far from here that he and Hershel discovered earlier in the summer. They went several hundred feet into it, but they had to stop because of the dust."

"One would rather expect it to be dusty."

"It's the major deterrent to exploration," Miriam said, beckoning him to follow her as she scrambled down the slope. "The caves are filled with bat guano, which has turned to powder over the centuries. Most of the discoveries have been accidental, or fortuitously near the entrance. The first Dead Sea Scroll was found almost forty years ago by a couple of shepherd boys, and many of the larger caves have been explored since then. The archaeologists are in agreement that there are dozens more with manuscripts or artifacts in them, but it takes money to excavate. The scrolls stay undisturbed for the most part. It's sad to think of the potential in these caves."

Theo was too breathless to ask further questions. Loose rocks skittered under their feet and dust drifted behind them as they alternately stumbled and slid down the mountainside. Miriam at last stopped and pointed over the edge of a jutting rock.

"I think the cave is just below us, but I'm not sure," she said. "Why don't you wait here while I find a way to get down without breaking both of our necks?"

Theo caught her elbow before she could disappear down a particularly perilous path. "I might as well join you in your impetuous folly," he panted. "A gentleman never allows a lady to break her neck by herself."

"Such gallantry," she murmured with a charming, if facetious, flutter of her eyelashes. "It's been quite a long time since I've had a male escort, except for Gideon. And he hasn't shown any chivalry since he was twelve years old."

Theo did not mention Yussef's vague insinuations. His purported gallantry precluded it. He settled for a nod and followed her as she eased down a crumbling path of loose rocks to a narrow ledge.

"Ah, I was right," she called, leaning out to peer around a corner. "It's tight here, but we can make it—I think." She promptly disappeared from sight.

"I certainly hope so," Theo said to the ledge and hundred-foot slope dotted with jagged rocks and dried weeds. He closed his eyes for a second, then took a breath, dug his fingers into the rock, and stepped around the corner. When nothing dreadful happened, he looked up in triumph.

Miriam was waiting in front of a hole about the size of the jeep. Her face was pink from the exertion, and alive with excitement. She might have been thirty years younger, pausing from labor to study the new fields of the kibbutz. It was difficult to stop several feet away with a questioning smile, but of course he did.

"Then this is it? Congratulations," he said. "Or perhaps 'Eureka!' might be more appropriate? Do you think we'll discover some vital scroll that answers the last remaining questions about Biblical times?"

"If we do, we can't tell anyone. The government is very strict about protecting the archaeological sites until they've been examined by authorized people. It's against the law to possess a metal detector, and a more serious crime than possession of a mere machine gun or box of grenades. Israel is rife with amateur archaeologists, but they have to be careful and report any finds that might be significant. Then the university people swoop out, put up barbed wire fences, and spend twenty years digging with spoons."

"If I discover the definitive scroll, I promise not to touch it," Theo said, enchanted by the sparkles of sunlight that seemed to explode in her hair as she moved.

"We're more likely to discover several feet of powdered

bat guano. I don't know how Gideon found this particular cave; it's not visible from above, and the wadi below is inaccessible." She stopped, her head tilted as she frowned. "There's something on a rock down there, but I can't see what it is."

Theo leaned over as far as he felt was prudent. "I also see it." After a moment of silence, he added, "It appears to be a body."

"How could it be? This cave is in the middle of the desert, for God's sake!" she protested. "No one comes here. You must be mistaken, Theo; it's more likely an old newspaper."

He shook his head. "I'm afraid there's a body in the wadi, Miriam. From the looks of it, a very dead body."

"That's a poor joke."

"If it were a joke, it would indeed be poor," he said, moving nearer to steady her should she threaten to topple. One body in the wadi was more than enough. "You take the jeep back to the kibbutz and call the authorities. I'll wait here."

"By yourself? I wouldn't want something to happen to you."

"Nor would I. I shall take every precaution in your absence," he said firmly.

Miriam blinked in surprise. "Yes, I suppose that's what we ought to do if it truly is a . . . body. Sometimes rock climbers do come here to try the walls of the wadis, and aren't found for weeks. Most probably, this will turn out to be some college student at the end of a frayed rope." She made a small noise in her throat, as if trying to laugh. It was more of a sob. "It should take almost an hour to drive back to the kibbutz and return. Are you sure you're willing to stay here alone?"

He assured her that he would, and waited until she reluctantly vanished up the mountainside. Then, after he heard the jeep grumble to life and subsequently fade from hearing, he began a descent toward the rag doll sprawled on the rocks below. He did it without dislodging more than a few rocks, and his pace might have rivaled that of a mountain goat in a marathon.

Had Miriam been there to see him, she would have been more than a little bewildered by the transformation. As it was, Theo was watched only by a hawk high in the cloudless sky. The body in the wadi was past watching anything.

Chapter 9

"She's been dead for more than twenty-four hours," the police lieutenant announced icily. "Rigor mortis has passed, and animals have already disturbed the body. I should estimate as much as thirty-six hours. It is interesting that no one at Kibbutz Mishkan was aware of her disappearance for so long."

Miriam was slumped on a rock, her face ashen. She touched her hair with a trembling hand, then jerked it away and forced it to her lap. In a controlled voice, she said, "Essie has disappeared before, Lieutenant Gili, and we've been looking for her this time for two days. She's always been—well, a bit odd. Our kibbutz doctor and a Tel Aviv psychiatrist both examined her, and periodically suggested medication or temporary restraints, but in general we allowed her to drift about freely. She was not a criminal or a political prisoner, for God's sake. She once told me that she went to the desert to listen for instructions."

"Instructions? From whom would she hear instructions, Mrs. Adler? Did she have secret meetings with someone?"

Theo forced himself to listen in silence. The police lieutenant had made it clear that he was in command of the scene, and that he would welcome no interference from the spectators. A squadron of uniformed officers searched the mountainside both above and below the site of the body. Thus far no one had discovered anything worthy of mention. The hawk had left an hour ago.

Miriam seemed to shrink into the rock. "Essie heard directly from God, or at least she thought she did—and that He listened to her as well. It was a harmless sort of mental disorder."

"Her death did not lack harm!" Lieutenant Gili snapped. "It was an unfortunate accident that she should fall to her death in the desert, without anyone to hear her cries or help her. She should not have wandered about the desert as if she were a bare-footed bedouin. The desert is filled with dangers. She was a young girl. The two are like oil and vinegar—they do not mix."

"Oil and water," Theo said to no one in particular. To his immediate regret, he realized the lieutenant had swung around to glower at him. "Oil and vinegar make salad dressing," he explained with an apologetic shrug. "Vinaigrette, I believe it's called."

"Why did you approach the body, Mr. Bloomer? Your presence has complicated the job for my men, who must now identify and dismiss your footsteps, along with those of the desert scavengers."

Theo resisted the urge to hang his head. Miriam needed protection from the arrogant little man with the oversized mustache and hooded, reptilian eyes. "I felt it my duty to confirm that she was dead," he said calmly. "Then I moved away as carefully as possible and waited for your arrival, Lieutenant Gili. I regret any inconvenience to your men."

"You could not see from a distance that the young woman was dead? I myself could see the condition of the corpse from the ledge above our heads. But this is to be expected, since I am trained to be observant, and you are a mere civilian and a tourist with no experience in these things. I have had the rank of detective for over ten years, and I have studied forensics with one of the best—"

"Could you stop this childish nonsense!" Miriam inter-

rupted, rising to her feet. Her hands were clenched at her sides, as if to keep herself from scratching the detective's face. "The poor child is dead; her body has been lying there God knows how many hours, while animals ripped at her. She was a dear and harmless person who deserved better than this. I would like to return home to call a general assembly so that I can tell the others of the accident. May I leave, Lieutenant Gili, or shall I sit here while you strut about recounting the highlights of your résumé?"

The mustache trembled, and Theo could have sworn a forked tongue shot out for a fraction of a second. Narrowing his eyes to slits, the lieutenant said, "When I have completed the official examination of the scene of the accident, I myself shall inform you and permit you to leave. Until then, you and Mr. Bloomer will retire here."

Theo climbed on a metaphorical white horse and donned an equally metaphorical white Stetson. "If it was an accident, why should the lady and I be forced to sit in the hot sun any longer? She may be on the verge of a heat stroke. Are you willing to take responsibility?"

Gili balanced on the balls of his feet, no doubt wishing he were several inches taller than Theo so that he could peer down with disdain. As it was, he had to settle for a shrug. "You can take the lady up to the jeep, but stay there until I give you permission to leave the scene. One of my men will accompany you."

"Thank you, Lieutenant Gili," Miriam said, smiling faintly at Theo. "What about the—the body? Will it be taken to Jericho? When can we make funeral arrangements?"

"I must complete my investigation. You will wait in your jeep and I will speak to you when I am readied." The lieutenant turned away to bellow at the officers worming their way down the wadi.

Theo helped Miriam climb up the path to the ledge, and then up the wider path to the jeep. It was parked squarely in the sun. The young officer who trailed after them agreed that the shade might be more comfortable—if they promised not to escape—and allowed them to sit beneath a granite overhang that provided some relief.

"I just cannot believe it," Miriam said, sighing. "Poor Essie has been roaming the desert alone for years. Although she never told anyone, we all knew she had secret hideaways all over the area for whatever crazy rituals she performed. Why would she fall?"

"Perhaps it was dark," Theo suggested. "The desert must be quite dangerous when one cannot see loose rocks. She simply lost her footing and fell off the ledge."

"There weren't any loose rocks on the ledge. If it had been anyone but Essie, I could agree with your theory, Theo. But Essie was a damned gazelle." Miriam blinked furiously as her eyes welled with tears. "I don't know why this had to happen," she added in a broken voice. "I should have found her sooner. Her poor face, after the animals . . ."

Theo handed her his folded handkerchief, and tactfully looked away until she had dealt with her tears before saying, "There were no loose rocks on the ledge. I will admit that I also looked. But I do think you're overestimating her skill in moving about the desert. It is possible that she lost her balance on the ledge and tumbled over before she could recover. Or she might have—"

"Why was she here? I didn't think anyone knew about the cave except for Gideon and Hershel. They never would have mentioned it to Essie."

"Essie did rather glide about like a shadow. Gideon and Hershel might have said something without realizing she was within earshot." He thought about her unsolicited version of

133

a conversation in the kitchen. "People did, I suspect, fail to notice Essie."

"I suppose so," Miriam said, unconvinced. "I'll ask Gideon if he said anything to anyone about the cave, although I doubt that he did. The only reason he told me was that I happened to see him covered with the powdered guano. He wasn't pleased to delay a shower long enough to tell me about the cave."

"When was that?"

"I don't remember, Theo. Two or three months ago, right after they returned from the university. I wouldn't have taken much interest in it if he and Hershel hadn't seemed so secretive about it. Motherly concern—or an effort to have a polite conversation with a surly son."

"They must have done a preliminary exploration. In that Hershel's an archaeologist, he would have been excited about the possibility of finding a scroll."

Miriam leaned back against the rock and shook her head. "The boys have been crawling around caves since they were ten years old, and the only thing they ever found was a piece of bone. It turned out to be from a donkey. They were devastated. If Hershel had thought this particular cave had any promise, he would have been on the telephone to the university in Tel Aviv two minutes later. He knows the law, and so does Gideon."

Lieutenant Gili's scarlet face popped over the edge of the path. "I have ordered my men to remove the body, Mrs. Adler. You must wait until it is released, and then you will be allowed to make the proper arrangements."

"Released? Does that mean there is to be an autopsy?"

"In all cases of violent death, we must satisfy ourselves that we have arrived at the truth. In this case," he added, punching a button on his chest with his thumb, "I have already determined that the woman died of a tragic accident. Had she not been encouraged to enter the desert alone—without a companion or safety equipment—she would not at this moment be dead. Your kibbutz has been negligible."

For a brief moment, Miriam looked as if she might protest. But she lowered her eyes and said, "I suppose you're right, Lieutenant Gili. Essie was disturbed, but we thought she was happiest when she was alone with her voices. It was negligent of us."

"Yes," Gili said. A smile twitched the mustache. "I found a little trinket in the girl's hand," he continued, now the ever-gracious victor. "You or her relatives might want to keep it as a memory." He pulled a thin gold chain out of his pocket and handed it to Miriam.

Theo studied it as it hung from her fingers. The chain was made of delicate, curved links. A heart-shaped locket swung back and forth at the end. With a sinking feeling in his stomach, he suddenly realized whose picture would be found inside the locket. The face of a handsomely aristocratic boy standing in front of a yacht, Cape Cod in the background.

Dear Biff, future fiancé whose virtues included impeccable breeding and well-aged money, had presented it to Dorrie after an especially meaningful regatta victory. It had been dutifully cherished since then, either from tenderness or from the desire to publicize the relationship to nubile competitors.

In any case, it belonged to Dorrie, whose welfare was in his hands. Whose future was to be determined by his ability to restore her to her proper environment. Whose mother would be incensed if Dorrie were involved in anything so tasteless as murder.

Miriam stared at the locket as though Gili had handed her

135

a thin, golden viper. "In Essie's hand? How could that be, Lieutenant Gili?"

Lieutenant Gili shrugged, still riding on his momentary victory. "Some boy from her past, Mrs. Adler. It is of no consequence to my investigation. Young men do present romantic babbles upon occasion. It gives them an advantage when wishing to take advantage of a maiden's modesty. Open it so that we can see the rogue."

Theo winced. Dorrie hadn't presented the locket to Essie in a burst of generosity, nor had she hiked into the desert to drop the locket on the ledge. Caldicotts went from pram (with aproned nannies) to limousine (with uniformed chauffeurs), but they walked only across tennis courts and French restaurants. That left two equally unpleasant theories. Either Dorrie had come to the cave with someone—such as Gideon—or Essie had taken the locket while cleaning Dorrie's room.

He felt an elbow nudge him. Miriam showed him Biff's minute round face, then snapped it closed and returned it to the lieutenant. "I've never seen the boy," she said dully.

Gili let the locket dangle in a hypnotic sway. "And you, Mr. Bloomer? Have you any idea who the boy might be?"

"I've never met him," he replied evenly. Aware that Gili's eyes were bright with suspicion, he added, "I am beginning to feel faint. It must be the heat—and the shock of finding the body. I'd better return to my room to rest."

Miriam looked sympathetic, Gili merely supercilious. For the moment, it didn't matter. Theo needed to speak to Dorrie.

Chapter 10

When they returned to Kibbutz Mishkan, Miriam went to call a general assembly of the members to tell them about Essie. Theo went to find Dorrie. The sun was high above his head, and the heat severe. She would not be any place that wasn't air conditioned, any more than she would be collecting turkey droppings or bagging dates. Unthinkable.

He tapped on her door and waited. When the door opened, he stepped back in surprise. The thing that stared back at him had Dorrie's blue eyes, but the rest of its face was covered with a black veneer that was not Dorrie's carefully monitored complexion. The turban looked familiar, but not enough so to convince Theo that he hadn't stumbled onto a movie set.

"I—I thought—the wrong room, so sorry—I," he sputtered helplessly.

"Uncle Theo?" A slit formed in the black mask. The voice was Dorrie's, if not the face.

"My dear, what has happened? Are you ill?" Theo nervously approached to peer at her coal-black cheeks and forehead. "Is this some sort of medication?"

"Oh, the mud, I'd forgotten about that. Come on in, Uncle Theo; you're as pale as a jib sheet. It must be the sun." She stepped back and held the door open. "It's perfectly safe," she coaxed, a mischievous smile dimpling the mud.

Theo allowed himself to be escorted into the lair and situated in a chair. Dorrie, or what he could identify of her, sat down across from him and said, "Please let me get you a glass of water, Uncle Theo. I am concerned about your pallor."

That certainly wasn't her problem. He dutifully sipped from an encrusted glass until he felt more composed, then said, "I do not wish to offend you with personal remarks, Dorrie, but your appearance is—less than normal. What is the purpose of smearing that particular substance on your face? Are you intending to appear in a minstrel show?"

The mask crinkled in amusement. "It's a mud pack, a facial. There's some weird sort of black mud found only on the shore of the Dead Sea, and it's supposed to do miraculous things for one's skin. Which is not to say my skin wasn't clear before I put it on, but I thought I'd try it anyway. You never know when a pimple might decide to explode. I'll wash it off now if it disturbs you, although I really ought to leave it on for—" she consulted her twenty-four carat wristwatch "—nine and one-half more minutes."

"I would appreciate a premature cleansing, Dorrie. Something has happened, and I must speak to you about it. I'm not sure I can ignore your appearance in order to do so."

The blue eyes narrowed above the black nose. "Give me a minute, Uncle Theo." She went into the bathroom.

While Theo listened to the sound of water gurgling in the sink, accompanied by a few coos of admiration for the end result of the peculiar treatment, he gazed around her room. The bed was unmade; the dresser littered with the same paraphernalia. More clothes had been discarded in untidy piles on the floor. A fashion magazine lay on the floor near the bed, its cover girl beaming steadily through a soda bottle.

Dorrie came out of the bathroom with rosy cheeks. "What happened that's more important than eleven dollars worth of mud?"

He told her about the discovery of Essie's body in the wadi

below the cave. "How horrible," she said, stepping distractedly on the cover girl's chin as she sank down on the edge of the bed. "Poor Essie may have been a loon, but she tried her best. What happened to her?"

"According to the police, it was an accident. They are presuming she fell off a ledge in front of a cave. Have you ever been there, Dorrie?" Theo squinted at her through his bifocals.

"In this heat? I'll trust you're joking, Uncle Theo; I've barely made it to the dining room and the beach. I certainly haven't been crawling around some miserable cave with a bunch of snakes and bats. The idea is repugnant."

"That presents an unfortunate complication, I fear. Your locket was found in Essie's hand."

"You must be kidding! My locket is in my jewelry box, which is around here somewhere." She began to dig through an alpine mass of clothes, muttering to herself as blouses and frilly underthings flew over her shoulder. "Here it is! See, Uncle Theo, my locket is—gone." She closed the box and sat back on her heels. "I don't remember too well, but I think it was here the last time I looked."

"I recognized Biff's picture," Theo said as he removed a satin stalactite from his foot with two fingers and dropped it beside his chair. "I should have immediately told Lieutenant Gili to whom it belonged, but I wanted to speak to you first."

"You don't think I pushed Essie off the side of a mountain, do you? I haven't gone outside the fence since I arrived two weeks ago, except for an ungodly trip to Masada. I now understand why all those Jews killed themselves; I seriously considered it myself after two excruciating hours with a pedantic guide who knew every last detail about every last old rock. He and Simmons would make perfect pen pals, if not bedfellows. In any case, why would I want to hurt Essie? She was schizo, but that was hardly my problem."

"I know that, and I know you had nothing to do with her accident. However, you will have to tell the lieutenant that the locket belongs to you."

"But he'll want to know why she had it—and I have no idea," she protested, sprawling across the bed with an exasperated expression. "It will be utterly dreadful. I think I'll pack my suitcases and hijack the next camel out of here. To hell with Judith; she can stay here with her beloved until her skin flakes off and blows away."

Theo tried for a stern tone. "You have an obligation to assist the police in their inquiries, Dorrie. When was the last time Essie cleaned your room? I would imagine she simply saw the locket lying about and picked it up without thinking."

"Two days ago, I think, but—" Dorrie clamped her mouth shut and rolled over so that her face was hidden. "You're probably right, Uncle Theo," she added in a muffled voice. "Essie saw the locket lying on a table and lifted it. Biff has exquisite taste; it runs in his family. The locket is charming, and she was attracted to the glitter. That's what I'll tell the horrid policeman."

"The horrid policeman is at the kibbutz to talk to various people. Shall I accompany you, my dear?" The only way to be sure she did not carry through with the camel threat. At least one Caldicott ancestor was hanged for piracy, although he reputedly preferred rum and distaff slaves to camels. And despite Nadine's refusal to acknowledge the rumor, great-granduncle Bloomer had left the world under similar circumstances.

Dorrie was on her feet, arms akimbo.

"Now? I really don't have anything to wear on short notice, and I don't have any makeup on whatsoever. I'm sorry, but I simply cannot be seen like this. It's out of the question."

"Come along, Dorrie. As Francis Bacon said, 'No pleasure is comparable to the standing upon of the vantage ground of truth.' You'll feel much better after you talk to the police."

The turban was unwound with deliberate slowness, and the hair fluffed into a semblance of its usual artlessness. Then, muttering under her breath, she snatched up a pair of sunglasses, and crammed them in place. "I'm going, I'm going. But as the bishop said to the hooker, 'It's not all it's purported to be.' I just hope no one sees me without mascara; I feel naked."

Lieutenant Gili was holding court in the dining room. Behind him the uniformed officers formed a row of sweaty, well-ripened courtiers. The kibbutzniks, gray and stunned, were huddled in small groups around the room. Hadassah and Naomi, the young women from the laundry, were there, as were the factory supervisor, the bartender, the waitresses from the restaurant and the other kibbutzniks Theo had seen leading quiet, contented lives behind the rolls of concertina wire. As any extended family might do, they had drawn together in a moment of grief.

Theo nudged Dorrie forward. Gili made several scratches on a pad, then glanced up impatiently. "Who are you?" he barked. "Do you have information about the unfortunate accident?"

Dorrie tightened her lips. "I am Theodora Caldicott, a guest in this country. Who are you?"

"I am the head of the police for this district, and I repeat, have you information, or have you a desire to waste my time with some personal problem about your passport? For that, you must go to the office in Jerusalem and stand in many lines, Miss Caldicott. I am too busy to concern myself with petty matters."

Theo considered rescuing Gili from the impending onslaught of Connecticut snobbery, but could think of no good reason to do so. Instead he went across the room to speak to Miriam. "Did you tell everyone about Essie?"

"Yes, and everyone was upset. I wish that pompous little *bulbanik* would leave so that we can decide about the funeral and all. He's convinced it was an accident, and he has no reason to remain here berating us about our so-called negligibles. No one's arguing."

"Bulbanik?" Theo said.

"A Yiddish Mrs. Malaprop. He's driving everyone crazy. Thank God he didn't try to interrogate Essie's parents."

"Have they been told?"

"I told them myself. Essie's mother had to be put in the infirmary, and her father is likely to join her any time. They're both in their sixties; Essie was an unexpected afterthought. I hope the shock doesn't kill them." Miriam gnawed on her lip for a moment, then said, "Why did you bring Dorrie here, Theo? Surely she knows nothing about Essie's mystic desert forays."

Before he could answer, angry shouting broke out behind him. Gili's face was as purple as an aconite, and droplets of spittle flew from his mouth as he slammed a fist on the table. Dorrie held her ground, smiling demurely but with visible satisfaction.

"I have no interest in your father's Washington friends!" Gili foamed, the purple taking a cerise turn. "I do not intend to telephone your president to confirm his interest in your welfare, nor do I care if he is your godfather's third cousin! You—you—you are under arrest!"

Dorrie held out her wrists, very much a candidate for martyrdom, if not direct sainthood. "Drag me away, little man. You'll live to regret it, but not for long."

Theo decided to intervene before Gili could arrange a firing squad in one corner of the room, which he seemed to be considering. "Lieutenant Gili, what seems to be the problem with my niece?"

"Your niece? I should have realized that you—you were reprehensible for this, Mr. Bloomer! This—this woman has the chutzpah to suggest that I—"

"Did she tell you about the locket? I imagine that Essie took it while she was cleaning the room, and the theft has no significance. However, Dorrie felt it was her duty to tell you that it was hers, in case it affects your investigation."

Gili had managed to temper his tantrum during the short speech. His mustache still jerked convulsively, and one eyelid seemed to be controlled by an invisible thread, but his face had returned to a more normal color. "She told me that it was stolen from her room, yes. I have no reason to continue further with the detail, but of course I cannot return the locket until after the case has been officially closed."

"I want my locket," Dorrie said politely.

"Out of the question! It will be returned to you when I say the case is closed, and not before then. I shall not arrest you for interference—at the moment." Gili beckoned to his men. "I am finished with my questions. We shall return to headquarters so that I can inform my superior of the convulsions I have reached."

Once they were gone, sans prisoner, Theo returned to Miriam's side, where he was beginning to sense he belonged. "The locket is Dorrie's, as you must have heard. I should have mentioned it earlier, but I felt that I should . . . ah, clarify its recent history."

"I talked to Gideon before the meeting," Miriam admitted

ruefully. "I knew he was not involved, but parental obligations forced me to confirm it first. Gideon can be blunt when he feels attacked."

"Did he remember mentioning the cave in front of Essie?"

"No, but Hershel thought they might have discussed it over dinner several weeks ago, and Essie was helping serve at the time. He remembered only because she later dropped a platter on her foot and went screeching out of the dining hall. She probably overheard them and decided to explore the cave when she had a chance."

"Very likely," Theo murmured. "Did you ask if they had found anything in the cave?"

"Hershel admitted that they thought so at first, but when they finally dug their way in, it turned out to be a newspaper from last fall. That went over as well as the donkey bone did. They said they hadn't bothered to do any further exploration since then."

Theo looked around the room for the disillusioned spelunkers. Gideon, Hershel, and Ilana were sitting at a distant table, their heads almost touching as they conversed. Although the words were inaudible, Theo could read the intensity from his position. Gideon looked angry; the other two pale but composed. Essie had been with them in the children's house; no doubt the tragedy was more painful for them than for the other kibbutzniks.

"In any case, I doubt we'll see any more of Lieutenant Gili," Miriam was saying in a relieved voice. "The newspaper will carry a stern reminder about the dangers of the desert, and that will be the end of it. For once there aren't any political ramifications. Just a sad and tragic accident."

They talked for a few minutes, and then Theo left to fetch Dorrie. She was near the door, deep in conversation with Judith.

"But, Dorrie," Judith was protesting as he approached them, "you were wearing your locket that day. Don't you remember—you took it off to swim and put it in your bag?"

Dorrie glanced up to meet Theo's eyes, then looked back at Judith's earnest blinks. "No, you're wrong about that, Judith. You're totally confused," she said coldly.

"No, I'm not. We all went swimming, and you said something about not wanting the locket to turn green and melt. I remember it very clearly." More earnest blinks.

"You were fawning over Hershel the entire time we were there. I doubt you saw anything but his manly bulge in that skimpy bathing suit," Dorrie countered. "That kind of suit may be appropriate for Cannes or Nice, but one would hardly confuse this place with the French Riviera." She flared her nostrils to emphasize her point. "It must have taken him an hour to wiggle into it, and three to get it off. I must say that I was appalled."

So was Theo, although he kept his mouth closed.

Chapter 11

Dorrie left to barricade herself in her room with a gloomy comment about incipient roots; Theo suspected she was not referring to subterranean plant structures. Miriam disappeared to check on Essie's parents. The kibbutzniks drifted away, still murmuring unhappily and looking like leftovers from the bottom shelf of the refrigerator. Theo tried to capture Judith before she could escape from the dining hall, but she insisted that she had to return to the children's house.

Theo read, napped, ate a solitary dinner, and retired to the lobby to watch the evening news. No footage of terrorist bombings was shown; instead, he was treated to a view of jet planes streaming over a desert, spewing lethal black pellets with the abandon of an airborn bunny. Lebanon, he presumed. He then watched as a bulldozer flattened a series of mean hovels, while the newscaster commented from an unseen vantage point. The bartender, who had come over during the scene, clucked his tongue and murmured a few words under his breath. At Theo's suggestion, he returned to the bar for a bottle of beer, then sat down on the couch.

Theo ascertained that his host was one Shel Greenberg, father of three and a recent grandfather. A snapshot of a pink bundle was produced and admired. He learned that Shel had lived on the kibbutz for nineteen years, that his daughter was a lawyer in Jerusalem and one of his sons an engineer in San Francisco. The other son was finishing his final year in the army, after which he planned to break his mother's heart by

146

opening a dance studio. Mrs. Greenberg felt the family needed a doctor, or at least an orthodontist in case the newest Greenberg's baby teeth were not properly aligned.

"But what's a father to do!" Shel concluded, throwing up his hands. "No matter how we try, our children insist on growing up and leaving us. You have children, Theo?"

Theo produced a snapshot of his night-blooming cereus and explained his omnipresent concern that it might bloom without him. He sighed, Shel sighed, and they both settled back in the cushions for a moment of introspective silence.

Having pondered the mysteries of plant behavior, Theo returned himself to the more immediate situation. "Those bulldozers on the news rather puzzled me. Everyone seemed inordinately serious about the removal of a few houses. Is that to be the site of a new school or shopping area?"

"Those were terrorists' houses. The soldiers destroy the houses as a deterrent to further acts of terrorism. Today in Safad a Jewish shopkeeper was killed by a gang of Arabs. As soon as the murderers were arrested, their houses were demolished. Reprisal comes swiftly."

"Before a trial?"

"They will receive a fair trial in front of a magistrate, then they will be imprisoned for their crimes. Israel is a democracy. Even Arabs have rights, too many rights some people say. They are allowed to move about freely, to buy and sell property and operate businesses, to meet in secret to plot violence against us. They aren't permitted to serve in the army or to vote but other than that they have all the privileges of any citizen."

"Have the police made any progress with the Hebron bombing two days ago? Has anyone been arrested?"

The bartender shrugged. "The Sons of Light do only what the rest of us would like to do. They aren't criminals; they're patriots who are still fighting the war—and they deserve medals. The Arabs have sworn to push us into the sea, and they've been trying for almost forty years. We can't sit back and wait."

"You have no problem with children being murdered in the name of patriotism?" Theo asked.

"My brother was killed in nineteen sixty-seven. I knew one of the men murdered at the Egyptian border last year. I've listened to the children singing folk songs in the bomb shelters while the Syrians tried to turn Kibbutz Mishkan into a pile of rubble. The Camp David meetings may have eased the situation temporarily, but now the PLO factions can't even agree on how best to destroy us. We're three million Jews surrounded by a hundred million hostile Arabs. What should we do? If I were twenty years younger, I'd join the Sons of Light myself, but they don't need fat old men with trembling hands and high blood pressure."

Theo had listened to the speech with a troubled frown. Again and again he heard the same passion, the attachment to the land that transcended patriotism. Was this a phenomenon of kibbutz life, he wondered, or a generality that could be extended to all the Jews in Israel? Had Essie felt it as strongly as, say, Miriam?

Shel mentioned a collection of dirty glasses awaiting him behind the bar. He fiddled with the television knobs to produce an ancient movie that was, if not particularly fascinating, at least in English. Theo dozed through the final shoot-out and went to bed.

He was awakened by a peremptory knock on the door. After a certain amount of fumbling to find his watch, he determined that it was shortly after midnight. He threw on a robe and hurried to the door. "Yes?" he said, envisioning the worst.

Ilana seemed oblivious to the time. Her eyes were clear and snapping as she said, "You have an overseas call, Mr. Bloomer. You will have to take it in the lobby."

She marched away before Theo could reply. He pulled clothes on over his pajamas and hurried after her, his slippers pattering on the sidewalk in gentle applause. She had already taken position behind the counter in the lobby when he opened the door.

"Here's the receiver. Sorry there's no privacy," she said. She did not sound regretful.

Theo grabbed the receiver. "Hello? Hello? Operator, are you there? This is Theo Bloomer."

"Well, Theo, I am waiting for a report. You have been in that commune for several days. Do make an effort to be concise; I have a bridge game in less than an hour."

"Do you know what time it is, Nadine?" Theo said peevishly. "You have roused me from sleep, forced me to dash to the lobby in my pajamas—"

"In your pajamas, Theo? It is a very peculiar place if you are encouraged to wander about in your nightclothes. I hope Dorrie is more aware of proprieties than you seem to be."

"Nadine, I am about to lose my temper. Do you—"

"Have you shaken sense into Dorrie? The fall semester will be upon us before we know it, and the girl hasn't even bought any new clothes. Also, Biff is beside himself with worry. Dorrie sent him a postcard—of all things. Four years of deportment classes and the girl still can't write a proper note. When I think of the money I spent on engraved stationery for her, I want to sob. I just want to sob my heart out, Theo."

"Nadine," Theo tried once more, "do you realize what time it is?"

A pause was followed by a gasp. "Oh God, the girls will be

livid if I'm late! The traffic on the way to the club has gotten to the point that I'd rather wade through marmalade than battle the stoplights in town, which is why I implored Pookie to pick me up. Charles lost his temper in front of the post office the other day and simply sat on the horn of the Mercedes until everyone had the common decency to move."

"It is the middle of the night, Nadine." He caught Ilana's eye and shrugged. She gazed back with the warmth of a porcelain cat on a mantel. He added, "As much as I enjoy hearing about the traffic congestion five thousand miles away, I'd prefer to do so at a more civilized hour."

"I am paying for the call," Nadine reminded him huffily, "and it's hardly worth the expense to listen to your obsessive desire to discuss the time. Now, what progress have you made with Dorrie? Shall I arrange to meet your flight tomorrow or the next day?"

"Possibly," Theo said. "She's less enchanted with the kibbutz than she avowed, and most likely is amenable to coming home in time for school. I'll talk to her when the sun rises."

"Oh dear, Pookie's in the driveway, and I don't want to keep her waiting. Last week she backed over the azaleas in a fit of impatience, and the gardener fell over dead with a stroke. He was a wonderful gardener, and Charles was furious with both of them. Let me know when your flight arrives."

The receiver buzzed in his ear like a misshapen mosquito. He handed it to Ilana, who replaced it behind the counter without comment. Theo decided to ignore the pajama cuffs creeping down his ankles and see if she could be provoked into conversation.

"I don't believe we've been properly introduced, Ilana. I'm Theo Bloomer, although I gather you are aware of that. I'm sorry the telephone call caused such a panic. My sister is

150

more concerned with bridge games than time zones."

Ilana did not smile at the attempted pleasantry. "I do not panic. It is my duty to awaken guests for telephone calls. We do not have the resources to transfer calls to the rooms."

"Oh," Theo replied, unable to compose anything wittier. He tried once again. "It must be tiresome to be here alone all night. Do you watch television or read?"

"Do I watch television or read? The kibbutz has entrusted me with the duty, and I have accepted it. Distraction I do not allow myself. Should I fail to remain alert, something might occur to endanger the kibbutz. We are all responsible for the well-being of the community; personal considerations must be kept in a proper perspective. From this we are strong."

Her strengths did not include small talk, Theo decided in the wake of her stern lecture. One last try, and then he would return to bed.

"I'm impressed by what I've seen thus far," he said. "I understand that you were born here?"

Her grim expression softened a bit. "Yes, my parents emigrated from New York when the kibbutz was organized. Like many others, they came here to escape the decadence and possessive society that ignored the needs of many to satisfy a few. Here we share everything. The kibbutz meets our basic needs: clothing, shelter, medical attention, education, and so forth. In your country, the workers have nothing except blisters for their backbreaking labor, and—"

"Indeed," Theo said, edging towards the door. It was not the hour for a symposium on Marxism, any more than it was for a telephone call from Nadine. Ilana's face was flushed with ardor; she was on the verge of bursting into an anthem extolling the glory of the workers, should he offer encouragement. He did not. "I think I'll return to bed, but thank you for the explanation."

151

"Wait, Mr. Bloomer, I have a question to ask you."

Intrigued, Theo halted. "Yes, Ilana?"

"Is your niece Dorrie intending to return to her decadent life as you said on the telephone, or was that a ruse?"

"I think Dorrie and I will leave within a day or two. She has been reared in a different environment, and she is aware that she would not be happy at Kibbutz Mishkan."

Ilana smiled, albeit briefly and scornfully. "No, she is too soft to live here. In America all the teenage children have cars of their own, stereo equipment, swimming pools, and thousands of dollars to spend however they wish. Here, we have a few personal possessions only. When we graduate from the secondary school, we must serve in the army." The smile flicked by again. "Dorrie would not enjoy her two years in the army. I was a munitions instructor on the Golan. I am not large, but I am with good muscles."

"So I see," Theo said with proper awe. "Your assessment is accurate; Dorrie would not enjoy the army. But I must go to bed now, so good night."

"One further question, Mr. Bloomer," she called to his back.

Theo considered a comment on her lack of vigilance during lengthy conversations held at ungodly hours, but instead turned around with a patient smile. "One final question."

"What of Judith Feldheim? Will she too leave the kibbutz to return to her decadent life in America, or will she stay to marry Hershel and have babies?"

"That I do not know, Ilana. She seems to feel a strong attachment to the kibbutz, although I cannot comment on her relationship with Hershel. You could ask her, I suppose."

"I grew up with Hershel," Ilana continued, "and am much like a sister would be, even if he is a klutz. I do not wish to see him hurt; he is unhappy already. But if Judith marries him and brings much money, then he would be happy again."

Theo swallowed unhappily at the necessity of further gossip, but he felt he ought to correct her fallacy. "Judith is not from a wealthy family, nor does she have money of her own."

"That is not right, Mr. Bloomer. She and Dorrie attend a very expensive school where tuition is high. When Gideon and Hershel met them, the girls were staying in a fancy-shmancy hotel. The coffee in the café cost several dollars for one cup. How else could Judith do such things?"

"She attends her school on a scholarship, Ilana. The tour was financed by a small annuity, which I fear has been depleted. Hershel surely knows about Judith's personal history and doesn't expect her to send for a suitcase of money. Her dowry won't buy any tractors for Kibbutz Mishkan."

"You are teasing me?" Ilana said, the smile a distant memory. Her expression was cold, as though she suspected him of ulterior motives or a streak of viciousness. "Judith must be rich to go about Europe instead of working. American girls are all rich. Dorrie is rich, too. I myself have seen her luggage and clothing."

Theo shrugged and tried once more to leave. "I really don't know any more about it. Good night, Ilana."

A growl drifted out the door with him, but he did not stop to comment. Ilana could believe what she wished. Theo believed in sleep.

The next morning after breakfast, he went to the lobby ostensibly to browse through the gift shop. A dozen postcards and a scarf (which Nadine would profusely thank him for and immediately give to her maid) later, he caught himself drifting toward the office for a chat with Miriam. He might be leaving within a matter of days, he told himself righteously.

153

He could at least say good-bye.

Miriam was on the telephone when he stopped in the doorway. The swirl of freckles on her cheeks contrasted harshly with her white face, and her eyes were bright with desperation. She snapped a word of agreement, then replaced the receiver with a clatter.

"That was the insufferable Gili," she told Theo. "He's coming back this morning and wants everyone to wait in the dining hall. I can hardly bear to face another general assembly."

"Does he have further information about Essie's accident?"

She shook her head. "He wouldn't say what it was about, but he oozed sarcasm. Oh, Theo, this is turning into a nightmare! Why can't we just bury the girl and let her rest in peace?"

The night-blooming cereus no longer rested in peace. The deep orange interior began to struggle against the gray-green prison walls in a slow but persistent rhythm.

Chapter 12

Lieutenant Gili reminded Theo of a plastic punching bag, inflated with hot, moist air and swelled with importance. One swift prick with a pin and he would rocket to the ceiling in a wonderful whoosh. The dining hall buzzed as he swaggered to the front of the room, trailed by the omnipresent bevy of uniformed attendants.

"Is everyone here?" he barked at Miriam. When she nodded, he looked at them with withering contempt. "Then I shall tell you what our medical examiner has determined from his careful and professional autopsy of the body of Ester Kelman."

The buzzing grew louder, then fell off under Gili's cold stare. Theo, in a corner with Miriam, searched for Dorrie and Judith, but could not find them among the two hundred or so people hunched at tables or shifting uneasily along the walls. He had knocked on his niece's door and told her of the meeting. Her muffled response had seemed to imply she understood and would appear. Perhaps, he told himself with a sigh, he should have persisted.

"Ester Kelman," Gili announced, pausing briefly to relish his momentary power over the open-mouthed audience, "died of internal injuries from a fall of approximately one hundred feet. Although there was much damage during the fall, there was also a bruise on the back of her neck that cannot be explained by the impaction. A black and blue mark, the size of the base of a hand." Gili raised his hand and slapped the indicated area. "Therefore, I have decided to investigate further, here at Kibbutz Mishkan, to see if anyone might have had reason to wish the girl dead. I no longer accept that her death was an accident. It was murder."

This time the buzz could not be contained. Theo wished he could take Miriam's hand in his own; her eyes were squeezed close and her shoulders trembling. But Yussef's sharp gaze from across the table warned him that an innocent display of support would be misinterpreted, at best. Theo did not want to be responsible for stirring up gossip, even if it were baseless. Regrettably baseless.

Gili ordered them to be available to be questioned, and then dismissed them with a snort. Most of the kibbutzniks hurried away to tend turkeys, children, dirty laundry, or whatever they tended within the complex. No one was smiling.

The occupants at the corner table dallied. Yussef had selected a bright yellow shirt and a gold chain for his morning attire, a gaudy dandelion that would soon go to seed, and noticeably incongruous among the more dignified hybrids. The woman next to him was more of a thistle, Theo decided after a brief survey. Her face was long, her nose hooked at the end, her upper lip quivering with contempt at some inner thought. A bristly thistle (*Carduus acanthoides*), he amended to himself, wondering if this were the errant Sarah who had, presumably, finally returned from Jericho. Miriam confirmed his hypothesis with a belated introduction.

"So you're little Dorrie's uncle," Sarah said. Her voice was as contemptuous as her eyes, as if his relationship constituted a particularly heinous crime. Before he could apologize for the inadvertent consanguinity, she turned on Yussef. "That police person has lost his senses. I am sorry about Essie, but I have no time to answer a lot of stupid questions about her accident. I know nothing."

"How true," Yussef agreed sweetly. "But, my dearest, we must all cooperate with the little man so that he can satisfy himself and leave us to our work. The accounts are scheduled to go into the computer at the end of next week, but they won't be ready if I don't finish them. I will have to work late for the next few nights."

"And also on the accounts." She gave him an icy smile.

Ilana appeared behind Miriam. "Sarah, what am I to do about the duty roster if everyone must return for interrogation? Someone must remain with the children, and also with the turkeys. The factory has an important order that must go out today, and the line supervisors are grumbling with resentment over the disruption. Likewise the agricultural supervisors."

Sarah stood up. "Come to my office, Ilana, and we'll see what we can do about it. Essie is as much trouble dead as she was alive."

On that irritable note the two disappeared out the door. Yussef patted Miriam's hand and said, "You are taking this much too seriously, my darling. Your shoulders are taut and your sweet, graceful neck so tense with worries. Why don't you allow me to give you a private massage in my office?"

"No, thank you," she answered in a distracted voice, to Theo's relief. "Gili's command performance is going to drive the guest house staff absolutely crazy, and I have not yet found someone with time to clean the lobby and rooms." She turned to Theo. "When did Essie last do your room? Are you knee-deep in dirty towels and dust?"

Pained at her assumption that he might coexist with squalor, Theo assured her that he was not. "Essie brought towels the day I arrived, but not since then," he added. "When was she last seen at the kibbutz?"

Miriam sighed. "She dropped a tray in the dining hall the

night you arrived, and I spoke to her about her behavior with guests later in the evening. She was not seen the next day. She never appeared to clean the guest rooms, nor to do the floors in the lobby."

Yussef made a strangled noise, as if he had inhaled an insect. It might have been a sign of internal amusement, but Theo heard himself mentally opting for a tsetse fly. Yussef finally managed to clear his throat. "You ought to ask Gideon when he last saw the girl. They had quite a lengthy conversation that night outside the dining hall."

"That is absurd," Miriam said. "No one has had a conversation with Essie in ten years. I made an effort every now and then, but her responses were inchoate at best, and more often incomprehensible. How could anyone, including my impatient son, have a conversation with her?"

"I saw them together on the night in question, well after midnight. Gideon was doing most of the talking, but Essie was flapping her hands hard enough to take off, and offering obscure observations about hers being less than his. If they were discussing IQs, I would have been hard pressed to argue with her. Or genitalia, as improbable as it seems. Why don't you come to my office, darling Miriam, so that I can relate the precise words?" The eyebrows wiggled up and down.

"I think not," Miriam said. "At the moment I need a maid, and I'd better see to it before Gili catches up with me." She wandered out with a worried look, leaving Theo and Yussef at the table. Yussef converted his leer to a man-to-man smile. "The women are upset that their schedules are razed. It's difficult to be as flexible as we are."

"Miriam found the body yesterday, as I'm sure you know. She has every right to be distraught. If we hadn't happened to climb down the hillside to find a particular cave, the body might have been undiscovered for several weeks. Miriam was very aware what might have happened to it. Aware—and appalled."

"She's more worried about Gideon. She told me a few days ago—before you arrived—that he was becoming more and more agitated about the political situation with the Arabs. There was violence in Hebron earlier in the summer, and she said he still growls about it."

"Surely she doesn't think that Gideon . . . ?"

"Blew a wall down on a group of children in Hebron?" He ended the sentence with a snort of derision. "I doubt it. Miriam's too devoted a mother to think such thoughts about her only offspring. She's concerned that his idle talk will get him into trouble. That's all."

Theo pursed his lips. "You saw Gideon with Essie the night she disappeared?"

"They were outside the dining hall and making a great deal of noise. I went to my office window to watch because I was concerned. Gideon sounded frustrated, but I could sympathize with that. It must have been as gratifying as a conversation with a bedouin."

"Essie kept insisting 'hers was less than his'? You had no idea what they were talking about?"

"No." Yussef yawned and stood up. "To tell the truth, I wasn't interested in Essie's ravings. Everything about her was less, in one way or another. Gideon seemed to agree, so I returned to my diligent efforts to balance the books and pay the government its just dues. Render unto Caesar, and so forth."

"Why were you there past midnight?" Theo asked with a mildly interested smile. "That seems rather late to be working on the accounts."

"It does, doesn't it? Oy vey, the work never stops. See you at the inquisition, old man."

Yussef sauntered away, leaving Theo to simmer at the

"old man" remark. Yussef was as old as he, or within a year or two. His anachronistic choice of clothing did give him an appearance of youth, but it was a flimsy, pitiable façade. Theo looked down at his pale gray suit and discreet tie. Starched white shirt. Shiny shoes. Creased trousers. The perfect image of a retired school teacher or an accountant.

"Or a florist," he murmured as he started for the door.

Lieutenant Gili stepped into his path. "Mr. Bloomer, I must have a word with you. I do not like the necessity, but there it is. It is out of my fingers. Follow me."

They went into a small room. The walls were hidden behind shelves filled with paper supplies and crates of condiments for the dining hall. Gray-headed mops and blond brooms were propped in the corner. It smelled of detergent, ammonia, and dust. As Gili sighed, the aroma of an *Allium giganteum,* a.k.a. garlic, infused the mixture. Theo considered utilizing his handkerchief as a primitive gas mask, but reluctantly left it in his pocket.

Gili held out his hand. In it lay the locket and chain. "Return this to Miss Caldicott. I have given it much thought, and I no longer require it as evidence in my investigation."

"Of course, Lieutenant," Theo said, putting it in his pocket as quickly as possible. Out of sight, out of Gili's mind, or so Theo hoped. "Then you do not intend to speak to Dorrie in person?"

Gili sullenly studied a mop in the corner. "No, Mr. Bloomer, I do not require further assistance from her. Ester Kelman took the locket like a common thief, and Miss Caldicott is no longer considered a suspect in the case."

Theo wondered if telegrams had flown across the ocean all night or if a telephone call to the American Embassy in Tel Aviv had sufficed. Charles was not one of Theo's more cherished in-laws, but he did have his uses. Dorrie had not exaggerated family ties.

"I am delighted to hear that," he said, edging toward the door. "Then if you have nothing further to add, I'll take this to Dorrie and tell her the good news."

"Before you do so, Mr. Bloomer, you yourself must answer a few questions about your involvement with Ester Kelman," Gili said. "Your statement will be written down so that you may sign it in front of witnesses."

"My involvement? I had no involvement with the girl," Theo protested. "I saw her once in the lobby, and again in my room, but I hardly exchanged more than a few words with her."

Gili's mustache resembled an agitated caterpillar. "In your room, yes. The girl was seen entering your room at approximately four o'clock three days ago. What exactly happened in your bedroom, Mr. Bloomer?" He leaned forward.

On one hand, the insinuation was flattering; on the other, it was monstrously insulting. Theo opted for the latter. "Essie was nearly forty years younger than I, and only a few years older than my niece. Your remark is offensive—and pointless. You have yet to produce any evidence that Essie did not fall off the ledge because of a twisted ankle or a loose rock. She certainly might have bruised her neck on the way down. On a rock the size of the base of one's hand." Theo did not slap the indicated area, despite an urge to do so.

"You do not expect me to share my professional acumen with a civilian, do you? You would be unable to utilize, or even understand, the nuisances that have led to my conclusion," Gili huffed. His khaki breast brought to mind a belligerent rooster atop a fencepost. No one would sleep through the impending crow. "In any case, you must give a statement to Corporal Amitan. I can no longer waste my valuable time by speaking to you."

Theo found himself in the company of mops. After a farewell nod, he left the utility room and, conveniently unable to identify Corporal Amitan amidst the troops, returned to his room and sat down on the edge of his bed to think. The trip to Israel was not at all what he had anticipated, or what he would have preferred, given options. A quiet talk with Dorrie and a quick round of the tourist sights in Jerusalem had been the extent of his expectations. Murder had not been included in the abbreviated itinerary.

Could Lieutenant Gili be correct? Had Essie tumbled off the ledge in a burst of mystical revelation, or had someone been near enough to add a bit of impetus? And if so, who would bother? Essie was a blithe spirit with a brain of gossamer. Hardly a threat.

Driven by instinct, Theo made the bed and tidied up the room, returning the glass on the bedside table to the bathroom, where he paused to rinse it out and leave it upended to dry. Essie's death was nothing more than an accident, he concluded as he lifted his eyes to gaze at the hairless circle on the top of his head. It glinted as eagerly as the wet glass on the counter.

"Old man!" he grumbled to his reflection, then went back into the bedroom. He was still grumbling when he heard a tap on the door.

Dorrie and Judith entered, both looking worried.

"Uncle Theo," Dorrie said, "what happened in the meeting at the dining hall? There were all sorts of veiled comments in the restaurant, but nobody would talk to us. Has someone decided that Essie's death was not an accident?"

Theo repeated what Lieutenant Gili had said, then took the locket from his pocket and returned it to Dorrie. She smiled at Judith.

"I told you it wasn't important," she said lightly.

Judith slumped down in a chair. "I suppose you're right,

Dorrie. Essie probably came in during the night and took the locket. Now you can pack and hurry back home in time for a shopping spree at Bonwit Teller and the dances at the country club."

"Shall I make reservations?" Theo said, encouraged by Dorrie's indecisive frown. "Your mother called earlier to ask which flight we would be on."

Dorrie's forehead smoothed as she arrived at a decision. "No, you can't make reservations until Judith agrees to come with us. Mother won't mind sitting at the airport for a few days; she can rope in strangers for a bridge game while she waits."

"Dorrie!" Judith and Theo said in unison.

"I won't go without you," she said to Judith. Despite the dulcet tone, the Caldicott jaw was extended to its utmost.

Judith glowered. "Damn it, Dorrie, why not?"

"I'm just too worried about the situation." Dorrie was still serene, with a gracious, forgiving smile for the frustrated outburst. Judith snuffled menacingly, like a bulldog with a choice bone. Dorrie's dimples deepened.

Theo decided to enter the conversation at his own risk. "What exactly worries you, Dorrie? The fact that Judith will fall behind in her studies, or the fact that she wishes to live in Israel on a kibbutz? It is not a sign of dementia." Miriam had done so.

Dorrie chewed her bottom lip as if from a concerted attempt at self-analysis, but Theo was not impressed. Caldicotts did not second-guess themselves, or display doubt. She was, he suspected, merely stalling for effect.

"Well," she said at last, "I suppose I'm worried that Judith might get hurt if she stays here. After all, people do set off bombs, shoot each other, and steal jewelry. I don't want to be tacky about it, but it could be dangerous."

163

Theo found himself in agreement, although he could not have explained the vague and undelineated feeling. From Judith's scowl, he could see that she did not agree. He rather wished she did.

Chapter 13

After further futile arguments that failed to alleviate the problem, Judith invited Theo and Dorrie to join her in the communal dining hall for dinner that evening. Theo accepted with alacrity, Dorrie with an off-handed nod. Judith left in a flurry of frustrated mutters that included allusions to mules and their progenitors.

Theo gazed at the problem, which was preoccupied with an insect bite on its arm. "Let's talk about the locket," he suggested amiably.

"Oh, Uncle Theo, it's all so boring. The day you arrived and the last day Essie cleaned my room—I had on the locket. It was so incredibly romantic of Biff to buy it for me. I happened to spot a similar one in the Tiffany catalogue and almost fell over dead when I saw the price. Which is not to say he shouldn't have spent the money; he could hardly give me a hideous knickknack made out of plastic." She paused for a shudder, then continued. "Anyway, I try to remember to wear it when it goes with my outfit, and I did have it on because I was wearing a darling cornflower-blue sundress that matches my eyes."

"Did you wear the locket all day and to bed that night?"

"Don't be silly. It would have cut my neck to ribbons and I would have been forced to spend the rest of my life in turtlenecks. I distinctly remember putting everything in my jewelry box before I performed an emergency pedicure and went to bed." She held out her foot in mute proof.

Theo closed his eyes and forced himself to recall the scene in the restaurant. "You were not wearing a blue sundress at dinner," he said, tugging thoughtfully at the tip of his beard. "You were wearing a T-shirt and shorts."

"I had to change for dinner, didn't I? It's one of the highlights of my day, and let me tell you, they're few and far between. But how totally unlike me to forget what I was wearing. You're right about the T-shirt, Uncle Theo. I wonder what happened to my locket?" She wrinkled her nose at him.

"Let's continue to think about the day of my arrival. What did you do from when you awoke to when you saw me in the restaurant?"

"To be brutal, this place is not the Cape in July. I washed out a few things, then studied Vogue until lunch time. I'm afraid to say it, but the new fall colors are drab beyond description. Later in the afternoon Judith and I went for a swim with her wonderful new friends, who discussed jeeps and turkey crates the entire time. I felt as if I were trapped at one of Mother's insufferable bridge parties."

"But Essie did clean your room?"

"To the best of her ability—which is limited to straightening the bedspread and dumping towels on the floor. I tried to be nice, but she was too spooky for words. I told you how she implied that I was cheap! There was nothing I could do but hide out in the bathroom with Vogue until she was gone. I wore the sundress and the locket to lunch, so Essie couldn't have taken it that morning."

"The next morning we did not have breakfast together," Theo said, trying to reconstruct days glazed by jet lag. "I went on a tour of the kibbutz with Miriam, and I presumed you were asleep. Could someone have entered your room while you were sleeping?"

Dorrie shook her head. "I did take a long shower when I got up, Uncle Theo, but the door was locked. You're the only person who's been in my room, except for Judith—who looks much better in white gold. The other calls attention to her sallow tinge. Isn't that criminal?"

"No one else has entered your room?" Theo persisted, refusing to be sidetracked into a discussion of the finer, if felonious, implications of Judith's skin coloring.

"Well, that same morning Sarah came by to see if I could fill in for a sick teacher, but I was more than a little horrified at the idea of wiping snotty noses and changing icky diapers. It will be different with my own children." Her expression made it clear that future little Caldicotts would not need assistance with their noses, since that portion of their anatomy would be at all times impeccable and quite adorable.

"Was Sarah alone in your room at any time?"

"I could hardly stand around dripping at her, although she deserved far worse. But she certainly did not have the opportunity to search my room for stray bits of jewelry. Oh, and Gideon came by to ripple his biceps at me. Egotistical men can be so juvenile. If I wanted to watch undulating flesh, I'd order tomato aspic and poke it with a salad fork. I let him know in no uncertain terms that I was less than impressed."

"Surely he did more than—ah ripple at you, Dorrie."

"It was bizarre. First he told me about the bombing in Hebron, as if I cared. Then he said that his mother had sent him to see if Essie had been there, but he was rippling away at a hundred miles an hour and flashing boyish smiles like Mr. Macho Incarnate. I said that she hadn't and politely suggested he have an internist run a test for degenerative muscle diseases—since his seemed to have gone amok. After a teensy moment of tension, he asked if Essie had said anything the day before about not coming again."

"And you said . . . ?" Theo said, struggling not to wince at Dorrie's guileless narrative.

"I said she hadn't. I dutifully repeated Essie's comments and he agreed that they made no sense whatsoever, but he didn't look pleased when I told him that I really needed to get back to more vital matters, such as shaving my legs. He stomped away without a single word of thanks." She tossed her hair back with a practiced hand and returned her attention to the microscopic red bump on her arm. "Do they have scorpions or tarantulas in Israel?"

"I shall make inquiries," he said. "Let us concern ourselves with the morning in question. Everyone finally left so that you could dress. Did you wear the locket that day?"

Dorrie stared at him. "Not with the silver buttons on my blouse, Uncle Theo! I wore adorable silver stud earrings and a matching chain that Daddy bought me for my birthday. This place may not be the Cape, but it's not some primitive outpost in Zambia."

Theo was forced to agree.

That evening he, Judith, and Dorrie met near the front door of the dining hall. They entered the stream of kibbutzniks that flowed past a steamtable and a second table covered with pitchers and coffee pots. When they had filled their trays, Judith followed a zigzag path to a table where Hershel and Gideon sat.

After a round of mumbled greetings, they all began to eat. Theo found the food palatable, and better than that which was served to tourists in the restaurant. The silence, as cheerful as a sky dark with storm clouds, was less palatable. He decided to attempt a round of pleasantries, beginning with Gideon.

"I didn't know spaghetti was kosher," he commented.

"Why not?"

Theo straightened his napkin and moved on to Hershel. "I understand that you and Judith met in Athens. Were you there to visit the archaeological sites out of professional curiosity?"

Hershel's thin shoulders curled as if Theo had squeezed his ribcage. "It wasn't professional. I went with Gideon," he answered through a mouthful of spaghetti. He gave his companion a panicked look, as if Theo now held his lungs in a tight grasp.

Gideon twirled a mass of strands around his fork until it resembled a fist of blood-drenched worms. "Yeah, that's right." He shoved the fork in his mouth.

Not yet prepared to accept defeat, Theo waited until Gideon put down his fork. "Was your trip sponsored by the kibbutz?"

"No. Unlike some people, we don't have money tucked away in trunks in the attic so that we can drive around Europe in an air-conditioned bus. Hershel and I saved our military allotment for a post-graduation trip. Do you find all this pertinent, Mr. Bloomer?"

Defeat loomed in the immediate future, but Theo bravely persisted. "I understood from your mother that each kibbutznik is entitled to travel if he wishes. Won't you receive some sort of travel allowance every year?"

The reference to his mother seemed to stir up some distant social training. Gideon managed a grim smile. "After two or three years, we'll be able to do more traveling. Right now all we can afford is Athens. In fact, we may be going back in a few weeks. Isn't that right, Hershel?" He jabbed his companion with a well-aimed elbow. "Don't you want to go back to Athens?"

Hershel gasped, then began to jerk his head back and forth in protest. "You said that we weren't going back," he said in a plaintive whine. "You said that the second—"

The elbow struck again. Laughing (very loudly, Theo thought), Gideon said, "Hershel didn't like the primitive accommodations, but we couldn't afford to stay in pricey hotels; we slept on the floor at a hostel. We had to cook our own food or eat sandwiches, and we hitchhiked around. Not exactly the grand tour. It was just coincidence that we met Dorrie and Judith."

Judith gazed devotedly at Hershel. "Or as they say in the Middle East, sweet kismet."

The object of her sibilance turned the color of the spaghetti sauce on his chin and ducked his head. "Yeah," he said, "we were almost broke by then. We were planning to leave that day."

Dorrie put down her fork to stare at Hershel. "While we were sitting at the café in Athens, I saw you and Gideon come out of an antiquities shop. If you were so occupied with survival, how could you possibly lose precious minutes shopping for souvenirs?"

Hershel gulped at Gideon, who said, "We weren't shopping. Browsing is less expensive than sleeping in a hotel or sitting in a theater watching a play by Aristophanes. Of course you were on a cultural tour with your playmates from school."

"The prices in those shops were higher than a week in the hotel, which was a haven for roaches," Dorrie sniffed.

"But at least it had running water so you could shave your legs every thirty minutes." Gideon's eyes were glittering, and his lips clamped together tighter than a fiddlehead fern that had just popped up. "Doesn't that make it preferable to a filthy floor in a hostel?"

"Barely!" Dorrie snapped. "At least the hotel maid in Athens didn't slink around muttering about crypts and sex. You ought to stay there some time. If you have a fetish about hairy legs, I'm sure she'd be delighted to show you hers. If you plead, she might even give you a glimpse of her underarms."

"We didn't have the luxury of maid service at the hostel, so we didn't have the opportunity to listen to cryptic remarks about sex or study anyone's sweaty armpits," Gideon snarled. Beside him, Hershel choked on a strand of spaghetti as he bobbled his head.

Dorrie winced at the crude anatomical reference, since Caldicotts did not acknowledge the existence of such things as glands or excessive moisture. "But you did buy something at the antiquities shop. I saw the package, and in fact Hershel asked Judith to smuggle it through customs for him! She wasn't supposed to tell me—but she did." The unspoken "So there!" echoed in the abrupt silence. Gideon turned the glare on Judith, who hunched her shoulders and slithered down in her chair as she blinked helplessly at her beloved.

After a moment of hasty mastication, Hershel said, "It was just a small present for one of my professors at the university, who's keen on Hellenic pottery. I asked Judith to carry it so that I wouldn't get tangled up in customs. It was a small favor, that's all." A long speech, the longest Theo had heard from him.

Dorrie responded with a sugary smile. "I fail to under-stand how you can be too broke to eat one minute, and be buying souvenirs the next. It must be difficult to keep your story straight."

"Who said we didn't eat?" Gideon said in a shrill yelp.

"You did," she crowed in triumph. "Didn't you hear those precise words earlier, Uncle Theo? How the poor, destitute boys had to sleep on the cold, hard floor and scavenge food from garbage cans? It almost moved me to tears."

"The only thing that ever moved you was a Mercedes!"

"You are an arrogant toad, Gideon Adler. Someone ought to wipe that smirk off your face once and for all. If I could bear the sight of blood, I'd do it myself!"

"You and the Islamic Liberation Front?" he jeered. "You two little rich girls couldn't kill a fly without a butler to hand you the fly swatter and sweep up afterward!"

"I am more than capable of flattening you," Dorrie said, now composed and as icy as only a Caldicott could be in the face of unseemly behavior. "If a butler appears, you'd better cling to the ceiling and pray your sticky feet don't fail you. Otherwise, splat!"

Gideon's face paled. "Splat," he hissed under his breath, his mouth forming each sound with ominous deliberation.

"That's right." The sugary smile widened.

Theo discovered that the spaghetti, by now somewhat congealed, was quite tasty. Dorrie and Gideon huffed at each other for a few more seconds, then snatched up their forks and began to eat. Judith and Hershel had finished, and were holding hands across the table with soulful expressions, her transgression apparently forgiven. Theo found it touching, if naive.

As soon as he could politely excuse himself, he did so. As he left the table, he saw Naomi at the next table, her napkin propitiously positioned to muffle a giggle. Shel, the bartender and news commentator, shrugged in sympathy. He recognized other faces from the factory, all studiously blank. An amateur but promising ventriloquist produced a faint rendition of a fly meeting death. His ears as pink as petunia petals, Theo hurried across the room to join Miriam at a far table.

She was hunched over a coffee cup. A plate of food had been pushed aside.

"I was invited to dine with Judith, but the atmosphere was—ah, on the turbulent side," he said. "May I join you?"

She responded with a faint smile and a wave at the empty chair across the table. "Excuse me, Theo, I was in another world—one where maids stand around pleading to scrub floors. I'm terribly sorry about Essie, but as Sarah said, she seems to be more trouble dead than she was alive. I think I'm going mad, and what's worse, I think I prefer it. Did I see you and the girls at a table with Hershel and Gideon?"

"You did. Did you not also hear us?"

She made a wry face. "Everyone did, I'm afraid. Gideon and Dorrie were not exactly restrained. What on earth provoked all the shouting and foaming?"

"It had its origin the morning you so graciously offered to show me around the kibbutz. Gideon came by Dorrie's room to look for Essie on your behalf, and to—ah, ripple at Dorrie, who responded as only a Caldicott can. I fear his male ego was wounded, and has not yet recovered."

"No more," she said weakly. "I can't find a maid, I can't control my son, and I can't stand to think about any of the above. Lock me up and swallow the key, please."

"Would it help to talk about it?"

"It would, but not here. I'd better have a word with Gideon, and then we can take a walk to the beach."

She crossed the room and yanked Gideon aside for a terse conversation. In the interim, Theo carried his tray to a conveyor belt and watched as it was whisked into the mouth of an aluminum carnivore with a clattering digestive tract. He then joined Miriam at the door and they strolled down the sidewalk.

The stars hung dully above the thick blanket of heat, as if

173

depressed by their inability to do better. The air was motionless. Theo daringly took off his jacket and draped it over one arm. When no retribution came, he loosened his tie and unbuttoned his collar. Again, lightning failed to strike.

They sat down on a bench under a spray of palm trees. Theo waited in silence, worried by Miriam's lack of vitality and the absence of her customary smiles. She had returned to her bleak thoughts, if her sighs were indicative, and her shoulders drooped like unwatered roses.

"I hope you're not distressed that you have not been able to find a replacement for Essie," he said at last. "There are only two guests, Miriam. We can survive nicely without a maid." He could, anyway. With any luck, Dorrie wouldn't even notice.

"There are three as of this afternoon," she said with a grimace. "A Mr. Sitermann from Dallas checked in for a week, and will be in the room next to yours. He explained in great detail that he would have preferred to stay at the kibbutz at Ein Gedi, but our prices were lower. Perhaps you two can swim together."

Theo refused to be distracted. "Even with three guests, the guest house can do without a maid until you find someone. You really shouldn't worry about it. You ate nothing at dinner, and—"

"Israel's getting to you," she interrupted lightly. "You're the one who sounds like a Jewish mother. I solemnly promise to eat something later."

Theo hoped the darkness would hide his flushed cheeks. He straightened his bifocals and cleared his throat before saying, "I did not intend to take a proprietary position in regard to your personal life, Miriam. I am—well, I will admit that I am concerned about you."

"I'll be fine once things have returned to normal and we're rid of Gili. Every time I see him, I remember Essie's face after the animals . . . found her. No one should be treated like that. I'm terrified that it will happen again—to someone as innocent as Essie. This has to stop, Theo."

Theo watched in dismay as she buried her face in her hands. It wouldn't do to pat her shoulder, or even offer a few words of comfort. They had met only a few days ago, and he could hardly think that she would welcome such brazen behavior on his part. However tempting it seemed. Instead, when she lifted her head, he told her what Dorrie had admitted about the locket.

"Then Essie didn't take it the last day she cleaned," Miriam said in a low voice. "How could that be, Theo? Dorrie didn't imply she'd ever been to the cave, did she?"

"Not in my wildest imagination could I envision Dorrie making her way down the mountainside. She hasn't been more than fifteen feet from an air conditioner since she arrived, except for meals, one tour, and brief bouts of sunbathing. Someone else must have entered her room while she was out."

Miriam's voice was no louder than the tiny waves of the Dead Sea. "No one else has a key. Essie used the master key from my office when she cleaned the guests' rooms, then returned it immediately. I keep it in a locked drawer. I didn't want her to lose it on one of her nocturnal jaunts."

"Then no one could have borrowed it?"

"I could have, Theo."

It was too late to change the subject, so he bravely forged ahead. "Did Gili manage to establish Essie's movements before she disappeared?"

She gave a short laugh. "Lieutenant Gili has decided to keep me informed of all his progress so that I can be impressed by the keen logic of his mind. He admitted that he had minor difficulties with poor Essie's movement, but that's not surprising—she wafted about like a dandelion seed in the wind. According to the official report, Essie left my apartment at about ten o'clock. I'm afraid I had scolded her rather sternly about her behavior with the guests. Gideon saw her several hours later near the dining hall, and sent her home. No one saw her after that."

"And that was after midnight," Theo said. It was, he realized, the same night he had encountered Gideon, Hershel and Ilana on the beach. Had he heard Essie drifting by seconds before that? Or had it been Yussef on his unexplained mission? Was there always so much traffic on the beach of the Dead Sea? "Was Gideon positive she was going toward the dining hall? Could she have been coming from it?"

"Does that matter?"

Theo sighed. "I don't know. Did Gideon say what he was doing at the time he met Essie?"

"Ilana was on security duty that night, and I would guess he had been walking around the perimeter with her to keep her company. They were furious with each other early that day over some silly incident, but they seemed to have worked it out." She gave him a sharp look. "Why, Theo? Do you think Gideon has something to do with this?"

"No, of course not," Theo said hastily. "I did happen to see him a few minutes before he met Essie, when he, Hershel and Ilana were patrolling the beach together."

"The boys went back to their apartments and went to bed. Ilana spent the night alone at the gatehouse. If you're hoping for tidy alibis, I'm sorry to disappoint you, Theo—but no one seems to have one . . . including me."

"I never—not for a moment, I can assure you—would even begin to presume that—well, that you might—" Theo sputtered, aghast—"have any reason, or are the sort of person—the sort of—"

"No, of course not," Miriam murmured. "To continue with the official report, Essie did not appear at the guest house the next morning. Anya went over to check on her a few minutes before noon, but no one was there. When she came back, she told me that Essie's room looked as if it had been searched; I thought the idea was absurd but suggested it be reported to Gili anyway."

"Did he think anything had been taken?"

She shook her head. "He was quite rude about it. Essie's room was a total mess, very dusty and disorganized; it would be impossible to be sure if something were missing. Someone could have taken a feather or a scrap of shiny paper, I suppose. Other than her treasures, Essie had only standard clothes and furniture provided by the kibbutz. She had nothing that would be of interest to anyone but a pack rat or a small child."

Unless she had added a locket to her collection, Theo told himself in a thoroughly muddled voice. "So Gideon was the last to see Essie until you and I happened to find her in the wadi. Could she have gone through the gate without being seen?"

"Ilana swore that Essie didn't leave that way. However, all the kibbutz children know of secret exits. It's our fault; we encourage independence at birth, and then are dismayed when they take us up on the challenge. Even Essie, in her own pitiful way."

"Did Gideon notice anything about Essie's demeanor to suggest she was upset or would leave the kibbutz shortly thereafter?"

"He said she was agitated, so I suppose I hurt her feelings. I must have driven her away from the kibbutz. Oh, God, I feel so guilty about it." She again buried her face, and Theo could only listen as the sobs drifted across the water.

177

Chapter 14

The next morning, Theo learned that Gideon was dead. According to Judith, who brought the news to the restaurant, the body had been found near the edge of the Dead Sea. Lieutenant Gili seemed to have no illusions that it was an accident, she explained in a teary, breathless rush before departing for the children's house. Runny noses did not, she called over her shoulder, stop flowing for murder.

Theo put down his coffee cup and sagged back in the chair. When he felt able, he signed a tab and left the restaurant to find Miriam. He was blocked by a robust bulk in the doorway.

"Sitermann," the man announced, sticking out his hand. "I'm from Dallas, Texas, US of America." His battered, genial face did appear to have spent a great deal of time at home on the range; his nose had been broken more than once and his bushy gray eyebrows were thick enough to shade most of his face from a blazing sun. He wore a white suit more suitable for the tropics, a shirt unbuttoned most of the way to his waist, and a tangle of gold chains around his neck. A horoscope medallion glinted from its hiding place among abundant silver chest hairs. Sitermann was proud to be a ram.

Theo paused for a numbing handshake, murmured his own name, and attempted to sidle around his fellow guest. Pleasantries seemed distasteful. He wanted to find Miriam and do what he could for her. Sitermann wasn't finished, however.

"Hey, how long you been here, Bloomer?" he said, sidling with Theo as though the two were engaged in a grotesque pas de deux in the doorway.

"Merely a few days." Theo feinted to the left, but Sitermann was quicker.

"Have you been in the Dead Sea yet? My chiropractor back home swears the water is miracle juice, but I'm not sure about it. Anything named 'dead' doesn't sound too healthy to me. Hey, why don't you stay and have a cuppa coffee with me, Bloomer? You can tell me if you think the salt water will cure my damned lumbago."

"I really must go, Mr. Sitermann. Another time, perhaps." Theo feinted to the right, but again found his nose inches from that of the agile Sitermann. Over the man's shoulder he caught a glimpse of Miriam as she moved across the lobby and vanished behind a corner of the registration desk. "Damn," he said under his breath.

"Hey, old buddy, don't get all offended," Sitermann said. He stepped aside with a wounded look, his hands held up in a gesture of contrition. The end of his nose glowed like a Chinese lantern (*Physalis alkekengi franchetii*). "I just thought us two Yanks ought to stick together, but I didn't mean to cause you to take offense. Back home in Texas we allow a man a lot of acreage as long as he gives fair warning."

"I am not offended; I have an urgent errand, Mr. Sitermann. Why don't we have a meal together later in the day?" Where had Miriam gone? Would she stay at her desk in a display of bravery, or return home to mourn? What could he possibly say that would not be sadly inadequate in such circumstances?

"Sure we will, Bloomer," Sitermann boomed, his weathered face restored to wrinkles of amiability. "After I get something to eat, I guess I'll stick a pinky in the water down there

179

on the beach. Did you hear about the local boy what got hisself killed? They say someone stuck a knife between his ribs in just the right spot, terrorist-style. Jordan's right across the water, eleven miles, you know. It's damned creepy if you ask me."

"Then I shall not, Mr. Sitermann. Perhaps I'll see you at lunch." Theo darted through the doorway, then went across the lobby to Miriam's office. Unoccupied. He left the lobby and hurried down the walk toward her home, for once unaware of the omnipresent heat and the perspiration coursing down his back like tears.

Hershel opened the front door. "Mr. Bloomer," he acknowledged weakly. His face was white, his eyes dulled by shock and grief. His throat rippled as if he had swallowed a yo-yo.

"I heard about Gideon. Miriam was in the lobby earlier, but she left before I could speak to her. Did she come back here?"

"She's here, but she doesn't want to see anyone. I'll tell her that you came by." He tried to close the door, but a well-polished shoe had rooted on the doorsill.

"Then why don't you step outside and tell me exactly what happened?" Theo commanded in a quiet voice. "All I've heard is gossip and speculation. There must be more to the story."

Hershel glanced over his shoulder for help. Finding none, he reluctantly joined Theo on the sidewalk. "Yussef found the body early this morning when he went for a swim. Nobody knows why Gideon was there, or how long he'd been there, but probably since midnight. He was—there was a lot of blood. Lieutenant Gili came in less than an hour, and has been prowling around the beach, sifting sand and stuff. That's all I know, Mr. Bloomer." He gulped several times and looked yearningly at the door.

Theo caught Hershel's arm. "What about the weapon?"

"They found it next to the body. It was an ordinary kitchen knife. Everybody has a couple of them in his house—they're sort of standard issue. You can buy one anywhere in Israel. The lieutenant said the fingerprints were badly smeared, and he wasn't about to have one of his men fingerprint two hundred people, anyway."

"Has Gili interviewed Miriam yet?"

A squawk from behind Theo interrupted the conversation. Gili rocked on his heels, his hands behind his back as if he hoped to be mistaken for General Patton by a horde of cheering, if invisible, troops. "Not of yet, Mr. Bloomer," he said coldly.

Theo released Hershel, who skittered into the house and closed the door. "Ah, Lieutenant Gili, I've heard about the most recent tragedy. You must be growing tired of the kibbutz."

"I have been here too many days already, and I am tired of leaving my cool office for this wretched place to ask questions of these wretched kibbutzniks. First the Kelman girl, and now this latest tragedy. If I were in your socks, Mr. Bloomer, I would leave before some accident befell me." The dark eyes seemed to bulge outward as he licked his lips, and the mustache threatened to fly off his lip. Groucho Marx could not have done it better. "But, of course," he added with visible relish, "you cannot."

"And why is that, Lieutenant Gili?"

"Because I will not permit it, Mr. Bloomer."

"And why is that, Lieutenant Gili?" Theo said with more patience than he felt the man merited.

"Because your niece, Miss Theodora Caldicott of Connecticut, is a suspect in the death of Gideon Adler—and of

181

Ester Kelman." Gili sounded very pleased with himself and excited at the prospect of avenging his earlier defeat. "I have sent two of my men to bring her to me for questioning."

"That is absurd! Dorrie doesn't have anything to do with this—this mess. She's a tourist, for pity's sake, and not some Jordanian secret agent sent to Israel to decimate the population!"

Gili stiffened; the mustache froze in mid-twitch at a perilous angle. "What do you know of Jordanian secret agents?"

"I know only what I read in the newspapers," Theo said, "and that is all Dorrie knows. She is barely acquainted with these people. Why would she—"

"Enough, Mr. Bloomer. I must speak to Mrs. Adler to see when last she saw her son, then I shall interrogate your niece and her friend Judith Feldheim from Brooklyn, New York. I have had a report that there was an argument last night between Miss Caldicott and the victim, and now the presence of her necklace in Ester Kelman's hand takes an ominous turn. I am determined to hear what was passed in the vicious argument."

"Come now, Lieutenant, I was present at the table when the purported argument occurred. It was merely a childish spat over accommodations in Athens."

"I shall have to hear their statements before I arrive at a conclusion. In the meantime, please wait in the communal dining hall. Corporal Amitan has not yet taken your statement, and he is agog to do so. You hurt his feelings when you avoided him yesterday; Amitan is a sensitive man."

"I should first like to offer my condolences to Mrs. Adler," Theo murmured without moving. "Then I shall rush to the dining hall to soothe poor Corporal Amitan's feelings and tell him everything I know. He will surely recover from the previous slight."

"Mrs. Adler will be occupied—with me," Gili said. "You must wait until I have interviewed her and taken a statement. Go, Mr. Bloomer, before I order someone to assist you in leaving."

Theo went. At the dining hall, he virtuously scanned the room for a corporal with a sensitive face, but saw no one who met the criterion. Most of the kibbutzniks sat at tables, brooding or talking in low voices. Dorrie had not yet arrived with her escort service, nor had Judith. When Yussef waved from a corner table, Theo joined him.

Yussef had on a dark violet shirt in honor of the occasion. His face was too strained to produce his customary smirk, or even a supercilious grin. "You heard?" he asked Theo.

"Judith came to the restaurant to tell me. I went by Miriam's to offer whatever help I could, but Gili stormed in ahead of me." Theo stared at the formica surface. "She must be devastated."

"She is holding up well," Yussef said. "Sarah stayed with her for a few hours, while the beach was searched and the body sent away to be autopsied. Not that there was any doubt about the cause of death . . ."

"You found the body, didn't you? It must have been a bad shock, especially when you were expecting a peaceful swim by yourself."

"It was—a shock, yes. I'd known Gideon since he was a baby, and Miriam is very dear to me, very dear."

Theo didn't doubt that. "Hershel was with Miriam when I arrived; he looked quite washed out and upset. He and Gideon were close, I understand, along with Ilana and Essie."

"Gideon was the leader of their little gang, the one with the mischievous ideas and the chutzpah to stage their pranks." After a pause, he added, "He was murdered by someone on the kibbutz. The gates are guarded at all times; no one can wander in without a verifiable reason. Every car and truck is stopped to be searched."

"He was found on the beach. Couldn't someone have come across the Dead Sea by boat?" A Jordanian secret agent, for instance.

Before Yussef could answer, Ilana and Sarah joined the two men. Ilana looked stunned, as if she had been brutally and unexpectedly punched in the abdomen. Sarah was less visibly distressed, although her jaw was clenched and her lips pulled in tightly.

Theo met Ilana's eyes. "I'm dreadfully sorry about Gideon, Ilana. I realize that he was very special to you."

She stiffened. "Yes, Mr. Bloomer, and I shall avenge his death. He was good and kind and strong; he should not have been killed. The ones who did it will suffer at my hands, as Gideon suffered at theirs."

"Then you know who is responsible?"

"Palestinian terrorists. This is how they kill innocent people—knifing them without a second thought, as though their victims were diseased dogs to be put out of misery. I shall put many Arabs out of their misery." Ilana spun on her heel and marched away, her shoulders squared and her head erect.

Sarah watched her with a frown. "Yussef, I think she's likely to do something that will cause much grief to all of us, but most of all to herself. Go catch up with her and talk some sense into her before she blows up Jericho or drives into Hebron with a gun."

"I can't leave the dining hall until Gili returns," Yussef said, sounding obscurely relieved. "You'll have to talk to her."

"I'll speak to her," Theo said. "At the moment, she won't

be permitted to leave the kibbutz, so she won't get into trouble. When she's had an opportunity to calm down, I'll find her." Figuring out what he would say to her would provide the challenge.

The murmurs around them broke off as Gili, Miriam, and Hershel came into the room. Miriam was pale but composed; Hershel seemed thinner, if possible, and thoroughly limp. Gili, however, moved with the brisk precision of a windup toy as he joined a khakied minion at the front of the room.

Miriam was immediately surrounded by her fellow kibbutzniks. After she accepted their condolences and disentangled herself, she sat down beside Sarah. "I'm fine," she said before anyone could ask the obvious. "Gili was reasonably decent about his questions, although he seemed disappointed by my lack of knowledge concerning Gideon's movements. Gideon was not a schoolboy; he was twenty-five years old and his life has been apart from mine since he was a newborn baby and I put him in the children's house."

"What could you tell Gili about Gideon's movements?" Theo prodded softly. He heard a snort from Yussef, but did not look away from Miriam's ashen face.

"I saw Gideon yesterday after Lieutenant Gili left," she said. "We talked for a long time about—politics, and I almost believed he intended to behave in a more responsible manner. He seemed calmer, anyway, and I felt encouraged." She looked away for a minute, as though she were reliving her last conversation with her son. "Gideon's room was searched, or at least that's what Gili thinks. Ilana wasn't certain; Hershel didn't think so. I haven't been in his room in months."

The envisioned chaos brought Dorrie to mind. She was to have been fetched, Theo thought guiltily, a situation she would not take kindly despite the implication that her presence was of monumental importance. He looked around once again for his niece, who at that moment entered the dining room between two burly officers.

Theo excused himself and crossed the room. "Are you unharmed?" he asked, ignoring the menacing towers on either side of her.

For a moment, she looked like a frightened child. "I'm okay. I'm terribly sorry about Gideon. I truly am, and I wish I hadn't been so bitchy last night. For all his arrogance, he wasn't so bad, although he seemed a bit berserko last night. I just snapped at him because I wanted him to tell Hershel to send Judith home."

"I understand," Theo said comfortingly, "and I'm relieved to see that you're okay."

The frightened child vanished under a blast of Caldicottian disdain. "Attila Gili sent these two barbarians to drag me here, but other than that I'm dandy, Uncle Theo. It was so entertaining to be watched as I dressed and did my makeup; in fact, it was amusingly kinky. The barbarians don't speak English, so they couldn't do more than grunt and goggle as if they'd never seen lipliner before. What is this about?"

Theo winced. "Lieutenant Gili thinks you have information about Gideon's death. I tried to tell him that you—"

"What am I purported to know—who killed him? That's nonsense, Uncle Theo! I wasn't there; I was in my room, washing my hair and trying for the millionth time to do something about my nails."

Theo avoided the increasingly dark looks from both sides as he dropped his voice to a whisper. "You returned to your room last night after dinner, and remained there until this morning when the two officers came for you? Nobody came by for a chat?"

Dorrie fluffed her hair off her neck. "That's right. I did my hair with this divine avocado gook that I bought at Bloomie's before I went to Greece, then I worked very diligently on my cuticles. I can prove that I was in my room all night," she ended in triumph, holding out ten shapely, shiny fingernails. "This does take time."

"I can see that," Theo said. He wondered if Gili would agree with her ironclad alibi.

The previous evening, Nadine Caldicott, née Bloomer, had driven by Theo's small clapboard house, fully intending to stop and water the houseplants as she had solemnly promised. And if Pookie hadn't snarled about the time, she certainly would have done so.

Chapter 15

Theo did not have the opportunity to discover Gili's reaction to the well-polished alibi. Dorrie was whisked away to the upstairs lounge amidst a great deal of grousing and glaring from all parties concerned. The kibbutzniks gaped at the drama, then turned on Theo with speculative expressions, centimeters away from overt hostility. An understandable reaction, but nevertheless discomfitting for its object.

Time for an exit. Smiling vaguely (as if his niece had not been taken away as a prime suspect in the murder of the son of two founding kibbutzniks), Theo sauntered out of the dining hall and went down the sidewalk to the children's house. Judith was in her corner of the playground, her combatants occupied with tricycles and sand castles. The branches above her cast dappled shadows on her noticeably morose posture. He went through the gate to join her.

"Gili seems to think Dorrie might have been involved in Gideon's murder," he told her. "She's been taken away to be questioned."

Behind her glasses, Judith's eyes were wary. "I know, since I'm scheduled for an interview as soon as someone can cover for me. But Gili won't detain her for long. Dorrie doesn't know the capital of Israel. How could she tell him anything?"

"I know her better than that," Theo countered mildly. "The preppy pose has never impressed me. Dorrie is intelligent, thoughtful, and observant, even if she pretends to be more interested in polo players and shampoo. You know that as well as I, Judith."

"I guess I do." She sighed.

"I need your help. There is a reason behind her obstinate refusal to leave without you. Whatever she's holding back endangers not only herself, but also the welfare of the kibbutz. Someone is a murderer. Surely you care about exposing him so that Kibbutz Mishkan can return to normal."

"The kibbutz is important to me, Mr. Bloomer. Even though I've been raised in foster homes where I was coerced into whichever religion the household preferred, I've always known that I was Jewish. This is my home—it has to be. This is where I belong now, and I'd do anything to protect it."

"Or to protect Hershel?"

She gave him a quick look, then turned back to stare at her dusty charges in the sandbox. "Hershel doesn't have anything to do with this and he doesn't need protection. He may seem inept and graceless to you, but he isn't that way when we're together. He's shy. He comes from a disrupted family environment that has sapped his confidence and left deep emotional scars. He's afraid that others will desert him just as his parents did. In that sense, he does need protection—from further pain."

Theo gravely nodded at what he presumed was standard Intro to Sociology rhetoric. "Then you are still determined to stay at Kibbutz Mishkan, despite the recent violence?"

"Of course I am," she said, emphasizing her determination with a series of earnest blinks. "Hershel needs me, as does the kibbutz. Here I'm not just an orphan watching from the fringe of the group, nor am I a poor little scholarship girl who doesn't know Perrier from soda pop. I'm needed—and I'm I going to stay."

"And marry Hershel," he added encouragingly. "You two

have talked about your pasts and know everything about each other."

She looked down, but not quickly enough to hide the dull red glow on her cheeks. "Of course, we do. Honesty is vital to every new relationship."

"He must have been impressed that you had earned an academic scholarship to such a prestigious East Coast school. Tuition for four years at Wellesley probably rivals the income of the kibbutz." Theo realized he was taking Essie's advice about fishing. Carping, in particular, seemed apropos. "That and the dorm must cost—"

"I did not want to intimidate him," she interrupted. "A communal social organization stresses intergroup dynamics over individual accomplishments. I'll tell him later when it won't be so threatening to his fragile male ego. As I told you, Hershel is a very delicate person with inner doubts about his own worth. He has only recently begun to consider a career in archaeology. Before he met me, he was too intimidated ever to agree to move away from the kibbutz. Now he—he has mentioned it several times."

It was impressive. Theo gave her a moment to brush away a tear or two, then said, "And you have no idea why Dorrie is so adamant about not leaving without you? She has behaved very oddly about this."

"Misguided loyalty," Judith pronounced in a cool tone. "She has some screwy idea that I don't know how to deal with men. I may have had a few minor problems with latent transvestites and married men, but that was last year. I am more in touch with my feelings now and capable of making critical life decisions for myself."

Sarah appeared at the gate. "Judith, I realize this is a bad time for all of us, but I must discuss this requisition with you. My accounts indicate that the children's house has already purchased new bedding, enough for the entire Israeli army from the looks of it."

"No, Sarah, we don't have any new furniture at all. The mattresses are army surplus, and about to split at the seams. Most of the bed frames are falling apart."

"Here's the voucher," Sarah said as she fluttered a paper. "You should have had over forty new sets of bedding arrive three weeks ago. You'll have to show me what you do have so that I can run down the requisition and try to sort this out."

Shrugging at Theo, Judith took Sarah into the concrete structure to confer with the other members of the staff and inspect the furnishings. A small, black-haired child approached Theo, intent on mayhem. Theo retreated, locking the gate securely before walking toward the beach. A toothless, lispy threat drifted after him.

Orange tape delineated the area where Gideon's body had been found. An officer watched Theo through mirrored sunglasses, clearly optimistic that he might be obliged to use force if the area were invaded by tourists, no matter how mild or innocently curious.

Theo prudently circled the area and went to the edge of the water. Sitermann floated twenty feet from shore, his face scarlet but happy. "Damnedest thing, Bloomer," he yelled. "You can't sink out here, you know. It's like being in bed with a warm lady's body all over you, just a-ticklin' and a-strokin' with all her fingers. It stinks worse than a squashed armadillo, but you get used to it after a few minutes, and I can tell my lumbago loves it. Hey, why don't you get your bathing suit and join me?"

"Not now, thank you." Theo gazed pensively at the bobbling figure, then picked up Sitermann's jacket and took a wallet out of the pocket.

"Bloomer! What the blazes do you think you're doing?"

191

Joan Hess

Sitermann bellowed with the fury of a bullock facing steerhood. "That's my jacket—and my wallet! Put it down, or I'll call a cop! Hey, Bloomer!" He began to paddle toward the shore, still roaring as Theo methodically examined the contents of the wallet and replaced it in the jacket.

"Okay, Bloomer, you're in big-ass trouble now," Sitermann growled. He limped across the last of the shallow water, then hopped about, either in agitation or in response to the hot rocks, until he reached his sandals. "You'd better have a damned good explanation for this; in Texas, we shoot rustlers for less!"

"But not in Washington, DC, in a nice, suburban setting. You really shouldn't have carried photographs. I'm afraid I recognized the neighborhood, since I once knew a gentleman who resided on your street. A lovely area, if I recall, and convenient to the downtown area. You shouldn't have slathered on the cowboy cover with such a heavy hand."

"What does that mean, Bloomer?"

"It means CIA, Sitermann. It means that you're an employee of our beloved Central Intelligence Agency, or, in simpler terms, that you're a common garden variety spy."

Sitermann snatched up his clothes and checked to see that his wallet was in his pocket. "I thought I did a fairly good Texas accent," he said without rancor—or accent. "Out of curiosity, why didn't you buy it, Bloomer?"

"I've had a little experience in intelligence work. Nothing like yours, of course, but I did develop an ear for it. Your accent was quite consistent, by the way."

"You're a retired florist from some tedious little Midwest town, Bloomer. You sold the shop several years ago and returned to Connecticut, where you were to the manor born. Your sister Nadine Caldicott is married to a surgeon with a golf handicap of four and a reputation for hefty contributions

192

to right-wing Republican candidates. Your niece, Theodora, was named after you, and she—"

"Must we, Sitermann?"

"—attends Wellesley, where she majors in sociology and dates a young man with a metallic blue Mercedes convertible, paid up to the last penny. His name is Bedford—"

"I know all this, Sitermann," Theo said, turning around to leave. "When your mouth runs down, I'll be in the lobby of the guest house, drinking soda water and watching television. We'll chat, hey?"

Sitermann trotted up the walk to catch up with him. "I didn't mean to show off, Bloomer. I guess I hoped it would intimidate you. Sorry about that. The bottom line, however, is that we have nothing in your dossier to indicate any involvement with intelligence work. I'm surprised anyone would take you after your less-than-glorious showing in Hollywood."

Theo hastened his pace. "That was forty years ago, and I do not care to discuss it with you. I want to know why you're here at Kibbutz Mishkan, Sitermann—or whatever your name is."

"It's Sitermann, and my assignment is classified."

They entered the lobby and ordered drinks at the bar. Theo took the soda water and sat down on a sofa. The spy followed with a hefty slug of bourbon. Theo felt responsible for driving him to drink so early in the day, and vaguely penitent. Having one's cover blown was unnerving, at best.

He gave Sitermann a smile of apology, then said, "You really ought to explain, classified or not. I'm hardly Jordanian secret service or KGB. If you refuse, I'll be obliged to tell Gili all about your fluctuating accent and covert credentials."

"That's blackmail, Bloomer."

"I believe it is, Sitermann."

Sitermann drained his glass and fetched another drink

from the bar. When he returned, he said, "I don't particularly desire involvement with the Israeli Criminal Investigation— or the Mossad, for that matter. It isn't very nice of you to threaten me."

"Spying isn't very nice, either."

"It pays well, though." Sitermann blinked at the empty glass in his hand, as if unable to determine its purpose or origin. "Anyway, I'm tracing a packet of explosives. We're on to this dealer in Athens named Popadoupolis who sells plasticine and other nasty stuff to anyone with money. We usually recognize all his customers, but this last time it was a pimply kid who looked like he ought to be at home playing with his chemistry set. Not at all our typical courier."

"Oh, dear," Theo said under his breath, dismayed but not especially surprised. Dorrie's peculiar argument with Gideon and Hershel had hinted at some mystery about the package. He wondered how much she suspected—and how much Judith knew.

"Yeah," Sitermann continued morosely, "I got sent to see who the kid was and who ended up with the explosives. I didn't think it would be used before I could get airline reservations! These damned amateur terrorists behave like children with a new toy. They open it up and start looking for a handy building to demolish, just to clap and giggle over the sound effects."

Theo felt as if he ought to apologize for the terrorists' impetuousness. He settled for a shrug. "So the explosives came here, and then were used in Hebron against the Arabs. Do you have any idea who actually planted the explosives?"

"No," Sitermann sighed. "But the local chaps have had their eye on Adler, Waskow, and the girl—Ilana Tor. She's trained in munitions, courtesy of the Israeli army, and capable of handling the technicalities. Hell of a job for a woman."

"Is there any proof that they . . . ?"

"Can't tell you; I'd get flack from seven different directions. It's a damned shame your niece got herself involved, Bloomer."

"My niece is not involved. Judith unwittingly provided a means of transporting the package from Athens, but both of the girls were convinced it contained a piece of pottery."

"Maybe it did. Then again, maybe I'll sprout wings and learn to keep kosher. Want a drink? I'll put it on my expense account." He started for the bar without waiting for a response.

"What about Gideon's death?" Theo said to the spy's back. "Who's responsible for that?"

Sitermann perched on a barstool while he awaited his third shot of bourbon in as many minutes. "That's really none of my concern, Bloomer. I'm here to identify the terrorists and inform the locals, if I'm instructed to do so. Other than that, I'm just going to try to cure my lumbago. But you wanna know what I think about this murder?"

"That would be kind of you, Sitermann."

"I think that the girls—Dorrie and Judith—found out their new boyfriends were as crazy as loons, that the little package would get them in big trouble if anyone found out exactly who carried it through customs. The girls got peeved and decided to take revenge. One of them, anyway. After all, who'd suspect some pretty little filly of having a knife tucked in her brassiere?"

"You believe that Judith or Dorrie stabbed Gideon? That is unworthy of an intelligence agent, no matter how much bourbon he has consumed." Theo put down his glass and stood up. "Do you also believe the girls had something to do with Essie's death? How about the Easter Bunny and Santa Claus, Sitermann? Florida real estate?"

He left the lounge in an aura of outraged indignation. And Sitermann's loud guffaws.

Chapter 16

Theo went back to the dining hall and waited until Dorrie swept out, unencumbered but pinker than a dianthus (*calypso*). Ignoring her barrage of frigid comments about officious officials, he took her by the elbow and steered her to the sanctuary of his room.

Once she was settled in a chair, she managed a more decorous tone. "That man is intolerable. Do you know what he accused me of doing, Uncle Theo? He honestly thinks I'm some sort of POL agent. I don't even know what that stands for, much less if I'd care to support it!"

"I believe it's PLO," Theo said mildly, "and it stands for Palestine Liberation Organization, one of many groups that specialize in hijackings, political terrorism, and so forth in the name of peace. Yasir Arafat is the leader."

"Oh, right, he's the one who never shaves for press conferences. But I don't believe we've met." She nibbled on her lipstick for a moment. "Some busybody kibbutznik told Gili that I'd argued with Gideon at dinner last night. It was hardly worthy of a response, but the little man was such a boor about it that I finally told him what I could remember. He then had the audacity to ask me for an alibi. Can he do that without a warrant?"

Theo took off his bifocals and began to polish them with his handkerchief. "He seems to think he can, my dear. Were you able to convince him of your innocence?"

"I showed him my nails, but he wasn't impressed. They can't keep me here, can they? Mother promised me that I could use her credit cards to shop before school started, but at this rate all the racks will be literally denuded before I get there. I'll have to wear rags to school."

"I thought you were determined not to return without Judith?"

"Yeah," she said, frowning at the ceiling. "Judith came in while I was there, and she doesn't seem to be in as much trouble as I am—which is damned ironic, since I'm here only to look after her welfare. She said that she was with Hershel all last night. They left the dining hall together and went to his room for a glass of wine. Israeli wine, if you can imagine. Then they stayed up all night discussing the role of manual labor in the socialist structure, whether it was acceptable to hire peasants to dig potatoes or whatever it is they do around here. It must have been sheer rapture."

"So Judith and Hershel were together when Gideon was killed," Theo said. "By the way, I heard a bit of gossip about the package Judith was so kind as to smuggle through customs for the boys. It seems it was not a pot."

"I warned Judith not to take the package, but she was in the throes of passion, and would have carried Hershel on her back if he'd asked her. I told her it was dumb, not to mention incredibly naïve. I could just see her being thrown in prison with a bunch of Arabs for the rest of her life. Lice, rats, no hair-care products."

"What did you suspect was in the package, Dorrie?"

"I wasn't sure, but I didn't buy the story about Israeli citizens having trouble with customs. Gideon laid on a real snow job, but Hershel was itching in the background as if the package contained a baby nuclear bomb." She narrowed her eyes. "What was in the package?"

Omitting Sitermann's name but not his job description, he told her what he had learned in the lobby.

197

She produced an unseemly squeak. "We smuggled explosives into Israel and now the CIA is after us? I knew Judith was going to get us in terrible trouble! I knew it! I knew it! I knew it! But she said she felt like the heroine of a spy thriller, and that as long as we didn't actually know what was in the package, we were safe. She actually suggested we wear sunglasses and trench coats, for God's sake! Talk about an overdose of John Le Carré." She shook her head in despair. "Who paid for Hershel and Gideon's gay little shopping spree, assuming one cannot put explosives on American Express or Diners?"

"I don't know, Dorrie. The kibbutz allotment for personal expenses is quite small, and the boys have been out of the university only a few months. I doubt they could buy the explosives themselves."

"Oh, great, I always wanted to be in the middle of a full-fledged conspiracy. What happens to me now?"

"I am not sure. The CIA agent will not necessarily share information with Gili. It is possible that Judith's involvement will not come out, and nothing will happen to her—or to you. Once Gili abandons his absurd contention that you are a suspect, you and I will be free to return to Connecticut."

Dorrie shrugged, then announced that she could live no longer if she did not properly apply makeup and tend to her hair. Theo warned her to stay in her room, where he presumed she would be safe. After she left, he fluffed the cushion on the chair while he tried to decide how best to extradite his niece from the situation and get her back to Bloomingdale's before the racks were denuded. Nothing came to mind.

At noon he went to the restaurant and ate a light meal. Sitermann waved from a distant table, but did not blurt out any hearty invitations to join him. Theo would not have done so in any case. Spies were not always the best luncheon companions. Too devious.

Afterward he approached an unfamiliar gray-haired woman at the registration desk. "Please excuse me for disturbing you. I'm Theo Bloomer of Connecticut, currently a guest in your charming kibbutz. May I presume your name is Anya?"

"Anya Bittleman, formerly of Flatbush. So delighted to make your acquaintance, Mr. Theo Bloomer."

"It is entirely my pleasure, Mrs. Bittleman. I've been hoping to have the opportunity to speak to you."

She displayed two rows of dazzling porcelain teeth. "Which you are doing very nicely."

"Miriam has told me that you were upset the morning Essie failed to come to work. It must have made your day most complicated."

"Should I love having to mop the floors on my hands and knees? Who would, if I may be so bold as to ask?" Her smile deepened as she studied him through shrewd eyes.

"It hardly suits you," Theo said gallantly. He wiped his neck with his handkerchief, wondering if there might be a problem with the air conditioner. The lobby was usually quite cool. "I was told that you thought Essie's apartment had been searched, and that Lieutenant Gili failed to appreciate your perceptive comment."

Anya put her elbows on the counter and cupped her chin in her hands. "So you think I'm perceptive, Mr. Theo Bloomer? If my dead husband Arnold Bittleman could hear you, he would roll over in his solid oak coffin. He always said, 'Anya you are nothing but a nosy old woman.' When I see him, I'll remember to tell him what you said."

"I'm sure he was only teasing, Mrs. Bittleman. Why did you think the girl's apartment had been searched?"

"What would you think if you came home and found all of

your things on the floor? Your drawers emptied and your closets a disaster? Surely your wife is a better housekeeper than that, Mr. Theo Bloomer!"

Theo decided to allow Mrs. Bittleman to think the worst of the nonexistent Mrs. Bloomer. "Would it be possible for me to rent a jeep from the kibbutz?" he asked. "I was thinking I might drive around the region for a few hours."

Theo subsequently found himself in possession of a key, a handful of brochures, a tattered road map, and a dimpled wish for a pleasant day. He drove through the gate and followed the highway to the south end of the Dead Sea, glancing when he dared take his eyes off the road at the mountains and harsh, chiseled cliffs.

Before they had been distracted by the body in the wadi, Miriam had mentioned that there were caves that were likely to contain scrolls and artifacts. The idea still intrigued him. It was whimsical but possible that he might, should he indulge in a bit of spelunking, crawl into a fantastic discovery. The find would be invaluable, the finder renowned on archaeological circuits (but not on prime-time television, unless there was a reference to sex, preferably of a bizarre variety). In any case, Miriam might enjoy a second outing, if only to escape the well-intentioned solicitude and Hershel's gloomy presence. It would simply be a thoughtful gesture on his part. No one would think otherwise.

He arrived at an intersection of sorts, with a rough road snaking in a northwesterly direction. There were a few houses, an occasional bedouin tent, and a great expanse of desert. Thirty miles later he turned onto a modern highway that led to the outskirts of Hebron.

The traffic swept him into the center of town, where it promptly stranded him behind a donkey cart that had taken residence in the middle of the street. Between the animal's ears, Theo could see the narrow alleys of the market, populated by swarthy men in long robes; veiled women in bright, embroidered dresses; nimble children; and a few nervous tourists. Armed Israeli soldiers leaned against walls and perched on rooftops, their weapons pointedly displayed. Only the children smiled.

Theo parked in front of a café and sat back to look at the cacophony of shrill voices and colors. Several children eyed the jeep with mercenary glints, but were shooed away by a grinning man in a dirty white robe and a tattered *kaffiyeh,* held in place by a piece of twine. His face was unshaven, his eyes lined with red, his teeth stubbles of moss-coated bark.

"Shalom, mister. You want to visit Haram el-Khalil? I can show you, tell you many interesting things, show you the Machpelah Cave where our common ancestor Abraham is buried, and also Sarah, Isaac, Rebecca, and Jacob. A condo grave, ha, ha. If you like to see these things, Abbu will take you for an insignificant fee."

Theo gazed at the guide, and then at the urchins. "Will my jeep be safe here?"

Abbu beckoned to the boys. After a lively discussion, Theo was assured that the hubcaps of the jeep would be guarded for a mere handful of shekels. The two went into the massive building, and Theo was instructed in the intricacies of the architecture and history in a rapid succession of acidic sibilants and smiles. Exotic tendrils of incense tempered Abbu's more pungent emanation, and the chanting of ancient Arab prayers drowned out the steady camera clicks and the whines of unimpressed children. It was, as Abbu had promised, very interesting.

Once the guide wound up his spiel, Theo paid the fee and suggested they have a cold drink at the edge of the market.

"You want to buy real sheepskin jacket, sir? My wife's

brother makes them out of the finest sheep, using his own hands to—"

"I think not, Abbu. I am curious about the bombing incident that occurred earlier this week, however. Can you show me where it happened?"

"A very bad thing, the bomb. There is much bad blood between the Arabs and the Jews in Hebron, many bad things happen. Many Jews lived here, but were killed in nineteen twenty-nine. More bad things in the last few years. Now we have soldiers, but they cannot stop the fights." Abbu threw up his hands and sighed gustily. "No peace in Hebron, even for poor men like me who must count on the kindness of tourists who visit the mosque to feed my many children and animals."

Theo removed a bill from his wallet. "Could I persuade you to leave the mosque area for a few minutes?"

"Come along, sir, we will see the remains of the building where the children were killed." He darted down a narrow alley made more narrow by the stalls on both sides, the clothes hanging from hooks above doors, the omnipresent racks of postcards, and the vendors with great trays of looped bread, candies, and jewelry. Theo puffed along after him, embarrassed by the abusive squawks of the merchants as he failed to stop to admire their wares.

The market gave way to limestone walls and boxes of garbage. At last they arrived at a dirt street populated only by impassive, mustached women, howling babies in disposable diapers, goats, and chickens. Donkeys had left redolent proof that they traveled the street. Abbu pointed at a table spanning the gutter.

"That is my wife's cousin's restaurant, sir, a very fine restaurant. Would you like to have something to eat, maybe pita and humus or a very fine kosher pizza?"

Theo glanced through the open door and quickly averted his eyes. "I have no appetite at the moment. Where is the destroyed building?"

"Ah, yes, I am taking you there as quickly as I can," Abbu said in an offended voice. Hopes of a large tip erased the disappointment and he flashed mossy teeth. "It is difficult to take you there, since it is not very fine for tourists to be here. You are safe with Abbu."

They turned down one narrow street after another, until Theo was totally confused. Many of the houses could qualify as the one he sought; their rooflines tilted to odd angles and the masonry had been done with whimsy, if not drunken disregard. Abbu called to many of the people, who reluctantly returned the greeting as they stared at Theo. When they finally arrived at their destination, Theo was out of breath—and his element.

There was not much to see. The wall was down, its stones scattered like toy blocks. The interior of the building had already been looted for anything of value, leaving a shell of gaping holes. Theo suspected someone would soon find a way to steal those, too.

"See, sir," Abbu said, gesturing at the rubble with a proprietary air, "this is where the bomb went off, at this side. The wall fell inward, crushing the four innocent children who had the grave misfortune to be sitting there. Many others were hurt."

Theo winced. "Did anyone on the street see anything before the explosion? Perhaps a car that was unfamiliar, or a package?"

"The people who live here see very little of what goes on, sir. The soldiers asked them many questions, but they are too worried about buying food and clothing for their many children and animals. It is a very poor neighborhood here. The soldiers are not always welcome."

"Do you happen to have a relative that lives nearby, Abbu—a relative with a very fine memory, who might be persuaded to recount what he saw that night?"

Abbu slapped his forehead in dismay. "My father's brother's nephew does live nearby, sir. I had forgotten all about the boy, who works very hard in the market every day in order to support his many children and animals. Do you want to talk to him? It will be very difficult to find him, very difficult."

Shekels exchanged hands. Abbu agreed to take Theo to the boy's favorite post near the bus station, and they again went through the alleys under the grim scrutiny from doorways and paneless windows. Abbu at last spotted the relevant relative and loosed a guttural stream of invectives, orders and warnings, or so it seemed to Theo. The boy stared at Theo over a pyramid of soda pop cans.

Abbu gave Theo an ingratiating look. "As I promised, sir. He will cooperate if he can."

"Ask him if he saw anything before the explosion," Theo suggested.

More guttural conversation ensued, but this time the boy responded with a great deal of vehemence, punctuated by an arch of spittle aimed at a slinking dog. Abbu turned to Theo and said, "Yes, he saw a jeep in the street the night before, and since there are few cars, he looked at it with some curiosity."

"Can he describe the jeep?"

"He says not, but he is very worried that he will not sell his drinks if he wastes much time trying to remember what he saw. It has been many days, sir."

Minutes later Theo owned sixteen cans of expensive, tepid soda pop. The nephew, now released from the distraction of harassing potential buyers, pulled Abbu aside for a lengthy conversation. Abbu's hooded eyes drifted over the boy's shoulder to study Theo, but shifted back for the finale of spittle. Theo waited at a prudent distance.

Abbu slapped the nephew on the back, took a can of soda and tossed it to Theo. "These are yours now; you can drink as many as you desire. Shall I find a boy to carry them to your jeep? It will cost only a handful of shekels."

Theo insisted that the nephew retain ownership, despite Abbu's obvious disgust. As they walked back through the market, Theo asked what had been said about the mysterious jeep. Abbu stopped in the middle of the pedestrian traffic, his lips pulled back to expose his teeth. It did not have the warmth of his previous smiles.

"The boy looked very hard at the jeep. From what he told me, it was exactly like the one you are driving today, sir. Is not that very interesting, very interesting, indeed?"

"And the driver?"

Abbu held his ground, despite the thrusting crush of buyers and sellers. "It was not a bald man with glasses, or I would have put a knife between your shoulders. One of the wounded children was my brother's youngest daughter, a very fine girl."

"I'm sorry, Abbu. I want to find out who did this terrible thing, so that he will be charged by the police."

"The Jews will never arrest one of their own, no matter how bad the crime," Abbu said. "Especially when it was a woman."

"A woman?" Theo repeated, stunned. "Is your nephew quite sure about that? What did she look like?"

Abbu's shoulders rose and fell under the robe. Dust drifted from the folds. "He could not describe her. He says all Jews look alike, sir."

205

Chapter 17

Theo followed Abbu out of the market. As they approached the jeep, he saw a figure sitting on the passenger's side, a figure in a cowboy hat adorned with quail feathers and a rattlesnake skin. Bleached denim jeans and a plaid shirt with silver-rimmed buttons. Ornately carved leather boots, high-heeled and pointed at the toes. The only elements of costume absent were a guitar, battered saddlebags, and a horse tied in front of the saloon. More than a dozen awed children giggled in a nearby doorway.

"Sitermann," Theo said in greeting, "does Buffalo Bill know you escaped from the sideshow? I thought you had given up the Western motif." He tipped his squadron of car tenders, told them where they might receive a discounted soda, and shook hands with his guide. Folded bills were discreetly passed. Abbu wandered away to find another tourist, but the children remained, wide-eyed and open-mouthed. Hopalong Cassidy was not a frequent visitor to Hebron.

"Hey, Bloomer, I just thought I'd take a look at the sepulcher. I even bought myself one of them guidebooks. Did you know that Abraham is as important a dude to the Arabs as he is to the Jews? This thing started out as a grave, and Herod the Great built the boundary walls two thousand years ago. You know, I could get into this archaeology stuff."

Theo got into the jeep and started the engine, then turned to smile at the huddle of spectators. "He's not really a cowboy, children. He's a spy from the Central Intelligence—"

"Bloomer! For Christ's sake, you don't have to go around telling everybody! It's supposed to be our little secret." Sitermann threw a handful of coins to the children and grinned as they scrambled in the dust. "Hey, how about I keep you company on the way back to the kibbutz?"

"Why don't you saddle up Old Paint and gallop back to the bunkhouse?"

Sitermann punched him lightly on the arm. "Quit your teasing, Bloomer; I only put on this stuff to contribute to the local color. Did you find out anything about the bombing from these Arab guys in the funky bathrobes? Did they tell you about the jeep?"

Theo gritted his teeth as he drove away from the market. Once they were on the highway, he said, "Nothing that you were not already aware of, it seems. A jeep was noticed on the street, apparently one of those belonging to Kibbutz Mishkan. A woman driver, but no further description."

"I know who it was, so you can rest your britches. It was Ilana Tor. The two boys went with her, but waited at the edge of town in order not to arouse suspicion. A lone non-Arab woman in that part of town is curious, but two non-Arab men is a declaration of war. It's a nervous town, Hebron."

"So Gideon, Hershel, and Ilana are the charter members of the Sons of Light and were responsible for the explosion." He nodded to himself. The conclusion had been obvious all along. It did not, however, explain how they had paid for the explosive.

"Yep, they sure as hell were. They've pulled some other cute tricks as the Sons of Light, but this was their first biggie. Damned kids, they ought to know better than that."

"One would think so. How did they get through the gate that night?"

"Sympathetic guard, I reckon. You think this has anything

to do with Gili's murder investigation? I'm used to bombers—you could say it's my specialty. But I'd hate to shield an ordinary murderer."

"Why don't you tell him that you're a spy, then ask him?" Theo suggested, increasing the pressure on the gas peddle until they were bouncing wildly down the middle of the road. A dark-skinned shepherd in the middle of several dozen goats gave them a cold look. The goats did not. Theo waved anyway.

"Watch it, Bloom! We're going to end up in a ditch if you don't slow down. Hey, I mean it!"

Theo did as requested, noting with some satisfaction that the feathers on the cowboy hat were now, as Dorrie would say, denuded. They arrived at the kibbutz without further conversation. Theo left Sitermann to examine his hat and returned the keys to the lobby. He then walked down the sidewalk to Miriam's duplex.

She wasn't home. It was absurd to feel quite so disappointed; she was, after all, an adult woman with responsibilities. Grumbling anyway, Theo went to the dining hall to search for her. The downstairs was empty, so he continued up the stairs. The lounge was empty. Feeling less and less like a brilliant detective, he turned to leave, but the sound of angry voices stopped him.

They were coming from Yussef's office, muffled by the door but strident enough to be heard with clarity. Theo edged across the room to stand near the door and eavesdrop, judiciously telling himself that he was engaged in such lowly behavior for Miriam's sake.

"You lying bastard!" Sarah was not happy.

"I would never lie to you, my dear," Yussef whined. He wasn't especially happy, either.

"Forget that! I know what you're doing, and it's only a matter of time before everyone else figures it out. You're endangering the kibbutz, not to mention your family. When will it stop, Yussef?"

"You're beginning to froth about the mouth, my dear. Why don't you sit down so that we can discuss this without being heard in Jericho, or Toledo?" Yussef was still whining, but there was a cold edge to his voice. After a minute, he added, "Now that's much better, isn't it?"

"Go to hell. I'm leaving."

Theo scurried across the room and down the stairs. He kept up his pace until he was a goodly distance from the dining hall, then sat down on a bench to catch his breath. The snippet of conversation between the Navas was very interesting. If only he could decide what it meant.

Loosening his tie and unbuttoning the jacket of his suit, Theo settled back to ponder the implications. Could Yussef be involved with the Sons of Light in some obscure way? Sarah was not the sort to be sympathetic to a politically extreme cause, and certainly would not be delighted to find out her husband was. He shook his head as he tried to place Yussef in the role. Too dangerous. Murder? Probably not. Yussef was more concerned with wooing Miriam with wine and flattery. Where was she?

Theo repositioned his necktie and rose before his thoughts could linger on Miriam. Out of the question. Foolish, unwarranted, and presumptuous. Again. Self-discipline affixed as tightly as his necktie, he went to the children's house.

Judith was not conveniently situated in the playground.

From the interior of the building he could hear the usual toddler battle, complete with squeals and thuds. Several women's voices pleaded for detente, but none of them belonged to Judith. Unable to bring himself any closer to what promised disfigurement if not death, Theo went back to the guest rooms.

Where he found a tremulous Judith, sitting on the balcony outside his door. They went inside and sat down.

"Mr. Bloomer, I'd like to speak with you if it's not too much trouble. It's—it's about that package that I carried in my suitcase for Hershel. I talked to Dorrie, and she told me about the explosives and the CIA. What will they do to us?"

"It remains to be seen," he answered gravely. "Have you discussed it with Hershel?"

"He admitted that the package contained plasticine, an explosive. Hershel said he hated to have me carry it, but that tourists are never bothered coming into Israel. He was right about that. They just waved us through the gate. Hershel and Gideon were hung up in another line for almost an hour."

"Did he explain how they had the money to buy the explosives from an arms dealer in the first place?" Theo tried for an expression of mild curiosity.

"No, only that Gideon bought it in Athens and ordered Hershel to trick me into transporting it. Hershel said that he felt totally miserable about deceiving me, especially when we were on the brink of love, but that he couldn't dissuade Gideon. Gideon had the forcefulness of one of those evangelist preachers on television."

"So Hershel agreed, albeit reluctantly, to lie to you. I suppose he showed you the pot, then went away to wrap it? That was not wise of you, Judith."

"But I love him; I had to do it for him," she said. She tugged on the end of her thick braid; hairs sprouted like cilia on a begonia stalk. "For the first time in my life I felt terribly romantic and daring. I wanted to do something dangerous to let him know how much I loved him."

"I'm sure you did. The end result was rather grim, however." He briefly described his journey to Hebron and the information he had gleaned for the price of sixteen cans of soda pop.

"Hershel told me about it," she said in a low voice. "Ilana's as crazy as Gideon was. Hershel says that every time she sees an Arab woman in a veil, she gets very puffed up about feminists' rights and Third World mentalities. The whole thing was actually her fault, since she packed the explosives and left them too close to the wall. Hershel said that they agreed beforehand only to frighten the Arabs in the neighborhood so they'd stop bothering the Jews. He and Gideon were both upset about . . . what happened. We had a long talk so that I could assure him of his innate human worth."

Theo tried to imagine Hershel in earnest conversation with Judith, or anyone else. Apparently he had poured out his heart to his future wife without regard to his co-conspirators or lifetime loyalties. Like Bermuda grass, love did move in mysterious ways. "So they did not actually intend to cause any deaths?"

"Of course not, it was an accident. Poor Hershel has had a difficult life, and now he's found happiness. Please don't let anything happen to him because of this, Mr. Bloomer. You're the only one we can trust."

Tears welled in her eyes, then crept through her eyelashes and streamed down her face like glistening snail tracks. Her hands remained clasped together in front of her and her eyes locked on his. If she continued to lean forward on the edge of her chair, she was apt to end on her knees in front of him in the classic supplicant's pose. The idea was distressing.

"I'll do my best," he soberly assured her. "It's impossible to determine what will happen in the bombing investigation, but the identity of the conspirators may be brought to the attention of the Israeli intelligence." Delivered in person by Hopalong Cassidy. "It would be better for Hershel if he would come forward to confess."

"But he can't," she wailed. "Children were murdered. Even though it was Gideon's plan and Ilana's misjudgment, Hershel could end up in prison for years. He said he wouldn't ever tell the authorities about how the plasticine came into the country, but they might be able to make him talk. Ilana wouldn't hesitate to offer our heads on a platter. Gili will probably decide that Dorrie and I murdered Gideon and Essie to hide our involvement. We'll—we'll end up in prison, too."

"You have nothing to worry about, Judith. No one has mentioned any kind of motive in Essie's death; I'm beginning to feel it was an accident after all. As for Gideon's murder, Dorrie told me that you and Hershel were together all night, having a serious political discussion."

She cut off a muted moan to blink owlishly through her glasses. "That's right. It was intellectually enlightening. Hershel pointed out that not all work can be given equal importance, realistically, and the need for a balance of agriculture and industry has—"

"We can discuss that later, if you don't mind. Since you and Hershel can provide each other with alibis, you shouldn't worry about Gili."

"Oh, we can," she said gratefully. "I was with Hershel the night that—that awful things happened, so neither of us is guilty of anything worse than being in a bedroom together before we get married. And we would never engage in—" She halted and gave him a prim look. "Well, you know. But what about Dorrie?"

"Gili doesn't have a case against her. His accusations are based, I fear, on his desire to cause her as much inconvenience as possible, but he won't be able to maintain it much longer. And although she was with you when you came through customs, she didn't actually carry your suitcase or present a false declaration."

Judith took a breath. "She had my suitcase because she insisted on putting forty pounds of shoes in it, and I refused to carry it. I carried her makeup bag for her. It weighed thirty pounds."

"Oh, dear," Theo sighed, glumly imagining Nadine's face hovering inches above his head. "I think I'd better talk to Hershel about this, if you can persuade him to cooperate."

"I'll tell him as soon as I can, and thank you, Mr. Bloomer. I knew I could trust you."

Theo escorted her out while she continued her babble of gratitude and her promise to produce Hershel. She did not kiss his hand, although she did glance at it once or twice. Theo closed the door and leaned against it. The wisest thing to do was drag Dorrie to the airport and leave. Let Gili try an extradition order. Let Judith go into battle with Goliath, since her David was on the frail side. Let Miriam mourn for her son in dignified solitude.

"Phooey," Theo said to the bedroom.

Chapter 18

"Your dossier ought to be on the best-seller list," Sitermann said over dinner. "I stayed up half the night reading about you being blacklisted in Hollywood; McCarthy's boys must have decided you kept communists under your bed like some people do chinchillas. 'Course chinchillas prefer cages and they aren't red . . ." He chuckled at his wit, then stopped and added in an ostensibly sympathetic voice, "It was a shame about your wife, though. She just couldn't take the ostracism from her friends, hey?"

"That's correct," Theo said calmly. He'd known Sitermann would contact his home office, or that of the FBI. The contents of his file were not difficult to predict. "My wife was vulnerable, and she cared very deeply about the people she thought were her dearest friends. She killed herself three months after the hearing."

"Damned shame," Sitermann said. "But there's one little old pesky thing I'd like to ask, Bloom. I didn't find anything about your so-called 'intelligence work' in the dossier. Are you sure you weren't working for the bad guys?"

"Quite sure, but you'll have to take my word for it. I have a question for you, if you don't mind. Now that you know who bought the explosives and the intended use, do you have any idea who's been funding the group? If I remember with any accuracy, plasticine is expensive, and the boys claimed they were broke."

"Popadoupolis doesn't run a discount supermarket, that's

for sure. He owns a private island and a yacht, and probably a harem. One of these days we're going to have to do something about him. No, Bloom, I must admit that I hadn't given much thought to the finances. What do you think?"

"I find it interesting." He opted for a diversion. "What do you intend to do with your information about the bombing?"

Sitermann leaned back in his chair and stretched out his legs. "Well, it's not for me to say. I sent off a report while I was in Hebron, and now I sit tight until the upstairs boys decide what to do. They may want me to report to the Mossad, or just slip away into the night like one of those desert critters." Sitermann was once again a hardy Texan, although the accent came and went with the waitress.

"Lieutenant Gili might appreciate a glimpse of your report," Theo said, both civic-minded and secure. Sitermann would not, under any circumstances, share his knowledge with an Israeli policeman. That would be too cooperative, and spies detested the very word.

"Sure, Bloom, I'll consider it," Sitermann said. "I think I'm going to go skinny dip in the Dead Sea, put my manhood in the salt water and see what rises. You want to join me?"

"Thank you, but I think not. Dorrie's been in her room all day, and I'd best see how she is. Have a nice swim." Theo left the restaurant, but did not turn toward Dorrie's room. Later would be soon enough. He went to Miriam's duplex once again, feeling like a toy train on a circular track.

She opened the door almost immediately. "Theo, thank you so much for coming tonight. It's been such a dreadful day, with Gili hounding me and everyone trying to be supportive, that I was about to take a bottle of wine to bed with me. The kibbutz would have been scandalized if I'd shown up with a hangover in the morning."

They went into the living room. The furniture was slightly

worn, but comfortable and inviting. The few knickknacks were of good quality, obvious souvenirs of an earlier time. Framed photographs lined the walls, most of them centered on a handsome, dark-haired man and a young boy. The houseplants in ceramic pots gave him a warm (and admittedly silly) glow.

"I have a night-blooming cereus that may produce a flower soon," he told her, bending over a vine to pinch off a shriveled leaf. Too much water. "It's taken nearly five years to develop a single bud, and I'm hoping it will wait for my return."

"If it blooms while you're here . . ."

"Then I shall wait another five years." He placed the leaf in the saucer of the flowerpot. "Would you like me to open the wine and find some glasses?"

"Please," Miriam said. "The bottle's in the refrigerator and the glasses are above the sink. I should assume the role of hostess, but I'm just too tired." While he was in the kitchen, she called, "You're a patient man, Theo. Five years is a long time to wait for a flower; why not buy another plant?"

He returned, desired items in hand. "Why didn't those of you who founded the kibbutz pay someone to do the initial drudgery?"

"Good point," she sighed. She took the wineglass from him and drank deeply, then studied him across the rim. "I heard from my substitute at the registration desk that you rented a jeep from the kibbutz for the afternoon. Did you visit Masada?"

"I went to Hebron."

"Oh." A guarded expression spread across her face to encompass her mouth and ashen cheeks. "Did you tour Haram el-Khalil and the market? Some of my favorite glassware came from there."

216

"Haram el-Khalil was impressive, but so was the building that was destroyed several nights ago by the Sons of Light. My guide was able to find a witness who was on the street just before the explosion occurred."

Miriam put down the glass, ignoring the splash of wine on her hand. "What did the witness have to say, Theo—a bunch of anti-Jewish propaganda about terrorism without any justification whatsoever? It's remarkable how quickly previous acts of terrorism against Jews can be forgotten. But, of course, if you give an Arab enough money, he'll tell you anything you want to hear!"

"He described the jeep that was in the street the night before the bomb went off, and he also described the driver. It wasn't anything I wanted to hear, but I listened."

"And . . . ?" The defensive pose evaporated with the single word. "The jeep was from Kibbutz Mishkan, wasn't it?"

"But Gideon wasn't driving," he told her gently, wishing he were brave enough to put his arm around her shivering shoulders. "Ilana was the one who packed and placed the bomb next to the wall, Miriam. I'm afraid that Gideon was involved, and also Hershel, but neither of them went into the Arab neighborhood."

She sank back, her forehead propped by her hand and her face hidden. "Are you saying that to make me feel better, Theo? If Ilana drove, then Gideon gave her the instructions. He's hated the Arabs since his father was killed in the war, and he's always talked of revenge, as violent as possible. I tried to help him learn to live with his grief, but he's a sabra; I'm a transplanted American. He never believed I had a passion for Israel."

"But he was wrong, wasn't he?"

"I care very deeply about the kibbutz, and I'd gladly give up my life to ensure its continued existence. Sy's grave is near here, on the far side of the palm grove; Gideon's will be there, too. That's what I have left after living here thirty years—two graves and my husband's name." She gazed down at her hands.

Theo looked at her with compassion. She was calm, now, and lost in her thoughts. There was nothing he could say.

She broke the silence with a short laugh. "Do you know the Biblical story of Isaac and Abraham? God told Abraham to sacrifice his son, an innocent child, in order to prove his devotion. That's the essential relationship we Jews have had with God for four thousand years. He still demands we defend his name, and we still obey, despite our incessant kvetching. All for this tiny land surrounded by Arabs who'd like nothing better than to drive us into the sea." She shook her head as she stood up. "I'd better try to sleep now. Tomorrow I'll have to make arrangements for the funeral. Thank you for coming, Theo."

Theo joined her at the door, dismayed by her oppressive mood but unable to offer any encouragement. "Thank you for the wine," he said with a small bow. Her response was inaudible.

As he walked back toward the guesthouse, he pondered the story of the sacrifice. As a Sunday-school student, he had preferred the melodrama of giants and slings, of lions' dens and whale interiors, but he could remember the terrifying drawing of the bearded Abraham, knife poised above his head, and the cowering boy on a rock slab. He'd had nightmares for weeks afterward.

Dorrie came to her door in a bathrobe, her hair covered by a terry-cloth turban. "I washed my hair, but I haven't begun on the conditioner yet. I'm seriously considering a mixture of the honey-and-herbs with the avocado this time, unless that sounds too insane. What do you think?"

"A fine experiment, Dorrie. The result will provide us all with useful data. Are you feeling well, my dear? I noticed that you did not come to the restaurant for any meals, and I was worried that you might be depressed."

"I'm fat," she said irritably, slapping at her hip. "It's impossible to get any exercise here, since the nearest tennis court is probably a hundred miles away. It might as well be in Lebanon, for all the good it does me. I'm not stepping out of this room until I've lost half a pound, Uncle Theo, so it's no use pleading with me."

Theo did not plead. He bade her good night and started for his room, then stopped. He had promised Sarah Nava that he would try to reason with Ilana. With luck, he could find Ilana in the lobby of the guesthouse, and thus far she had proved more loquacious at night.

She was indeed at the registration desk, but her expression was less than affable. "Do you wish to make an overseas call, Mr. Bloomer?"

"I would like to speak with you for a moment. I went to Hebron today and made inquiries in the neighborhood where the explosion occurred. You were seen, Ilana. The conclusion is unavoidable."

"How very clever of you, Mr. Bloomer. I often wonder if I should have treated you as a spy when I first saw you on the beach, but it is too late for regrets. What will you do with your conclusion?"

Theo shook his head. "If I could discover what I did in less than an hour, the police will be able to duplicate my efforts without much problem. Other people have also arrived at the same conclusion. What you decide to do is your problem, Ilana. I cannot help you."

She glared defiantly across the desk. "I do not need your help. They will arrest me, drag me through a mockery of a

219

trial, and then throw me in prison. The sentence may be severe, but public sentiment favors those who make sacrifices for Israel. There will be demands made for clemency, and even pardons. I shall not stay long in prison."

"Even for murder?"

"Arabs," she said, shrugging. "I will be released within a matter of months, and then I shall return to the kibbutz and once again make war against the Arabs. I, Ilana Tor, will drive them across the Dead Sea and into the desert of Jordan."

"The murder of Arabs may not result in a lengthy sentence, but what about the murder of a fellow Israeli? Surely public sentiment will not swing in your favor?"

Ilana's black eyes glittered like those of a raven. "I have not murdered anyone, Mr. Bloomer. I left the bomb in a garbage can in order to teach the Arabs to leave the Jews in Hebron alone, and some Arabs were killed. As for a fellow Israeli—you have spent too many hours in the sun. Your brain is baked, Mr. Bloomer! Essie's death was an accident, caused by loose rocks and carelessness. Although I have not bothered to tell the little policeman, I know this to be true. And Gideon was killed by a terrorist, perhaps one who saw him in Hebron the night of the bombing. I shall take care of him soon."

Theo pensively tugged at his beard as he studied the girl. "How do you know what happened to Essie, Ilana?" he asked softly. "Were you there on the ledge when she fell?"

"I was on the second security shift that night. After we returned from Hebron, I stayed at the gate. Better you should keep your nose out of things you know nothing about."

She spun on her heel and marched into the office. The door slammed behind her with the crackle of a sonic boom. Theo sighed, then left the lobby for his room. As he neared the building, however, he gradually stopped to think. Ilana had admitted to the bombing, but that was hardly startling. He had learned nothing else from her, except that she was less than penitent and capable of mindless, destructive anger. But she had denied killing Gideon or Essie, and she hadn't waited long enough for Theo to politely inquire about the identity of the treasurer of the Sons of Light. He decided to investigate a possibility.

The dining hall was dim. Theo slipped between the tables and up the stairs, wishing he could be certain the building was as deserted as it felt. The lounge was empty. No light shone below the door to Yussef's office, and no glow came through the opaque glass. The door was locked.

After a glance over his shoulder, Theo took an odd-shaped piece of metal out of his pocket. Seconds later he was inside the office, the door closed and once again locked. Sitermann would have been proud of the performance, had he been watching from a dark corner.

Theo ascertained that Sitermann (or another stray spy) was not watching from a dark corner, then turned on a penlight to study the messy desk and filing cabinets behind it. The ledgers of the kibbutz's financial dealings would be more complex than those of a small florist shop, but likely to have the same structure. He hoped so.

The drawer of the filing cabinet opened with a squeak. Theo took out the first ledger and sat down to study the figures.

Chapter 19

It took several hours to wind a path through the ledgers, of which there were two superficially identical sets. The figures were in shekels, and therefore immense. The kibbutz bought raw materials for the factory, manufactured goods from a kibbutzim cooperative, and other necessities from various sources, including warehouses in Jerusalem and businesses in Jericho. They sold the cartons from the factory and excess produce from the agricultural endeavors. It was a more complex operation than Theo had realized.

The second set of figures was as tangled as a clematis vine. From what he could determine, monies from one account were transferred to a different account to cover temporary dearths caused by previous transfers, then sent into a financial labyrinth with no discernible exit. The remittances for one stack of invoices, all properly signed and cross-referenced, vanished into the same labyrinth. Some totals could be found in one set of books, but not the other. The exit was discovered, but only after another hour of tedious search.

Theo's eyes began to burn as he hunched over the columns. The penlight, although prudent, was hardly a reading light, and the knowledge that he might be caught in the midst of the unauthorized audit added to his worries. At last he replaced the ledgers where they had been, checked the desk for signs of his covert chore, and snapped off the light. He locked the office door behind him and started across the lounge, guided by the light from the dining hall below.

"Hey, Bloom, did you find anything useful?"

Theo turned back with an exasperated frown. "Sitermann, your propensity for inopportune appearances is growing tiresome. Have you ever considered simply announcing that you've arrived?"

Sitermann joined him and they went downstairs. "Please, I am a professional spy, and a good one, if I say so myself. I personally supervised a very sophisticated operation in East Berlin that resulted in the hostile termination of a nasty little mole and several of his species. I'm slated for a cozy desk job once I tidy up things around here, and a well-deserved raise. I wish you'd show a little more respect. How'd you get into the office?"

Theo fingered the thin metal tool in his pocket. "Through the door, Sitermann," he said patiently. "Spies prefer chimneys and tunnels, but we civilians just use doors. Boring, but pragmatic."

"The door was locked, and so were the filing cabinets."

"Were they?" Theo rubbed his forehead. "I don't recall having a problem. It's late; I'd better go to bed."

"You are beginning to interest me very much. I may have to do a little more research in your dossier. So what'd you find?"

"Two sets of books. Although I'm hardly an accountant, it looks as if Yussef Nava has been channeling kibbutz monies into a private account for years. His activity increased dramatically six months ago, probably when he learned of the impending computerization of the books. Miriam thought it had depressed him. On the contrary, it must have terrified him."

"What's he doing with the money?"

"What all good embezzlers do: he sends it to Switzerland. I found the number of his bank account in a notebook in one of the desk drawers."

"Those were locked, too."

"I'm afraid I didn't notice, but the light was not good. You might ask Mr. Nava about that in the morning, Sitermann."

"Do you think he's behind the Sons of Light?"

Theo shrugged. "He's taken nearly a quarter of a million dollars since he started pilfering, but it's all been deposited in a Swiss bank. There weren't any canceled checks lying about, so I don't know if he saved it for retirement or spent it on toys for terrorist tots."

"If he is giving money to the terrorists, he'd be concerned about hiding the connection. Maybe the girl Essie found out something to link him, and he had to push her into the wadi to silence her. Then Gideon got antsy, and he killed him, too. Nava was the first on the scene, you know."

"I know all of that, Sitermann, and I also know that I'd prefer bed to idle speculation. So if your curiosity is sated . . . ?"

"Sure, and, hey, thanks a lot. The CIA and I owe you one. Maybe the big boys will take you on, let you work for the good guys for a change."

"I shall stand by the mailbox every day in hopes of a letter in a plain brown wrapper," Theo said dryly. They had reached the balcony, and Sitermann moved toward his door. "A question for you, Sitermann, since I've been so gracious about sharing the fruits of my labor. Why did you sit in the lounge instead of coming into the office?"

"The door was locked," Sitermann said in a superficially scandalized voice. He laughed as he went into his room and closed the door.

It was well past three o'clock by the time Theo had changed into his pin-striped pajamas and brushed his teeth. He slipped into bed, turned off the bedside light and pulled the blanket to his chin. It was delightful. The sound of footsteps on the balcony, followed by a brisk rap on his door, was not.

The earlier expletive came to mind, as precise and succinct as it had been when Essie interrupted his nap. Once again Theo rejected it, pulled on his bathrobe, and went to the door. Once again Ilana stood at attention, her eyes flickering with malicious amusement as she announced the arrival of an overseas call.

"I was told that it was an emergency," she ended with a contemptuous sniff. "You must come quickly, Mr. Bloomer. The international operator is very short-tempered tonight."

Once again Theo watched her stomp away, then pulled trousers over his pajamas and flip-flopped to the lobby. Ilana smirked as he took the receiver and muttered his name.

"Theo, do you realize that I must pay for the time it takes you to answer the telephone? What on earth were you doing all that time—planting bulbs?"

"Nadine, it is three o'clock in the morning. It is too dark outside to plant bulbs, or anything else. I'm not even sure that they utilize bulbs; the soil is acidic."

"Theo, I feel as if you're not cooperating with me, that you're avoiding the subject with these odd little comments. You might show a little more concern about Dorrie's situation and less about the flora of that place. When are you to return home?"

"I'm not sure, but I believe we'll be allowed to leave within a few days." He bit his lip, but it was too late. Too late for telephone calls, and too late for discretion. He waited for the storm to break loose in all its hellish fury. After a stunned silence, it did.

"Allowed, Theo?" Nadine said in a mellifluous crescendo. The receiver began to vibrate against his ear. "Am I to presume my daughter is being held hostage by that group of—of left-wing socialists? What could they hope to gain from this outrageous scheme? What will Charles say when he receives a tacky note demanding ransom money? How could you permit such impertinence?"

"Not by the kibbutz," he explained over her arioso sputters and snorts. "There's been a minor incident here that has required our continued presence. Dorrie's not involved in any way, but the officials feel her observations might be of value."

"What does that mean, Theo?" she demanded, clearly not beguiled by the glib explanation.

"We'll be home within a few days. Did you water my plants, Nadine?"

"Of course I did, although it seemed absurd to waste my time going all the way to Handy Hollow in order to dump a cup of water on a collection of sticks and leaves. My silk flower arrangements are more attractive, and a great deal easier to tend. I simply have my girl dust them daily and vacuum them once a month. No water, no loose dirt, and no nasty little bugs."

"Bugs?" Theo echoed, alarmed. "Were there bugs on the plant on the windowsill in the kitchen? Did they resemble tiny red spiders?"

"I did not examine them, Theo. I'm confident that they will still be lurking about when you return home—in the next few days. How is Dorrie, by the way?"

"She's fine, as is her hair. I shall call as soon as Dorrie and I have arranged reservations home. As for now, I would like to return to bed and hope for a few hours of sleep, so—"

"I don't know how you can sleep at a time like this, Theo. Charles had been forced to answer several pointed questions from his associates, and he has felt quite uncomfortable. Furthermore, Biff's mother, a lovely woman from an old Boston family, called to inquire about Dorrie's preparations for school, then suggested a little tea party for the Wellesley girls in the neighborhood. I was unable to accept on Dorrie's behalf, but I must tell you it was very awkward, very awkward indeed. You must stop dawdling and do something. Dorrie's future is at stake!"

Theo said good-bye to an empty line, then handed the receiver to Ilana and started for the door. Red spider mites meant mortal danger for the night-blooming cereus. If he were home, he would spray with a strictly organic mixture of pepper and Tabasco, and gently cleanse the leaves with a damp towel. Nadine would not be pleased to do so for him in his absence. Dumping a cup of water, indeed!

"Good night, Mr. Bloomer," Ilana called to his back.

As long as he was awake . . . He turned back and said, "Who else knows the identity of the members of the Sons of Light? Is it common knowledge at Kibbutz Mishkan?"

She narrowed her eyes. "No one knows for sure, although some of the kibbutzniks may have suspicions. The night guard at the gate swore not to mention the jeep the other night. Miriam may have worried about it, but a mother has glass eyes and sees only what she cares to see. But soon everyone will know, and I shall be a hero in the war to protect Israel."

"But surely the person who provided the funds knew the identities of those involved."

"What person is that? I tell you, no one knew for sure that Gideon, Hershel, and I were the Sons of Light. We did not announce it because certain people would have tried to stop us to hamper our plans to eliminate the Palestinian terrorists."

"Explosives cost money. Unless you three saved your allowances since your collective childhood, you could not have bought the plasticine in Athens. Who gave you the money?"

"We did not have to take money from anyone. The Sons Of Light were not beggars. Gideon knew how to get the explosives."

"And now Hershel will take over the assignment?"

She laughed. "He is hopeless, the schlemiel. He mopes around Miriam's house, like a sad puppy with his tongue hanging out. He also hangs out his tongue for Judith, but with other purpose. Perhaps the rich American girl can teach him what to do with it. In any case, he was not a good defender of Israel. He does not have the nerve, and he would prefer to take his—" She stopped herself abruptly, then said, "He would prefer to be an archaeologist who digs with his fingernails."

"Then why did Gideon recruit him as a member?"

"Gideon took care of him like he would a baby brother. Behind Hershel's back, he would laugh and say mean things, but he was fond of him, and permitted him to tag along with us. Now Hershel is useless. He says he will not go to Athens. He wants to go to Tel Aviv and mope around the university."

"It is not surprising that Hershel is disturbed by the death of his best friend," Theo said.

"Oh, he is disturbed," she said sardonically, "but he is also relieved. The meshuggener!"

He slowly walked back to his room, thinking about Ilana's harsh assessment. She had the exterior of a cactus; that much was obvious. *Sabras,* according to Miriam, had a succulent interior, but he was not convinced Ilana carried through the analogy.

When he had asked about the source of financing for the explosives, she seemed offended at the idea that they were dependent on an outsider. But he did not believe that the three printed shekels in the basement or saved up their allowances.

Yussef Nava was the logical choice for financial backer. The money was available, and he was a kibbutznik with the same loyalties and passion for the land, even if he maintained a more urbane pose. A hefty draft from a Swiss bank would raise no eyebrows in an antiquities/explosives store. But it was hard to accept the theory.

He couldn't ask Miriam what she thought; the subject was much too painful for her. He couldn't ask Gideon, for obvious reasons, and he wouldn't find an answer with Ilana. Hershel was likely to stammer a denial. Yussef was not the sort to admit that he was a thief. He supposed he could talk to Sarah, on the chance she might still be angry enough to betray her husband. The very idea caused a shudder.

Or, more probably, it came from a noticeable lack of sleep. Theo intended to remedy the situation with all due haste.

Chapter 20

Lieutenant Gili strutted into the restaurant the following morning, his mustache waxed to pine-needle points and his uniform starched so rigidly that he crackled as he crossed the room.

"Mr. Bloomer," he said, "it has been brought to my attention that you have not yet given a statement to Corporal Amitan, who has dearly suffered for the undersight."

"My deepest apologies, Lieutenant Gili. I shall remedy the—ah, undersight at once."

"Ha! Now it is too late and your statement is of no importance." Gili flared his nostrils and turned away, looking as smug as a tick on the rump of a bloodhound, as Sitermann would undoubtedly wax innovative.

Theo felt mildly offended. "And why is that? Does that mean you have completed the investigation and identified the murderer?"

Gili swung back without a second's hesitation. "Yes, it does, Mr. Bloomer. My careful and professional investigation has raised many answers to the puzzling crime, and I am confident that I have arrived at the truth. The case is closed, and you and the young ladies are free to leave Israel. I would encourage you to do so with great haste."

"What answers did your investigation raise?" Theo asked. "Have you come to Kibbutz Mishkan to make an arrest?"

"Since you might profit from my experience and acumen, I shall tell you how I have solved this case." Gili swelled for a moment. "The girl Ester Kelman should not have been allowed to wander into the desert by herself—that was a crime. However, on my orders the medical examiner has reexamined the bruise and announced that it might have resulted from the fall. His previous examination was in arrears. I have therefore concluded that her death was an accident."

"Very astute, Lieutenant Gili," Theo said with all the admiration he could muster. "But Gideon Adler's death was not an accident, surely. What did you conclude about that?"

"Initially, I thought the murderer must have been within the confounds of the kibbutz, since the gate was guarded by those with army experience. I took many statements and pored into them for hours, seeking to find a motive for this tragedy. But many of those who were close to the young man had alibis, and the others lacked motives. It became clear to me that I should analyze the reports more carefully."

"Which you did," Theo said. He nodded encouragingly.

"I determined that the Adler youth was killed by a PLO agent, who swam across the Dead Sea from Jordan. By coincidence, my men found such a parsonage in Jericho, and after a few sessions of interrogation, the scum admitted everything. Even you must see, Bloomer, that the case is closed. I shall write a report about the negligence of the kibbutz in both permitting the girl to go in the desert and in not maintaining security on the beach. I myself shall dismiss the case from my mind and continue with my work at my office."

"But how could such a person find a knife, or escape from the kibbutz after committing the crime? He couldn't have gone through the gate, and the fence is surrounded by the security road. Surely he would have left footprints in the dirt?"

"Terrorists are very crafty, Mr. Bloomer, very crafty. Maybe Allah sprouted wings on the scum's backside. But I have solved the murder; you should be congratulating me rather than tying me up with these silly loose ends."

Theo promptly offered his warmest congratulations for the amazingly efficient and successful investigation. "Then you no longer are concerned about the argument my niece had with the victim?"

Gili closed his eyes. In a pained voice he said, "I know nothing of that. I suggest that you also forget about it, Mr. Bloomer—unless you wish to find the girl in serious turmoil. Take her away."

Theo left the interview with a frown. Something strange had happened to Gili's investigation, and he wondered if he could see signs of Sitermann's finger having dabbled in the pie. The CIA might have passed the report on to its Israeli counterpart, which might have then issued a tactful command to the police chief in Jericho. Someone had stopped Gili in mid-puff.

Pursing his lips, Theo went to Dorrie's room. She opened the door, a drowsy expression on her face. "Hi, Uncle Theo. What's the matter?" she said in a graveled monotone.

"Nothing, dear. I have good news. Lieutenant Gili has concluded the investigation and has encouraged us to leave for Connecticut as soon as we're able. I thought I'd call for reservations at once."

"What about Judith?" she said through a yawn. She gave him a mulish, if slightly unfocused, look.

"I spoke to her last night, and she seemed resolute about remaining at the kibbutz with Hershel. I doubt anyone can persuade her to leave. I will speak to her one final time, but she most likely will refuse to leave." As her jaw began to inch forward, he added, "Your mother called me several hours ago. Biff's mother is hoping to have an afternoon tea for the Wellesley girls." Devious, but potentially effective. Dorrie's eyelashes shot up. "When?"

"Your mother did not mention the date, but she implied

that you could attend if we came home in the immediate future. And," he said, lying through his teeth for a good cause, "she said there was a fantastic sale at Sak's. Forty percent off all the latest designer fashions. Racks and racks and racks of them, as yet untouched by human hands. She thought you'd be interested."

"Forty percent?" Interested, but not yet convinced.

Theo played his final, mendacious card with what he felt to be the epitome of sincerity. "I fear we won't be able to find seats in the tourist section on short notice, but I'm sure your father won't mind if we're forced to fly first-class. I understand they simply shove champagne and canapes at you the entire flight."

"Call the airlines; I'll pack." The door closed in his face.

He mentally ticked that off the list and went to find Judith. It wasn't going to be easy; however, he felt obliged to offer her a final opportunity to return to her studies. She was not at the children's house, he was told, but at her room in the apartment house where single adults were stored until they married and began to beget.

After several taps, Judith appeared and motioned him inside. She then closed the door and leaned against it. "Did Hershel come by to talk to you?"

"No, but I spoke to Lieutenant Gili, and he has closed the investigation. He made no mention of the incident in Hebron, so you need not worry about it. He did suggest several times that you and Dorrie leave Israel, though." Theo studied her gravely. "You must decide what you intend to do. I shall make reservations within the hour."

"Then he knows who murdered Essie and Gideon?"

Theo repeated the essence of the conversation. After a moment of silence, Judith said, "Then Dorrie has agreed to return to her tidy life in Connecticut? She's not going to continue with her demands that I abandon everything in order to occupy half of her dorm room—or even a quarter?" She did not sound as delighted as he had presumed she would, and her face was the color of antique venetian blinds. She swallowed several times, as if holding back a flow of words that threatened to erupt.

"With a bit of gentle persuasion, yes. I thought you would be relieved by her departure, Judith."

"I am, I am," she mumbled, plucking at the hem of her shirt. She looked up, blinking in great earnestness. "I really am, Mr. Bloomer. Kibbutz Mishkan is right for me; I can feel it more and more every day. The camaraderie, the sense of family, the commitment to a Jewish state. It's where I belong."

"With Hershel," he reminded her. Twelve hours ago she had proclaimed undying love. Now she had forgotten to include him in her vision of life on the kibbutz. Interesting.

"Yes, of course," she said. "I finally admitted everything about myself. When I was with Dorrie, it was fun to pretend I had old money and a twelve-room cottage on the Cape, but it was time to be honest with Hershel. He didn't care that Dorrie is the one with money and I'm dirt poor, Mr. Bloomer. He said not to think about it ever again."

"It is a more sensible beginning for a marriage," Theo murmured.

"I'll go by Dorrie's room later to say good-bye. We can still write, and it's not like I won't come to the States to visit her every few years. Uh, would you do a small favor for me, Mr. Bloomer?"

He nodded. She went into another room and returned with a well-used manila envelope. "This is a . . . present for Dorrie, but she mustn't open it until she's on the airplane. Could you keep it until then?"

"I shall be delighted," Theo said. He took the envelope and tucked it under his arm. "I wish you every happiness with your new life, Judith."

"Thanks. Hershel and I may decide together to move to Tel Aviv, or it may turn out that the kibbutz rejects me after I've lived here for a year. If that should happen, I'd have to return to school, wouldn't I?"

On that peculiar note, Theo left her and went to the lobby to call the airlines. Charles owed him the price of two first-class seats, if only because of the threat of red spider mites on the night-blooming cereus. And Dorrie would cause a scene worthy of her mother if he produced the more plebeian seat assignments once they were on the airplane. Having bolstered himself, he made the call. The voice at the other end of the line promised first-class seats on a flight the following day.

He then ticked Judith and reservations off the list. He knew that he needed to talk to Miriam before he left Kibbutz Mishkan. But before he did, he decided to see if he could learn anything more about Yussef's thievery and Sarah's knowledge of it. He owed that much to the kibbutz in exchange for its tolerance of Dorrie's presence, not always a pleasure for those within earshot of her.

Yussef was in his office, slumped behind the desk, a pencil clenched in his teeth. He removed it and began to roll it between his fingers as if making a cigarette. "So you're leaving, I hear on the kibbutz grapevine."

"Lieutenant Gili has closed the investigation, so there is no reason for me to stay any longer," Theo said agreeably. "He told me that Essie's death was an accident and that Gideon was killed by a PLO agent who swam across the Dead Sea. The man has confessed, according to Gili."

Yussef snorted. "I'm sure he did. He probably would have

confessed to being the Messiah, had Gili suggested it after a few hours in the basement. Ah, well, I'm glad that the ordeal is over. You must be heartened at the thought of leaving this hot, scrubby place for a more civilized climate. God, I hate the heat more than I do my lovely wife."

"I understand Switzerland has a lovely coolness this time of year, not to mention the delightful wines from neighboring countries. It may be eccentric of me, but I've always thought I'd like to live in a mountain chalet." Once one perfected the rhythm of lying, it was amazingly easy. With a bright smile, Theo sat back to study Yussef's reaction.

Yussef's tongue brushed over his lower lip. "Why not? Of course all that yodeling might get on your nerves."

"I think I could find a certain charm in it," Theo persisted. "Wouldn't you like to live in a country like Switzerland, Yussef? You and Sarah could enjoy the scenery as you grew old together."

"What makes you think I'd enjoy looking at anything with her? As long as we're indulging our fantasies, I can think of other women with a lot more, shall we say, promiscuous promise." He wiggled his eyebrows suggestively. "I bet you could, too."

Theo did not allow himself to respond to the insinuation. "Have you ever visited Switzerland?"

The pencil snapped in two. Yussef threw the pieces into a metal trashcan and stood up. "What are you getting at, Theo? I don't think you came by my office to discuss the glory of the Alpine climate. What do you want?"

"Do you happen to know a gentleman named Popadoupolis? He has a charming shop in Athens that carries a wide range of interesting antiquities . . . and other more volatile items."

"I've never been to Athens."

"But Mr. Popadoupolis conducts some of his business through couriers disguised as backpackers on budget tours. Perhaps you've dealt with him in that manner?"

Yussef moved around the desk, looking rather menacing despite the corn-cockle-pink shirt. "Does this have something to do with Gideon Adler's death, or has your mind already found a chalet in the Alps?"

"I believe it does," Theo said under his breath. He raised his voice to say, "You're absolutely right, Yussef. Gideon was murdered because, as you already knew, he was the guiding force of the Sons of Light. Someone had to stop him before he said too much."

"You're senile, old man, and if I weren't so amiable I'd knock your dentures across the room—and they'd still be in your mouth!"

"Let's not sink to verbal abuse," Theo said stiffly. "I could, if I wished, make several tacky remarks about the number of your Swiss bank account. Page three in the notebook, I believe."

"You've lost your wits," Yussef snarled. "That's not an account number; it's a—a telephone number for a cooperative wench in—in Tel Aviv. It's in my personal code, since a man's entitled to keep those sorts of secrets from his wife." Muttering to himself, he took the notebook out of his desk drawer and flipped it open. The page in question had been ripped out. The jagged margin was blank.

Yussef's face and neck turned gentian violet as he gripped a corner of the desk for support. His eyeballs seemed to bulge outward, until Theo felt they might pop with ghastly results. His lips opened and closed wordlessly, bubbles of saliva appearing at the corners then dribbling down to his chin. He clutched his chest, gurgled once, and toppled across the carpet.

"Oh, dear," Theo said. He stepped over the twitching body, took the notebook from the desktop, and tucked it in his pocket. He then hurried downstairs to find help for poor Yussef.

The spider mites, truly a florist's nightmare, were gone. The petals of the night-blooming cereus were no longer threatened by tiny teeth. They began to force a wider opening in the leaves of the bud. The performance could not be delayed much longer.

Chapter 21

"Oh, Theo," Miriam moaned across Yussef's hospital bed, "I don't know how much more I can take of this. There aren't so many Jews in Israel that Kibbutz Mishkan can afford to lose three in less than a week."

She stared intently at the grayish figure attached to numerous tubes, as if she were worried he might find a way to lose himself should her vigilance slip.

"The doctor seemed to think Yussef will recover," Theo said with an encouraging smile. "Has anyone informed Sarah about her husband's heart attack?"

"No one can find her. Ilana thought that Sarah mentioned a trip to Tel Aviv, and one of the cars is missing. She'll appear sometime, and then I'll tell her about it. At least none of us will be suspected of murdering Yussef," she added. A shaky attempt at a laugh followed, but her lips were white and too stiff to cooperate.

Theo saw no reason to expound on the scene that preceded Yussef's heart attack. "The investigation is over," he said gently. "Kibbutz Mishkan must forget it and think of the future. You'll have one new member—Judith Feldheim has decided to stay."

"With Hershel? He may not be here with her. Lately he's been saying things about returning to the university, for postgraduate work, I suppose. Does Judith know?"

A nurse shooed them out before he could answer. In the waiting room he briefly touched her shoulder and said,

"Dorrie and I are leaving tomorrow for home. An evening flight."

"I already knew, Theo. I saw the calls to the airlines logged in the book at the desk. Someone will add them to your room bill when you check out."

Theo thought of several things to say, but none of them were adequate. He finally settled for a timid, "May I write you a note when I arrive home?"

"Please do, and let me know if your night-blooming cereus had the courtesy to wait for you. I'd better go back to Yussef now; someone must sit with him until Sarah returns. Perhaps we can have a farewell glass of brandy tonight."

As he left the infirmary, Theo brought out the notebook and examined the page under the one that had been so rudely removed. A faint indentation was visible; it matched the number he had carefully copied the night before. He wrote the number on a second piece of paper and went toward his room. Spies had their uses; Sitermann could justify the expense of an international call, in that the money in the account seemed linked to the terrorism. Anyone who dreamt that a Swiss bank would keep secrets from the CIA also believed he could buy a dozen long-stemmed roses for as many dollars. On the afternoon of Saint Valentine's Day.

Sitermann took the number and promised to inquire about the account and its recent activity. "I hear you're leaving, Bloom," he added in a genial drawl. "Why don't you give me a call some time and we'll get together with a six-pack to hash over old times."

Theo nodded a vague agreement to the unsavory scenario and went down the balcony to his room to pack. It had been less than a week since Nadine had called with her demand that he rescue Dorrie from the kibbutz (or vice versa). Since his arrival, two people had died and one had

240

suffered a heart attack. He had had the dubious honor of dealing with one spy, two Wellesley coeds, and three Jewish terrorists. He found himself humming about partridges and pear trees as he took clothing from the closet and placed it in his suitcase.

The orderliness of his room reminded him of the chaos of Dorrie's room, which led his thoughts, with a few diversions of no significance, to the locket. Gili had simply dismissed it, but he hadn't known that Essie could not have taken it while cleaning rooms. She would have been attracted to it, and might have pocketed it—had it been there. But how had she ended up with it?

As he pondered what he felt was a minor puzzlement, there was a knock on the door. It was too reasonable a time for a call from Nadine; it had to be the spy.

"Fast work," he said as he opened the door for Sitermann. "I must admit I'm impressed."

"About goddam time." Sitermann came in and sat down on a corner of the bed. "I ran a check on the account, and guess what?"

"The account was closed a few hours ago," Theo guessed obligingly. He needed tissue paper to properly pack, if the trousers were to keep their creases. And he did not want to put unwrapped shoes—

"How the hell did you know? You asked me to check less than twenty minutes ago. If you already knew, you might have saved the taxpayers a few bucks on the telephone bill. Besides, getting information from those Swiss guys is harder than getting a vow of celibacy from a jackrabbit."

"I didn't know; I merely suspected as much. Sarah Nava learned about the existence of the account only yesterday, but that was time enough to make reservations and hop the first plane for Switzerland. I made only one telephone call to

241

the airline, but there was at least one more logged at the desk. The question is: Had there been a previous withdrawal that coincided with the time the explosives were purchased?"

"Nah, the money came in regularly, but there hadn't been any withdrawals in over two years. Your theory that Nava funded the terrorists didn't pan out; they had another source of income that I haven't identified. Maybe they found a gold mine in the desert." He stood up and looked in the mirror as he settled the hat on his head. "I've been ordered to forget about it and return to Washington for a debrief, so I'm not going to worry about it, myself. You're crushing the collars on those shirts, Bloom. My wife uses tissue paper."

Sitermann left, chuckling under his breath. Theo took out the shirts and rearranged them, but the collars were a lost cause unless Mrs. Sitermann appeared with a bundle of tissue paper. It did not seem likely. Abandoning the shirts, he sat down on the bed.

There were still several untidy problems. He considered the wisdom of telling Miriam to cancel the search for Sarah, but decided to wait until he heard an update on Yussef's condition. The news that Yussef no longer had a nest egg might produce a second, decidedly fatal, attack. That he no longer had a wife in residence might help him through it. Then again, the fury of the kibbutzniks when they learned of the theft might warrant a stroke. A medical dilemma best left in the greenhouse for the moment.

His thoughts returned to the locket. Tissue paper having not materialized, he packed everything he would not use the following day, then went to Dorrie's room and tapped on the door. She yanked it open seconds later.

"What? What?" she demanded in a harried voice.

Theo looked over her shoulder at the aftermath of a hurricane, coupled with an earthquake or two and a stampede of cattle. "How's the packing going, my dear? Can I be of assistance?"

"No thank you, I'll have it by tomorrow, Uncle Theo. It simply takes time to fit everything in, and I don't understand what possessed me to bring seven—count them—seven cocktail dresses on a tour of Greece!" Her eyes had the feverish look of a malaria victim, and the appropriate shade of gray glinted under her makeup. "Simmons almost expired when I suggested a martini in the lounge the first night out. You'd have thought I offered her a pinch of cocaine."

"Please allow me to ask a question before you return to your chore. Although I realize Essie's possession of your locket had no significance, it continues to puzzle me. You wore it the last morning Essie cleaned your room. You went to the beach with several individuals that afternoon, and Judith seemed to think you put your locket in your beach bag. What subsequently took place?"

"I am trying to remember how I packed nine pairs of shoes in three suitcases. I cannot divert myself in order to think about a little beach party," she said darkly. Her fingers tightened on the door as if to slam it in the face of so trivial a request. Packing was, he deduced, not among her many talents. A genetic problem. Her mother had once thrown a lamp through a bedroom window before a trip to Nassau. Charles had been furious.

"Take a deep breath and think for just a minute," Theo insisted with a façade of sympathy.

"Oh, I'll try," she muttered, "but it won't get the Guccis in the suitcases." She ran her hands through her hair and stared at the beach in the distance. "I went with Judith, and we met Gideon, Ilana, and Prince Charming in person. Gawd, now I remember, Uncle Theo! No one, not a single person, warned me not to shave my legs before I went to the beach, so of course I did. I deplore the very idea of stubbles, and I always shave my legs before going out. It's a policy of mine. Anyway, I floated out in the water, and three seconds later I thought I'd died and gone straight to hell."

"The salt water stung?" Theo said, slathering on more sympathy. "It must have been dreadful."

Rolling her eyes, she said, "The worst pain I've ever had, and everyone thought it was *trés amusant*. Even Judith had the nerve to giggle as I ran for the shower, as if she'd known what would happen. I could have murdered all four of them right then, and never given it a moment's thought. I probably should have."

"But you left your bag with your towel on the beach?"

"I did not take it with me to the shower, Uncle Theo. I was more concerned that my poor legs would flake away like onion skins. The Chinese ought to investigate that as a form of torture—they'd have more confessions than they'd know what to do with."

"Then the others were sitting together on the beach while you were at the shower halfway up the sidewalk?"

"Gideon and Hershel were in the water, jabbing each other with their elbows and making nursery-school wisecracks. Judith did come to see if I would survive," Dorrie admitted in a begrudging tone. "And Ilana came about five minutes later to see if she could rub an additional handful of verbal salt in my wounds. She's such a sweet girl; I must think of a little present for her when I get home. Maybe a whip and a monogrammed leather mask . . ."

Theo wished her success with the task of repacking her suitcases and went back to his room. If the young men had remained in the water, then only Ilana could have taken the locket from Dorrie's bag. But why would she subsequently give it to Essie? Essie had been too peculiar to take bribes—if she possessed any information of value—and she wouldn't have understood the premise in any case. Her strengths were mysticism and adenoidal mimicry rather than such mundane things as comprehension or deceit.

Aware that he was endangering his life, he returned to Dorrie's door. This time it took several minutes for her to respond, and in the interim he heard several shrill comments about disruptions. When the door swung open, he quickly said, "One final question, I promise, and then I will allow you to pack in peace. You mentioned a conversation with Essie the day before she disappeared. What precisely did she say?"

Dorrie's face was a masterful ice carving of patience at the splintering point. "I do not remember, Uncle Theo. It was some absurd, meaningless nasality that meant nothing to me, and I therefore did not take notes for my diary."

"It's vital that you try to remember," Theo said.

"Do you have any extra space in your suitcases?"

Unlike Essie, both Theo and Dorrie were acquainted with the delicate art of bribery. He mentally acknowledged the necessity of donating his pajamas to the state of Israel. "Yes, I can fit three pairs of shoes in my luggage, and perhaps a few other things. May I presume that your mind is now eased enough to recall the conversation in question?"

"Four pairs of shoes, a sweater, and my beach robe." When Theo nodded (farewell, cheap sandals), she said, "We've been over this before, and I told you that I was pained by it, but since you insist, Essie said I was cheap. She then threatened to run and bite me. It seemed an extreme reaction."

"Are you quite sure, my dear? That doesn't sound like the girl."

"Then she put some kind of weird gypsy curse on me. It was too silly to bother with, as I told you earlier, and I simply retreated to the bathroom. When she finished, I emerged and hustled her out of the room before she moved on to cursing my unborn children à la Rumpelstiltskin."

"A curse? That's even more peculiar. Please try to remember her exact words, Dorrie."

"She warned me that I was going to trip on my great aunt's crypt, if you must know. I was floored, just floored. What could I say in response—the family crypt is now under a shopping center and Daddy replanted Auntie amidst the booboisie in the local cemetery?"

"And that was all?" Theo said, trying to make sense of the senseless words. Essie must have been repeating something she had overheard, but the message had been severely muddled along the way.

"Only her name and sex," Dorrie sniffed, "an improbable combination at best. Now I really must return to the packing, if you're finished with all this. Why you find that poor girl's last words of any interest is beyond me, but—"

"Thank you, Dorrie." He went back to his room once again, wondering if there was an indentation on the balcony from his many sojourns between the rooms. He sat on the bed and repeated Dorrie's fragmented version of the conversation and one comment Essie had made to him, until he at last arrived at a possible interpretation. It explained much of what had occurred in the last few days, but finding a way to confirm it would be more challenging than the storage and safe passage of nine pairs of Guccis.

Chapter 22

Theo went alone to the restaurant for what he hoped would be the last dinner of leaden turkey and limp vegetables. As he entered the lobby, Ilana beckoned from the registration desk.

"You left this earlier," she said, flapping a manila envelope at him. "It was by the telephone; Miriam thought it was yours."

The present from Judith. He guiltily took it, then gave her a bland smile. "Thank you, Ilana, I had quite forgotten it in the excitement of making reservations. Dorrie and I will leave tomorrow afternoon. Would you be kind enough to arrange for a taxi to take us to the airport?"

"With great pleasure. Judith intends to stay?"

"Yes, she feels that Kibbutz Mishkan is her home, and the kibbutzniks the family she never had. I hope her expectations will prove true and that she will be happy here."

"Strong, she isn't, but she is intelligent enough. Maybe I will train her to make little packages for me."

"Then the Sons of Light will continue without its leader?"

"I shall change the name to the Daughters of Light," she said, letting the words roll off her tongue like malted milk balls. "The other name was insulting to me. Now I shall teach them that women can accomplish much violence in the name of retribution. Things will go boom, Mr. Bloomer." She sounded childishly pleased with the alliterative sound effects. "Boom!" she repeated softly. "Boom, boom!"

Theo was less pleased. "I understand from Lieutenant

Gili that the murder investigation is closed, and there has been no link to the terrorism. I imagine you'll be able to continue your acts of vengeance for a while longer." He blinked through his glasses at her, disturbed by the depth of her complacency. "One day, of course, you will be careless and the little package will explode in your hands."

"Or in Judith's hands."

"I wouldn't count on it," he said. "You may find yourself alone in your endeavor. Hershel seems to be interested in returning to the university to continue his work in archaeology."

"If he does, it will be with empty hands," she growled.

Theo again smiled, pleased with her inadvertent support of his theory. "You will arrange for the taxi after lunch tomorrow?"

"Immediately, Mr. Bloomer."

"By the way, Ilana, why did you give Dorrie's locket to Essie?"

She jerked to a halt and glared over her shoulder. "I did not," she said. She managed an even tone despite the sudden twitch of her shoulders, and her mouth remained slightly agape with what Theo hoped was debilitating astonishment.

"But you did steal it," he persisted. "You're the only one who could have taken it from Dorrie's beach bag while she was trying to save her legs from the Dead Sea."

"It was a tasteless display of vanity," Ilana growled, "and she did not care enough to keep it in the safe. I thought I could sell the locket and use the money for more important matters."

"Did you hope to sell it to Popadoupolis?"

She opened her mouth to retort, then caught herself and sullenly shook her head.

"I understand that Popadoupolis was always interested in

purchasing things. He might have considered the locket even though he specialized in antiquities."

"I have never met this Popadoupolis person, so I do not know what he might have considered," she said coldly. "Now I must make arrangements for the taxi so that you can leave tomorrow, Mr. Bloomer. I do not want to be the cause of a delay."

"So you stayed here while Gideon and Hershel went to Athens?" Theo said. He felt no remorse in continuing to badger a terrorist with notches in her belt. "They seemed to enjoy the vacation, didn't they? Coffee in sidewalk cafés, chats with pretty girls, amorous visits to hotel bedrooms . . ." As difficult as it was, Theo essayed a smirk that competed with any of Yussef's. It succeeded.

"They were not on vacation, Mr. Bloomer; they were there for the sole purpose of doing what they did. They picked up the girls to acquire a safe means of bringing the plasticine through customs. They made the trade—the deal—and left as quickly as possible."

"I gathered that they enjoyed themselves, despite the rushed itinerary," Theo said, nodding amiably.

"Why don't you ask Hershel if he enjoyed the trip?" she sneered. "He's been a senile *zeyde* since he came back. Moaning and whining, mumbling to himself. Hoo-ha!"

"What did you trade?"

"Better you should talk to the wall. I will tell you that it was not the locket. Your niece lied to you, for it was given back to her. Gideon was very mad at me for taking it, and he took it away from me to return to her. He accused me of jealousy—as if I wished I were like the stupid *shiksa!*" She abruptly spun around and went into the office. The door banged closed.

"Essie and sex, and a stroll at ten," Theo murmured to the wooden barrier.

"Essie and sex?" Miriam said from behind him. "That's the most unlikely thing I've heard in a long time, Theo. I doubt she ever figured out the intricacies of reproduction, much less how to enjoy them. Are you certain you have the right schizophrenic in mind?"

Theo gave her a pensive look. "No, I'm not at all certain that I do." He suggested they move to a sofa, then fetched brandy from the bar and returned to sit beside her. "May I presume that Yussef has regained consciousness?"

"Yes, for a few minutes. He asked me for something rather strange, Theo—a notebook. He was very agitated about it, and the doctor was alarmed. I went to Yussef's office and went through all the drawers and files, but I couldn't find the notebook that was so important. He was asleep when I returned, so I haven't told him."

Theo took the notebook out of his pocket and gave it to her, then told her the significance of the number that had been scrawled on one page. She downed the brandy in one gulp, choking on the last few drops.

"Oh, Theo, how can you say such a thing? Yussef's always been so loyal, so enthusiastic and involved with the kibbutz. He was the chairman for several years and our representative to the kibbutzim association. He never complained about the long hours with the ledgers or the tediousness of dealing with the nudniks in every bureaucratic division. I don't believe it."

"It's a matter of linens and bed frames," he said, wishing she were not so visibly shattered by the information. Old friends, he reminded himself in a resigned tone. He told her about the double set of books and his conclusion concerning the Swiss account.

Miriam sank into the sofa. "Poor Sarah, how can I tell her?"

Theo told her that Sarah—well, already knew about the

nest egg and had left Israel to deal with it. At this next recital of treachery, Miriam finished Theo's brandy and weakly requested another. He left her to assimilate the information and went to fulfill her request, but as he went across the lobby he saw a peculiar sight through the glass doors. Sitermann, stealthily approaching a jeep parked near a hibiscus. Sitermann, sliding into the driver's seat and disappearing under the steering wheel as if he had been sucked into an eddy. The same, popping back up, glancing around with noticeable furtiveness, and then driving out of the parking area with the scowl of a condor taking to wing. Very spyish stuff.

He returned with the two snifters and handed one to Miriam, who looked pinker and more composed.

"Thank you, Theo. I thought I knew Sarah and Yussef after twenty years of communal life. They never pretended to care for each other, but they did seem to care about the kibbutz and the future of Israel. Is no one what he claims to be?"

A touchy subject for Theo, very touchy. He thought for a moment and then said, "It is, I suppose, the nature of the beast to do whatever is necessary to survive, although the definitions of survival may vary. Essie, for instance, preferred to be overlooked so that she could keep her freedom. She was treated as a shadow, but she did listen to what occurred in her presence—not only listened but also absorbed and later repeated. Quite a bit got lost in the translation."

"Does that have something to do with the 'Essie and sex' remark you made earlier?"

"I think it does, if I've correctly deduced the original phrasing that led to her distorted version," Theo said humbly. "But other people have produced façades of equal deception. Yussef and Sarah are obvious candidates, as are Ilana and Hershel. Sitermann, our resident cowboy. Even Gideon played a role."

251

A spasm of pain flashed across her face. "Gideon never pretended not to be an outspoken radical who believed in violence as a means to insure the existence of Israel. I tried, Theo. God knows I tried to reason with him, to make him see that terrorism was not the solution, but I could never overcome the malignancy of hatred. I couldn't stop him from destroying himself."

"He was beyond help, I'm afraid. His behavior the night he argued with Dorrie was manic, and he sounded as if he felt omnipotent. The success of the bomb in Hebron must have triggered something within him. He seemed ready to blow up any and all of the West Bank Arabs. I suspect he would have tried to do so."

"I, too, heard hysteria in his voice," she said, looking away. "As you said, he was convinced of his power and willing to do anything to further his cause. He would have destroyed anything he felt threatened him. In that sense, one might say his death was a mitzvah." After a minute, she slowly turned her head to look at him through bleak eyes. "You don't think that Gili arrested the murderer, do you?"

"No, I must admit that I don't; there are too many loose ends his tidy, timely arrest cannot explain. I have a theory about much of what has happened—the trip to Athens, the financing for the explosives, the searches in certain rooms, the appearance of Dorrie's locket in Essie's hand, and the reason Essie was killed."

"I deserve to know. He was my son."

"I know," he said with great gentleness. He picked up Judith's package and stood up. "I must find Hershel at once. I'm worried that the violence is not yet concluded."

"More violence?" Miriam said, turning gray. "How can there be more violence?"

"I'm not sure that there will be, but I fear that Ilana has

taken on Gideon's megalomania. It may force Hershel into doing something drastic."

"Did Hershel—cause Essie's fall?"

"He's the odd man out in this whole scheme. Judith's analysis of him is probably close to the truth. He's shy, uncomfortable, and repressed, but capable of passion. The problem is that his passion is aimed in a tangential direction. He never wanted to bomb Arabs; he wanted recognition in his field. One chance has already passed, but he may believe he has a second chance for glory."

"Do you believe he killed Gideon?" she demanded.

"I don't know yet. But it is possible that we shouldn't have been referring to Jonathan and David," Theo said, looking down at her with a grave expression. "We may discover the story of Cain and Abel to be more fitting."

Chapter 23

Miriam told him that Hershel was at her house. The manila envelope clutched to his side, Theo left the lobby and walked down the sidewalk while he considered how best to confront Hershel. If the hypothesis were correct, the young man was under a great deal of stress. It might be thorny.

But it wasn't, for no one answered Theo's persistent knocks. He took the metal strip out of his pocket and entered Miriam's house. Once inside he stopped. The living room was strewn with magazines, papers, books from the shelves and pillows from the couch. The couch itself lay upended, its feet poking out. A table had been smashed. Shards of glass from picture frames were scattered on the carpet like a flower girl's droppings.

The kitchen had fared no better from what appeared to be a thorough but sloppy search. Flour lay in drifts along the wall; the refrigerator had been emptied, as had cabinets and broom closet. The bedroom and bathroom were equally disastrous.

Hershel was gone. Theo felt an urge to straighten up the house before leaving, if only to save Miriam from the dreadful sight, but willed himself to leave the evidence intact. Instead he sat down on the overturned sofa and pondered the scene with sober, unblinking eyes.

Someone still continued to search for something. Hershel was most likely the culprit, since he had been alone in the house. Theo could guess what Hershel might have been searching for—but not if he had found it.

Then again, Sitermann had been behaving oddly. Not oddly for a spy, perhaps, but oddly enough to arouse Theo's curiosity. However, Sitermann was capable of a more professional search—unless he had preferred it to look amateurish. He was not available for comment. Nor was Hershel, for that matter. And Ilana had left her post at the registration desk—if one were, in a manner of speaking, counting noses.

Despite his previous intentions, Theo straightened up the papers on the floor, returned the sofa to its feet, and clucked over the smashed end table. Then he locked the door behind him and walked slowly toward the lobby to tell Miriam about the destruction.

As he reached the building where the guest rooms were, he felt a sudden twinge of unease. He veered up the stairs and hurried along the balcony to Dorrie's room, scolding himself that he was behaving like an old maid who nightly checked under the bed for rapists. He knocked on her door, waited several minutes, then knocked once again in an increasingly heavy cadence.

After a quick glance over his shoulder, Theo let himself into the room. Which was empty of nieces, but not of clothes trampled on the floor, suitcases emptied and agape, Guccis tossed in corners, and plastic bottles on their sides like beached whales. In Miriam's house, it had been simple to determine there had been a search. In Dorrie's room, it did take a minute to determine that the chaos was not an intentional part of an obscure packing strategy.

He concluded that her room had been searched. Dorrie would never have permitted it, had she been in any condition to protest. Where was she now? Theo hurried to his room, this time utilizing the room key. His suitcases had been stacked near the door, but now they had fallen victim to the same, insane search. His pale brown suit, left in the closet for the following day, had been kicked into a corner. The mattress hung drunkenly over the bed frame, the covers pulled back to expose a slashed ribbon of cotton stuffing.

It was quite enough to produce a pained noise from Theo's throat. He picked up his trousers and rehung them in the closet, although the crease was forever ruined. His jacket had lost a button. The one dress shirt carefully set aside to wear on the airplane had been wadded into a ball and left on the bathroom floor. It was too much, it really was.

The expletive (twice repressed, but via great inner control) finally slipped out as he glowered at the contents of his suitcase, which had been neatly arranged to survive the simian treatment of airport employees. The word startled him back to reality. He realized he had been clutching Judith's present tightly enough to leave a wrinkle and hastily put it down as he hurried out of the room.

After a quick peek at Sitermann's room to see if it too had been searched (it hadn't), he went to Judith's room in the apartment house and banged on her door with an un-Bloomerish fist. Unlike the other players in the rapidly disintegrating drama, she opened the door at once.

"Mr. Bloomer, how nice of you to come by," she said. In spite of her smile, she looked very unhappy. Theo had presumed she would.

"Have you seen Dorrie?" he demanded.

"No, we were going to do lunch tomorrow before she left. Her idea of a meaningful farewell, I suppose. Isn't she in her room packing?" Judith stepped back and began to play with the hem of her shirt. "She brought an awful lot of clothes with her," she added in a thin voice, "and—"

"She has disappeared. Her room was searched, as was mine and Miriam's house. Where is Hershel?"

"I don't—I don't know. I saw him earlier. We talked for a few minutes, but he didn't say where he was going when he left." She looked up abruptly. "Why do you think Hershel knows where Dorrie might be?"

"Tell me again what happened the night Gideon was killed by a PLO agent from Jordan. You and Hershel had wine."

"We—uh, we talked about the socialist structure of the— of the kibbutz. I told you about that."

"And you and Hershel were together every minute? He never once left the room and all you did was talk politics?" He advanced slowly, stalking an admission.

She retreated, her head bobbing in small jerks. "No, we talked all night. That's all we did. I mean, we have—well, kissed each other a little bit, but we—we didn't—I wouldn't normally allow things to get out of hand, but—but . . ." She ran out of protests as she backed into the kitchen table. Her eyes filled with tears and her chin began to quiver helplessly. "It's nobody's business what we did that night, Mr. Bloomer. You have no right to insinuate that Hershel and I indulged in premarital cohabitation!"

"What happened afterward?" Theo persisted politely, if a shade remorselessly.

"I felt terribly guilty that we had allowed ourselves to be distracted by sexual desires," she said through a hiccup. "Hershel felt badly, too, and went to his room to find an aspirin for me. When he came back, he brought a bouquet of orange flowers. It was so sweet of him, and he's been a perfect gentleman ever since then."

Except when he dumped suitcases and slashed mattresses, Theo thought to himself. "How long was he out of your room, Judith?"

"I don't know—I was crying," she said, crying. "He was very gentle when he returned, though, and told me that he would always love and respect me, even though we had . . ." A wet, tremulous sigh served to describe the unspeakable. The tears eased to a steady dribble.

"And you have no idea where Hershel is now?"

"No," she sniffled. "We talked about what you said. He's not a terrorist. Gideon was the one who insisted that they do those terrible things, and Ilana always had to be the one to plant the bomb. Hershel said there was still a way to salvage his reputation, and I believed him."

If he could find what he needed . . . After a moment of thought, Theo ironically realized where the desired object was. "Then why did you steal the manila envelope from him and pretend it was a farewell card for Dorrie, not to be opened until she was in the airplane?"

"But I didn't steal that from Hershel. Gideon gave it to me the day after the bombing in Hebron, and asked me not to tell anyone, including Hershel and Ilana. He said it was an insurance policy."

"Why did you give it to me?"

She wrapped her arms around herself and dug her fingers into her shoulders. "Because I think it has something to do with the cave where Essie's body was found, but I was too frightened to tell anyone about it. Gideon's eyes were on fire when he made me promise not to say anything. He was cursing under his breath and saying terrible things, as if he were one of those crazy zealots from the Bible. Then he was murdered, which terrified me even more. I decided to get rid of it."

"By giving it to me?"

"I needed time to make a decision about it, but I was going to tell you before you left tomorrow. I wouldn't have let the envelope leave Israel."

"When Hershel was here earlier, did he demand to know if

you had anything that belonged to Gideon?"

She nodded.

"And you told him about the manila envelope?"

She nodded.

"And when he got angry, you had to tell him that you gave it to me for safekeeping?"

She nodded.

He could get nothing more from her other than a series of hiccups and a few mostly inarticulate words.

Chapter 24

Theo rushed back to the lobby. To his relief, Miriam was sitting on the sofa where he had left her earlier. She looked frail and tired, as if she were a biennial in its third year.

"Dorrie has disappeared," he said. "I need the keys to a jeep." When she opened her mouth to protest, he added, "I must insist on haste, Miriam. The keys and a description of the road that leads to the cave, please. Dorrie may be in danger."

"The keys are behind the desk, but I don't know how to describe the road. It's an unpaved road, like a dozen others. Shall I go with you?"

Minutes later, with Theo at the wheel, the jeep squealed through the kibbutz gate and roared down the highway. He tried to answer her questions, but the wind seemed to tear the words from his mouth to scatter behind them. They had passed several unpaved roads when Miriam tugged at his arm and pointed. "That's it," she shrieked over the wind. "I'll tell you when to park."

It was not necessary, for there were two red jeeps blocking the road above the cave. Theo shut off the engine and took out his handkerchief to wipe the dust off his bifocals.

"What is going on?" Miriam demanded. "Why are two of our jeeps already here, and why do you think Dorrie would drive one of them into the desert? Why is she in danger?"

He settled his bifocals in place. After he had blotted his forehead and refolded the handkerchief, he said, "Dorrie didn't drive; Hershel brought her, and under protest. The other jeep was—ah, borrowed by Sitermann, if I am correct in my assumptions. He was following the others to see what was happening and to ascertain if there were anything of interest in it for him. It's a very bad habit of his."

"Hershel forced Dorrie to come with him, and Sitermann stole a jeep to follow them? Theo, are you—"

"I fear I'll have to delay the explanation until I fetch Dorrie and see that she's unharmed," he said apologetically. "It would be better if you waited here, just in case there's a spot of trouble. Hershel may not agree to release Dorrie without some persuasion."

"Then I'm the one who ought to talk to him," she said. "You seem to think he murdered Gideon. A mother has some rights, one of which is confronting her son's murderer. I'm coming with you."

They slid down the path to the ledge above the cave, wincing as pebbles bounced ahead of them like pinging announcements of their imminent arrival. There was nothing to do about it, however, except wince. Theo stopped for a moment to take a small handgun out of his pocket, then motioned for Miriam to wait where she was.

"You have a gun," she whispered in a stunned voice.

"A little one, and only for emergencies," he said primly. "It really would be better if you waited here, Miriam. If you happen to hear any peculiar noises or shouts, you might consider the wisdom of returning to the kibbutz to telephone Lieutenant Gili."

"This is a dream, right?" She rubbed her temples with her fingertips. "You don't really have a gun, and Dorrie's in her room with black mud on her face and avocados in her hair."

"I wish it were," he answered as he inched toward the edge of the massive overhang, "but I do believe I hear Dorrie's voice. She would only come here in her worst nightmare, so we may have to accept the reality of it for the moment. If you'll excuse me . . . ?"

He dropped to a prone position and wiggled to the far edge to peer down at the entrance to the cave. He found himself looking at the tops of two heads, but neither belonged to his niece. The black hair was Hershel's; the sandstorm-and-split-ends was Ilana's. Frosted ash blond was not in sight.

"I have to find another scroll!" Hershel said, breathing heavily enough to blow down anyone's house—straw, sticks, or bricks. "The other one is gone—stolen—I don't know! I looked for it in Essie's room, and in Gideon's. I even looked at Miriam's house, in case Gideon had hidden it there. He knew I had to have it. Judith finally admitted that she gave it to the Bloomer guy. While I was searching his room, the girl must have heard me and come over to investigate. I grabbed her and made her let me in her room, but it wasn't there, either. Maybe he mailed it away or something! But it's gone and I have to find another one. I can still be famous." He choked on the final word and bent over in a paroxysm of coughs.

"Fame does not matter," Ilana said with a scornful laugh. "Forget the stupid scroll. We can get thousands of dollars from the rich little girl's uncle. This time I shall go to Athens to buy the explosives, and I won't come home with some princess who turns out to be a pauper."

Hershel groaned. "She told me she had two houses, a big car, a wealthy family. She lied to me, just like you and Gideon did. Everyone has lied to me, everyone! You made me sell the scroll to that arms dealer, but the next one was to be mine!" He again broke out in painful spasms of coughing, as if his throat were constricted by a brutally tight collar. "I want my scroll," he managed to say in a pitifully weak croak.

"Well, I certainly don't have it," came a righteous voice from the interior of the cave, "and it will take weeks for Uncle Theo to arrange a ransom payment. I am not a troglodyte who delights in nasty, cramped, filthy holes in mountainsides, and I have no intention of sitting in one while you wait for the money. It is time for all of us to behave in a more adult fashion. Why don't I just write you a check right now, and then you can drive me back to the kibbutz?"

Ilana and Hershel turned to stare into the cave. Theo himself felt rather taken aback by Dorrie's suggestion. Behind him Miriam muffled a laugh, albeit a semi-hysterical one.

Ilana was the first to recover. "Shut up, you spoiled child. We are soldiers, and if we want to hold you for three months in the cave, then we shall do it. And if you open your mouth again, you will find a dirty, greasy rag stuffed into it."

"I beg your pardon," Dorrie countered contemptuously. "That sort of thing went out with the Flintstones. Anyway, you haven't even got a dirty, greasy rag, and I wouldn't open my mouth in any case. This entire thing is too melodramatic for words."

Ilana growled, but managed to restrain herself as Hershel said, "I must go into the cave. The first two manuscripts dealt with the Essene sect's agricultural inventory, but there may be others with historical implications. I could find an early copy of a book of the Bible, I really could." He was pleading, his voice hoarse with raw emotion. He seemed to lean toward the entrance of the cave as though the hoped-for manuscripts held a magnetic pull on him.

"Essie and sex, Essene sect," Miriam whispered in a wondering tone.

Theo turned to nod at her. "My 'great aunt's crypt' is a 'great manuscript.' The reason for the 'trip' to Athens." Ignoring her bewildered look, he held a finger to his lips and returned his attention to the scene below him.

"Forget this petty desire for personal glory," Ilana snapped. "We must fight a war against one hundred million Arabs. There is no time for this childishness. The scroll you took Popadoupolis bought only enough plasticine for two bombs." Her head swiveled as she peered into the cave. "I have a brilliant idea how to utilize what we have left."

"Don't even think about it," Dorrie said from her invisible vantage point. "I hate firecrackers on the Fourth of July; they give me an absolute migraine. I refuse to be around real explosives."

Hershel followed Ilana's eyes, and apparently her mind. "No, Ilana, you aren't going to rig some kind of booby trap until I've explored the cave. I won't let you do it."

"Right on," encouraged the unseen voice from the cave.

Ilana snorted, then ducked her head and disappeared from Theo's view as she entered the cave. After a startled gulp, Hershel also disappeared, howling for her to stop. The ledge in front of the cave was, Theo realized, propitiously empty. Cautioning Miriam to remain still, he scuttled around, dangled his legs over the lip of the overhang, and let himself slither down.

He landed on the ledge with a muted thud. When nothing happened, he bent down to wave at Dorrie, who was tied up rather prettily and sitting just inside the entrance to the cave. "Are you okay?" he asked in a low voice.

She nodded, then wiggled around to show him her wrists, which were ringed with knots. "Not my idea of a bracelet," she whispered. "Cheap polyester rope!"

Theo scrabbled at the knots, keeping half of his attention on the inky interior of the cave. A flashlight splashed across one wall, then whipped away. Ilana and Hershel were at most twenty feet into the cave, arguing over their cache of explosives.

Dorrie would not be able to climb up the path with her hands behind her back; it was necessary to remain long enough to free them. At the sound of intensified anger from the blackness, he tripled his efforts, but he knew it would take at least another minute before he could unravel the professional work.

"I won't let you do this," Hershel screeched. His voice bounced off the walls of the cave, echoing in a ghostly wail of sheer desperation. "Put down that cap, Ilana."

"I do not care about the damned manuscripts," she answered in an equally hollowed voice. "I'm going to rig a bomb for that rich *shiksa*. One more word from her and she'll find herself under fifty feet of limestone."

"But my manuscripts . . ." Hershel croaked. The light began to dance around the cave, accompanied by thuds and gasps.

Dorrie looked at Theo over her shoulder. "I would like to believe that you are hurrying, Uncle Theo."

"I've almost got it," Theo said. He flinched at a sharp crack from the cave. A slap—or a gun. "One last knot, my dear, and we're up the hill."

"Put down that cap," Hershel howled.

"Give me the plasticine," Ilana growled.

"Could you please hurry?" Dorrie whispered.

"What's going on?" Miriam called.

"Need some help?" Sitermann drawled.

Theo looked in all the relevant directions, but before he could answer, there was a thunderous roar from within the cave. The noise grumbled and grew until it seemed to seize the sky. Clouds of suffocating white dust swept out of the cave in cottony swirls. Dorrie squeaked as he freed her wrists with a final jerk. The ledge crumbled under their feet and they began to tumble toward the wadi amidst an avalanche of rocks and dust. It was unsettling, to say the very least.

Chapter 25

"Your body's in the wadi, Bloom."

Theo opened his eyes to a view of Sitermann's grin. His ears reverberated in a high-pitched squeal, and the sky was filled with spiraling stars against a background of pulsating blues and reds. Patriotic but improbable, he decided as he pushed Sitermann aside and forced himself to sit up. Waves of nausea promptly struck, and it was several minutes before he dared try to speak. He passed the time with an inventory of his limbs, which were bruised but unbroken.

"Where's Dorrie?" he whispered at last.

"She'll be all right," Sitermann said. He put Theo's bifocals in place and chuckled. "You're the one with a lump where your forehead used to be. You're dustier than a groundhog's ass, and your britches lost their crease halfway down the mountainside. You better just sit for a minute until the stars fade and the little cuckoo stops serenading in your ear."

In that the analysis was accurate, Theo decided to follow the advice. He cautiously turned his head to look for Dorrie. She was leaning against a boulder, pale, coated with dust, bedraggled, and blessedly intact. She fluttered her fingers and produced a half-heartedly polite smile.

Theo did the same, then looked back at Sitermann. "I gather the explosive went off somewhere in the proximity of Ilana and Hershel. They are—buried?"

"A good fifty feet of limestone on top of them," Sitermann

agreed. The affable grin widened. "Speaking as a professional in this kind of thing, which of course I am, that was a real good one. I couldn't have done a whole lot better myself. It was so loud they probably heard it all the way to the kibbutz, if they didn't notice the clouds of bat dust. All in all, a damned fine production."

"And Miriam?"

"She's trying to get down to us, but she didn't take the express elevator. It'll be a few minutes, Bloom, before your lady friend arrives to hold your hand. Mine is less delicate, but it ought to suffice in the interim."

Theo stared at him. "What did you say?"

"I said that Miriam is—"

"No, not that," Theo said impatiently, "The comment about your hand being less delicate."

"Why don't you lie down for another minute or two, Bloom? I'm beginning to think you ended up with some bat dust between your ears. Maybe the paramedics can figure out how to get a stretcher down here so you won't have to crawl up the mountainside."

"Forget it, Sitermann; I'll be fine." He took out his handkerchief and did his best to tidy himself as he pondered Sitermann's comment. It was the confirming link in his theory of Essie's death, which had been an accident only in the sense that Essie had been unlucky enough to hear too much. She had been silenced, as had Gideon, although for another reason.

Once he had cleaned his bifocals, Theo searched the mountainside for Miriam. She was, as Sitermann had promised, climbing down as quickly as she could, and he could see the whiteness of her face and uneven, frantic pace. Behind her, centuries of dust still curled and danced in the sky like the mist on the surface of the Dead Sea.

Ignoring Sitermann's increasingly perplexed gaze, he tugged at his beard as he continued to watch Miriam. Her son had shared her passion for the land, more so than she had realized when she had talked of the second generation's desire for personal fulfillment. The passion had obsessed him. Ultimately, it had killed him.

"Have you decided on a concussion?" Sitermann asked.

"No," he sighed. "How did you happen to put yourself in the thick of things, by the way? Were you merely out rounding up errant steers for a rodeo, or were you following the others?"

"You ought to know me better than that by now, Bloom. I heard a ruckus in your room, so I borrowed a jeep and wandered along to see what all was going on and to keep an avuncular-type eye on your niece. I had an idea she wasn't real pleased about the trip out here, maybe because she was squawking louder than a prairie dog in heat. I was lurking behind a pile of rocks."

"May I presume you intended to make your presence known if Ilana and Hershel actually threatened Dorrie with physical violence?"

Sitermann gave him a wounded look. "You honestly think I'd let them harm a hair on the pretty little filly's head?"

The pretty little filly had been listening to the conversation. "Is this the so-called CIA agent, Uncle Theo? I find that rather hard to accept. I had always imagined the CIA to have a shade more savoir-faire, not to mention a more elegant wardrobe. And if he was there the entire time, while I was literally forced to inhale bat droppings while listening to Ilana and Hershel plot how best to persuade a mountain to drop on me—"

"You're basically correct, but we'll discuss it in depth on the flight home," Theo said. "At the moment, we need to deal

269

with the situation. Two young people have been killed—"

"And whose fault was that?" Dorrie inserted acidly.

"—and we must inform the authorities. It is, I fear, a tremendously complicated story. If you don't mind, I'm beginning to feel faint. I'd better save my strength to get up the mountain." He lay back and closed his eyes. It was as good a plan as any, and it proved successful.

Lieutenant Gili crossed his arms, uncrossed them, and crossed his legs. He then recrossed his arms and said (rather crossly), "Well, Mr. Bloomer, I cannot wait all day for you to explain what happened at the cave. My men have informed me that there is no possibility that the two inside the cave could have survived. Miss Caldicott refuses to speak. Mrs. Adler claims to be—to be addled." He stopped to laugh at his joke, then forced his mustache into alignment and added, "Mr. Sitermann says you're the only one who can explain. How long must we dilly, Mr. Bloomer?"

Theo shifted the icepack to the opposite slope of his forehead and peered around the room from under it. The lieutenant, his officers, the kibbutzniks, and the visitors were all gathered to hear what had taken place on the ledge in front of the cave. Hadassah and Naomi were there, no longer giggling. The bartender, the factory men, Anya, the nurse from the infirmary, and others whom he had met during the week were watching him, waiting to learn which member of the kibbutz had broken the fifth law of Moses. He could see the sorrow on their faces, sorrow that came from the knowledge that one of them had betrayed Kibbutz Mishkan and forever damaged the strong tie that kept so diverse a group of people together in a close bond.

Lieutenant Gili had ordered everyone except the children to attend the general assembly. Even Yussef had been escorted from his sickbed. He sat in a wheelchair, his drab green bathrobe nicely coordinated with his overall chlorophyllous complexion. Sarah had not yet returned from her excursion to Switzerland.

"It has been difficult for me to understand how the Jews feel about Israel," Theo began quietly. "It's a different kind of passion, based not only on an historical precedent, but also on a God-given right to be here. Because it is the Promised Land, its citizens are willing to make whatever sacrifice is needed."

He glanced at Miriam as he moved the ice pack to the other side. A dribble of water ran into his eye, and he hastily brushed it away. "As Miriam explained on my tour, the loyalty to the kibbutz strengthens the commitment even more. It is admirable, when tempered with reason. Miriam told me she would gladly die for the kibbutz. For someone, it became necessary to kill for it."

"Mr. Bloomer," Gili interrupted, his eyes rolling in a display of pained forbearance, "this is hardly earthquaking. Could you arrive at the point?"

"I shall try my best, Lieutenant Gili. The situation began when Ilana, Gideon, and Hershel returned from the university with a shared commitment to seek revenge against the Arabs. The major complication was money, but they lucked into a veritable gold mine—" he inclined his head at Sitermann—"in the desert: a cave with two ancient scrolls. A dealer in Athens traded explosives for one scroll, and they subsequently bombed the building in Hebron."

The kibbutzniks eyed each other, some shocked and others nodding as if they'd suspected some, if not all, of Theo's theory. Gili rose to rock on the balls of his feet. "Murder, Mr. Bloomer. The terrorism is not within my jurisdiction, or I would have solved it in a matter of days. If you

271

don't mind . . . ?" He sat down with a martyred sigh.

"On the day of the bombing each one of them had a problem. Ilana, already elated with anticipation, wanted to plan another bomb immediately afterward, then trade the remaining scroll for more explosives. Boom, boom, boom. Hershel wanted to take the scroll to the university so that he could be recognized as a great archaeologist. Gideon wanted to make sure no one found out about the cave, since he knew that removing antiquities would produce more disgrace and punishment than a minor bombing incident. If Hershel took the scroll to his professor, the location of the cave would no longer be a secret, and the scroll would be confiscated. Gideon decided to hide it in a most ironic place until Hershel calmed down.

"They had a rousing argument, which Essie happened to hear. She delightedly repeated what she could remember to anyone who would listen. Dorrie did, and so did I and that evening I told Miriam. Only later did I hear a more precise version of what Essie said to Dorrie. She had tried to say 'Essene sect,' although it did come out differently. She also mentioned the word 'cheap,' which referred to the jeep that was used to go to 'he runs to bite,' Hebron tonight, and the 'trip' to sell the 'great manuscript.' She even told me to take a scroll to Athens, which I erroneously interpreted as a suggestion to take a stroll at ten."

"I knew I wasn't cheap." Dorrie tossed her hair back and lifted her chin to offer a view of her slender neck. "I had never in my entire life been accused of that."

"You had no frame of reference," Theo said. "However, Miriam did, and she deciphered the words almost immediately."

She looked up with a bleak smile. "I had suspected something about the cave, and I did tell Gideon that Essie was mumbling to the guests. I—I didn't want anything to happen to him. It never occurred to me that he would take such drastic steps to silence her. Afterward, it was too late to do anything."

"It was," Theo agreed. "By coincidence, later that day Gideon managed to gain possession of Dorrie's locket, and he used it to lure Essie into the desert. He arranged to meet her after he returned from Hebron. Yussef heard her begging for 'my necklace' outside the dining hall. Ilana allowed the jeep through the gate, and later believed what Gideon told her about Essie's fall. But I fear it was a fabrication designed to appease the other members of his group—and to avoid retribution. Gideon drove Essie to a remote site in the desert. A blow on the back of her neck and she was gone. If the fall didn't kill her, exposure and scavengers would. His solution was effective, if psychotic."

"Aha!" Gili said. "Now we have solved the first murder, and very neatly. I can hardly arrest the young man, can I?" He gazed around the room with a triumphant smirk, as if awaiting applause. After a moment of silence, he looked at Theo. "Then who killed Gideon? I suppose you are going to tell me that the Dead Sea is haunted, as well as the cave above the wadi? I do not believe in ghosts."

"That was prickly," Theo said, again finding Miriam to study her with great sympathy. "Once I determined that Gideon murdered Essie, I wondered about motives. Ilana wasn't particularly perturbed about Essie's death; she believed Gideon's story. Hershel probably did, too, since he was used to being bullied. In any case, he was too busy wooing Judith for her supposed fortune. If he could persuade her to produce a hefty dowry, it could be used to purchase explosives. Then the others would allow him to take the second scroll to the university. No one would suspect the first scroll had been illegally removed from Israel, and he would be famous and respected."

This time it was Judith who produced the bleak smile. "He was upset when I admitted that I wasn't a typically wealthy Wellesley girl. He didn't want to stay at the kibbutz. All he could talk about was getting a university position and supervising digs." She hiccuped, but managed to hold back the tears. "Then I had to tell him that I would admit that I brought the explosives through customs."

"That is, of course, what instigated the scene at the cave," Theo said. "Hershel realized that the whole affair would be exposed. It would become known that he had smuggled an antiquity out of Israel, and he had only a small chance of avoiding professional ostracism. He needed the remaining scroll to produce with a flourish, as if that might serve as an act of contrition. He was unable to find it, since I was innocently carrying it around with me. He decided to hold Dorrie until I agreed to return the manuscript to him—or he found another one. It was illogical, but he was panicked beyond any point of logical analysis."

"That's right," Dorrie said. "I heard a dreadful thumping in your room, so I went over to see if you were having problems with my shoes. Hershel dragged me to my room and made me watch while he absolutely undid all my hours of work, then took me with him to a jeep near the beach. Ilana joined us and we drove to the cave like a little family on a Sunday-afternoon jaunt. All we needed was an old quilt and pimento cheese sandwiches."

"But why did you agree to be kidnapped?" Gili snorted, clearly tired of a minor role. "Surely in such a situation you should voice an obstruction?"

Eyelashes aflutter, Dorrie gave him a sweetly bewildered smile. "I haven't had your experience with these things, but I did notice that Hershel had a knife, Lieutenant Gili. I'm not mentally disabled."

Theo opted to continue before the discussion digressed into dangerous territory. "Ilana decided to forget the scroll and demand a ransom. If she needed to blow up the cave to do so, she was willing. Hershel fell apart. There was a scuffle, a lack of prudence with the plasticine, and—well, boom." He blinked ruefully at his choice of words. "The three terrorists paid for the deaths of the children in Hebron."

"But you have not yet told us who is responsible for the death of Gideon Adler," Gili said. "I think you do not know."

Theo laid the icepack on the table. "The Biblical references kept haunting me, but I'm afraid religion was never my strength. We had Ruth the loyal follower, and Jonathan and David, best friends and almost brothers. Then it seemed as if they might have been Cain and Abel. It was terribly confusing, but I kept coming back to what I was told was the essential allegory for the Jews: Abraham and Isaac. The ultimate sacrifice. The death of a child by his parent's hand."

Miriam met his eyes. "But God stopped Abraham before he killed his son, Theo."

"I wish He'd done the same for you," Theo replied gravely.

She stood up as if to leave. Several khakied officers moved behind her, and she sank back down. "I knew about the manuscripts in the cave, and I suspected that Gideon and Hershel had sold one in Athens to buy explosives. But they promised they would halt the violence. Why would I—do what you said?"

"Because you realized that Gideon killed Essie. A bomb in Hebron was disturbing, but murder was too much. The signs of his breakdown were increasingly hard to miss; he was telling everyone about the glorious defenders of Israel, and he

275

was close to actually boasting about his involvement in the Sons of Light. You suggested a picnic at the cave because you thought he might have taken Essie there, and you had to find out how far he would go."

"I—I did. I had to find out if he were crazed enough to leave her in the desert. I couldn't allow her to stay there—with the animals and the heat. The very idea was so dreadful. She didn't deserve that. He shouldn't have let her lie there by herself."

"Once we found Essie's body, you realized he was out of control, willing to do anything to continue with his war against the Arabs. Murder would disgrace his father's memory, and bring the police here to investigate and make arrests. It would all be made public: the bombing, the murder of an innocent girl, the theft from the state of Israel. He had to be stopped, for the sake of Kibbutz Mishkan."

"He was furious with Dorrie. The argument at dinner, the scene in her room a few days ago, the way he glowered at her—it all frightened me. I arranged to meet him later that night. He said that Dorrie had understood Essie's mutterings, that she would eventually put the words together and betray him to the authorities. I couldn't let him do something to Dorrie, Theo. He had to be stopped."

"I should say so," Dorrie contributed in a righteous voice.

Miriam continued to look at Theo. "It had to be a knife, so that God would understand why I had to do it. The kibbutz could never withstand the disgrace; the tourists would never come, the factory orders would dribble off, and finally the desert would reclaim the land. My husband sacrificed his life for it, and I couldn't let it return to wilderness. With no one to tend it, the grave would be covered with sand and weeds . . ."

"Not to mention other potential sacrifices," Dorrie muttered, but no one seemed to hear her.

Miriam took a deep breath and let it slide out between her lips. The half-smile was forever gone, along with the flecks of gold in her warm brown eyes and the husky amusement in her voice. All were gray, flat, as lifeless as the Dead Sea.

"You caused a widow's heart to sing for joy, Theo Bloomer of Connecticut," she whispered as the officers gently took her arms and helped her to her feet.

"It was my honor," Theo answered with a grave bow. Then she was gone.

Chapter 26

Theo buckled his seatbelt and tried to make himself comfortable between a gentleman with the girth of a Sumo wrestler and a child whose hands, face, clothing, and sharp little elbows were all covered with the remains of sticky red candy. Five hundred seats ahead of him Dorrie and Judith were sipping champagne and happily groaning about the new fall colors. There had been only two seats available in the first-class section.

"Please give your attention to the cabin attendant who will now demonstrate the safety features of our aircraft," a crackling voice commanded. The child began to whimper and complain of a tummyache. Despite the well-lit "No Smoking" sign, the wrestler lit a cigar. The seat in front of Theo tilted back far enough to endanger his nose.

"Looking forward to the movie, Bloom?"

Theo laughed. "Sitermann, you are a truly devious spy. Can't our government afford first-class tickets?"

"I thought we might play some penny-a-point gin rummy. Hell, we've got twelve hours of togetherness; maybe I'll win enough to buy a new hatband. By the way, did you hear about Sarah Nava and the Swiss banker?"

"I hope they'll be very happy together. The note enclosed with the cashier's check sounded quite optimistic."

"And they won't have to pinch centimes on a banker's salary. Neither will you, with that scroll worth millions— unless you were fool enough to give it back?"

"What do they teach in spy school these days? Of course, I

gave it back, Sitermann," Theo said, somewhat offended. "The kibbutz has already approached the university in Tel Aviv about accepting it, in exchange for a hefty contract to provide housing, meals, supplies, and labor for the dig, which will probably last for ten or twenty years. With all that anticipated income, someone found it prudent to assign Yussef to the back room of the turkey house."

"The archaeologists can swim in the Dead Sea every evening. I hope it does more for sore backs than it does for goddam lumbago. Hey, Bloom, did you visit Miriam in jail before you left?"

Theo shook his head.

Like a weathervane in a hurricane, the stewardess began swiveling in all directions to point at what the crackle insisted were emergency exits, sources of oxygen, and personal flotation devices. The child, retching happily, grabbed at the paper bag in front of the seat, and the cigar smoker began to cough through his pale blue miasma. The crackle grew louder and more strident. With obvious reluctance, the airplane shuddered into life and began to roll around the runways in search of a vacant strip.

Theo closed his eyes and forced himself to think about his night-blooming cereus on the kitchen window sill. Maybe, if environmental stimuli had been delicately balanced, if Nadine hadn't forgotten to water it, if red spider mites hadn't chewed the leaves, if it hadn't already bloomed and withered in lonely splendor, then maybe he would be there for a glimpse of the blossom. He certainly hoped so. It would be nice. Very nice indeed.

Pookie stared at the bud. "That looks exactly like a nasty green wart on a witch's chin; I am tempted to pinch it off. When is this idiotic thing supposed to bloom?"

"I really couldn't say," Nadine snorted, tapping a tattoo on the counter with the house key. "If you prefer, we can stand here all afternoon and hold our breaths—or we can go on to the club and play bridge until I have to leave for the airport. Theo has a rare talent for selecting the most incredibly inconvenient times."

The door slammed as they left. If a plant could look relieved, the cereus certainly would have as it returned to the business of preparing to bloom.